PRAISE FOF
(PREVIOUSLY
PRE.

C000295942

'Utterly unputdownable, the
but lyrically written, with vivid and striking lines that will ...o
in the reader's mind.'

—Daily Express

'Rosi fires on all cylinders in this stylish erotic thriller. A dark,
hugely enjoyable read that had me rooting for the cold-blooded
killer.'

—G.D. Abson, bestselling author of *Motherland* and *Black Wolf*

'Oh-my-word! A seriously dark, explicit, no-holds-barred novel
that will send shivers down your spine!'

—Noelle Holten, bestselling author of *Dead Inside* and
Dead Wrong

'One of the best books I have read this year. Simply outstanding.'
—Keri Beevis, bestselling author of *Dying To Tell* and
Deep Dark Secrets

'If you enjoyed *American Psycho*, you will love this!'
—A.J. Campbell, bestselling author of *Leave Well Alone* and
Don't Come Looking

PRETTY
EVIL

ALSO BY ZOE ROSI

Someone's Watching Me

PRETTY EVIL

ZOE ROSI

THOMAS & MERCER

Published by Thomas & Mercer, Seattle

First published as *Predator* by Bloodhound Books in 2020. This edition contains editorial revisions.

www.apub.com

Amazon, the Amazon logo, and Thomas & Mercer are trademarks of Amazon.com, Inc., or its affiliates.

ISBN-13: 9781542037167
ISBN-10: 1542037166

Cover design by The Brewster Project

Printed in the United States of America

PRETTY EVIL

Chapter One

The date rape drug he'd intended to give me has knocked him out so hard he's barely even flinched, despite being dragged to the top of a twelve-storey building, stripped naked and bound to a post.

His head lolls towards his chest. I stand back to admire him, taking in his slumped frame as he wilts against the pressure of his rope bindings. He looks Christ-like, vulnerable. His skin is grey in the murky moonlight. His body is incredible. Hardly surprising, since he seems to spend half his life at the gym. His stomach is taut, rippled with abs. His pecs are straight from a swimwear ad, his broad shoulders and ripped arms built like a boxer's. His biceps are strong, lined with veins that will soon cease to pump blood. He has the kind of arms that could pin you down so tightly you wouldn't be able to move a muscle. His hands are large – the least attractive part of him: dry, thick, stubby. They're the type of hands that could grip your wrists and stifle screams. Hands that could have killed me tonight. Hands that would have hurt me. Hands that would have held me in place while he raped me.

I let my eyes wander down to his cock, which would probably have been pounding away inside me around now if things had gone his way. I could tell pretty early into our date that he was a predator.

Perhaps it takes one to know one, but I could see it in his dark eyes and sly glances, the hungry way he took in my body, the type of questions he asked, his eagerness to buy me drinks. He probably didn't think I had it in me to notice. Of course he didn't. He just saw my shiny, sweeping hair, my lashes, my clothes, my smile. He saw what everybody else sees: my mask.

It's several hours earlier and we're one drink into our date. He's wearing a crisp navy shirt, and asking the kinds of questions that could pass for ordinary getting-to-know-you chit-chat, but actually provide highly useful nuggets of information for rapists. Do I have many friends locally? Am I close to my family? Do I live alone? Do I get on with my neighbours? He probably thinks he's coming across as interested in my life, rather than concerned about whether someone will hear a struggle or see him leaving the scene. He probably doesn't think I suspect a thing, but he doesn't know me.

I excuse myself to go to the toilet and deliberately leave my glass of Shiraz alone with him: a test. I can feel his eyes on me as I walk to the bathroom. I feel them land on my body, sliding over my hair, my waist, my arse, my legs. I turn to look at him over my shoulder. His gaze darts back up to my eyeline. I give him an indulgent, flirty smile and he winks. He literally winks.

I head through the door leading to the toilets, and once I'm on the other side, I shudder. *Eughhh.* I walk past the ladies' and slip through the fire escape at the end of the corridor instead. The air is cool as I step out into the alleyway where the bins are kept. I came here a few weeks ago and I remember the layout. It's a new place, not far from my flat.

I hold the fire escape door ajar and look around for something to jam it open with. I scan the ground, but I can't see anything. I reach into my handbag and pull out an eyeshadow palette. It's longish and narrow; it'll do. I wedge it between the doors and then I creep, ninja-like, to the front of the bar. I peer through a gap in the curtains and watch Julian. That's my date's name. Quite a nice name, actually. Wasted on someone like him.

For a minute, as I watch him sitting there, his back to me, staring into space, I wonder if maybe I've got this all wrong. He looks bored. My glass of Shiraz is untouched. Perhaps he's not going to tamper with it after all. Maybe all those questions came naturally to him, and he just has a unique interest in my neighbourly relations. But then, suddenly, he leans forward. He moves my drink closer to him. Here he goes. I was right. My gut's always right. Julian reaches into his jeans pocket and pulls something out. He looks around, checking no one's looking, and then he brings his hand up to my glass, swiftly dropping a pill into my wine. Done. In less than a second. He slides my glass back across the table, before reclining in his chair.

I knew it, but even my suspicions weren't enough to prepare me for this: the feeling. The prickling, cold, sinking, empty, suffocating feeling. The icy vice that constricts my heart, my throat, my lungs. Again. And again. And again.

I turn to head back to the fire escape. My shock is morphing into something different now: a lip-curling, snarling sense of disgust. The kind of disgust that makes your skin crawl.

'Fucking asshole. Fucking prick. Fucking, fucking prick,' I spit to myself as I pace down the alleyway. I knew Julian was a bad guy, but a *rapist*? How dare he?

I pull the fire escape door open, scoop my eyeshadow palette off the ground and slip back inside. For a moment, I pause in the corridor and catch my breath. Adrenaline is surging through me. Rage. A normal woman would call the police at this point. But a normal woman would never have been paranoid enough in the first place to pretend to go to the toilet, only to sneak out of the fire escape and spy through a window to watch what her date does when he has five minutes alone with her drink. Nope. A normal woman would have gone to the loo, done a pee and topped up her lipstick. Or she'd have texted a friend about her hot date, feeling giddy with hope and excitement.

Now, let's think about what would have happened to a normal woman.

A normal woman would have headed back to her date, smiling prettily, before sitting down and drinking her drugged drink. Then, a short while later, that normal woman would have started feeling far more drunk than she normally does after just a couple of drinks, but she'd probably blame herself. She'd wonder if maybe she'd drunk too much. Or maybe she'd blame herself for having not eaten earlier in the day because she didn't want to look fat in her dress. Or maybe she'd blame herself because that's just what she does; she blames herself. And then, just as she started to feel woozy and a bit confused, her date would take her outside for some fresh air and she'd be grateful to him. She'd think he was caring and responsible, when really, he was just whisking her out of sight, before she started to look less like she was drunk and more like she'd been drugged. And then the next thing she'd know, she'd be staggering into the back of a cab and her date would be asking her to tell the driver where she lived. And when she'd barely be able to get the words out and her date made a joke to the driver about how drunk she was, she'd feel small and embarrassed. And then she'd find herself slumping into her date's open arms, flopping against his big manly body, and she'd feel grateful once more that this man was taking care of her and getting her home safe.

And then, once the taxi slowed down and she blinked her eyes open and found they'd pulled up outside her flat, she'd notice in a fleeting moment of clarity that when the driver asked for the fare, her date thrust two crisp ten-pound notes towards him in a weirdly premeditated move, as though he'd known this moment was going to happen all along. As though he'd had the cash lined up, the plan set, and she'd feel something. Something. But then she'd be staggering out of the taxi, even sloppier than when she got in, and her legs would be buckling, and she'd cling to her date for support, her make-up now smudged, her eyes half-closed, her hair messy.

She'd look a state and he'd ask her which flat was hers, and she'd walk with him to her front door, to the flat where she lives alone. To the place that's full of books and cute knick-knacks from charity shops and colourful but inexpensive clothes. She'd unlock her front door, her hand sliding drunkenly over the lock, and she'd lead him into the place she's been using as a base to try to get ahead in life, and then he'd look around, keen-eyed, until he spotted her bedroom and he'd draw her in.

And then all of a sudden he'd be in her bedroom and she wouldn't be able to remember if she'd asked him back or not or quite how this happened, and it would all be moving so fast and her thoughts would be unable to keep up – they'd keep sliding away – and he'd be kissing her and she'd be unsure what was happening as he pulled off her dress and she'd wonder, did she ask for this? Does she want this? Has she been a 'slut' again? But the thoughts would be weak, they'd keep falling away and he'd be confident and he'd be certain and he'd be good-looking and he'd be pulling off her bra and taking off her knickers. He'd be pushing himself inside her.

The next day, he'd be gone by the time she woke up. She'd be blocked, unmatched, and she'd feel like such a state. She'd blame herself. She'd hate herself. She'd feel like a mess. She wouldn't want to leave the house.

That normal woman used to be me. But I'm not normal any more.

I'm better now. I'm *much* better.

I draw in a deep gulp of air and head to the toilets. They smell stale, musty. I flick on the lights and take in my reflection in the mottled mirror. My eyes are glassy, my expression blank.

I root around inside my handbag for my lipstick. There are two compartments to my Furla bag and they're a bit like me. In the front compartment, which is the one I open in public places, I have all the things you'd expect a woman to bring on a date: lipstick, make-up, phone, wallet, hairbrush, even condoms. When things go well, that's all I need. But the pocket that sits behind that one is a different story. That's where I keep my pepper spray, my flip knife, my handcuffs, my duct tape, my drugs.

I knew Julian would be bad, but I didn't expect him to be this predatory. I heard about him a few weeks ago. An article caught my eye in the local paper. Julian Taylor, a twenty-eight-year-old from Dulwich, south London, had been given a twelve-month suspended sentence for assaulting his girlfriend. She'd been left with a broken nose and needing stitches, traumatised, in a counselling programme, yet he was free to walk. Fucking joke. My blood boiled when I read the article. It contained a mugshot of Julian. A striking-looking guy, undeniably attractive with an endearing, feminine-looking beauty spot under his left eye. Then, one night, I was bored. Swiping on Tinder, I came across his profile. I sensed I knew him from somewhere. I wracked my brains. And it hit me: the guy in the mugshot. Gripped by morbid curiosity, I swiped right. We matched. He messaged and I humoured him, not really sure of my game plan. After a while, he asked if I wanted to meet for a drink, and I thought: why not? Why not get to know him a little better and see just how bad he is?

I pull off the cap of my lipstick and apply a slick of it to my lips. It's one I haven't used for a while. I glance at the label: Dangerous Liaison by Charlotte Tilbury. Ha! How apt. I press my lips together and pout in the mirror, before dropping the lipstick back in my bag.

I reach into the second compartment and twist open the top of a multivitamin bottle, which actually contains a couple of dozen tabs of Rohypnol I bought online a while ago, in anticipation of something like this. It was disturbingly easy to get my hands on them. Selling roofies is meant to be illegal in this country, but British law can't exactly stop sellers in Thailand and China shipping here. An eight-year-old with an iPad could find their online shops. Vendors brag about their products: 'Best date rape drug!' and 'Highest potency Rohypnol!' Their sales spiels include shit like, 'It won't matter if the police come, there won't be any trace in the body after 5–6 hours' and 'Guarantees complete amnesia. She won't remember a thing!'

Is it any wonder I've become the way I am? Seriously. How is it even possible to relax for a second in a world where men invent such a thing, where they buy it? How is it possible to not be raging?

I slip a pill into the front pocket of my handbag for easy access. My sinking, snarling sense of disgust turns into something else: excitement. Nothing's more fun than playing a player at their own game. Drugging the druggers. Abusing abusers. Controlling controllers. Don't worry, I'm not into raping rapists. Sometimes I murder them, but I'm not sure if Julian warrants the special treatment. I'll probably just get him into a drugged stupor, rough him up, leave him in a park somewhere, or an alleyway. He'll wake up tomorrow morning, bloodied and bruised, having been pissed on by drunks, shat on by pigeons, and he'll realise not all women are as weak and defenceless as he thought. He could do with a taste of his own medicine. Literally.

I pull my bag up on to my shoulder. I'm ready for action. I swagger back out into the bar.

Okay, that's a lie. I don't swagger, I walk daintily on my Zanotti heels while touching my hair. But inside I'm swaggering. Julian is sitting there, gazing into space, his eyes misted over.

I wonder what he's thinking about, if anything. 'Hey,' I say as I approach the table.

The focus comes back into his eyes. 'Hey,' he replies.

I bat my lashes a little as I sit down, as though I'm still attracted to him.

A silence passes between us.

'I'm starving,' I say with a sigh. 'Skipped dinner. Should have got a bag of crisps or something. Would you mind getting some from the bar? Don't make me stand any more in these heels, they're killing me!'

I gesture towards my six-inch stilettos. Julian looks at them, perplexed, clearly unable to relate to female shoe troubles. I imagine forcing one of the spiked heels into his eye, his aqueous humour making it shine.

I really need a moment alone with his drink.

'Please,' I implore. I move my foot closer and stroke my toes against his ankle. That should do it.

Julian's face softens.

'Sure,' he replies with a laugh, before getting up.

'Thanks, Julian!' I beam, smiling through my unease, as I pick up my wine and pretend to take a sip. The wine is wet against my upper lip. It sloshes against Dangerous Liaison like a wave.

I watch as Julian heads towards the bar.

I place my handbag on the table, using it as a screen for what I'm about to do (a perk of doing this as a woman!). I grab the pill from the front pocket, glance over my shoulder to see Julian leaning against the bar, his back to me, as Lawrence the barman roots around for a bag of crisps. I drop the pill into Julian's pint. Done. It disintegrates into the golden liquid, lost among the rivulets of tiny bubbles. Then I tip a third of my wine into a wilting aloe vera pot plant on the table, to make it look like I've been drinking.

Julian comes back with a tray laden with a bag of salt and vinegar crisps and two shots, messily poured. I try to look relaxed, hoping he isn't observant enough to notice the tiny red splashes on the aloe vera leaves.

'I got us some shots,' he says proudly.

'Nice!' I reach for one. We neck them. Tequila doesn't really make me wince, but I do a wince-face like a girl. Julian's eyes water and he winces too, using his pint as a chaser. He downs half of it in one go. Perfect. A lad. He doesn't seem to notice the strange taste. I guess in comparison to the tequila, his drugged pint probably tastes pretty good.

'Glad you're up for shots. My kind of girl!' Julian says as he thuds his beer back on to the table.

'They'll help us get to know each other better,' I purr, eyeing him sultrily and placing my elbows on the table in a way that pushes my breasts together, making my cleavage full.

Julian's eyes immediately wander south, like a moth to a flame. Two emotions pass over his face: desire and determination. Misty eyes, tense jaw. Then he glances towards my wine. My drugged fucking wine. I reach for the crisps instead, tearing the bag open.

'So, been on many Tinder dates then?' I ask as I pop a crisp into my mouth.

Like so many guys, Julian insists he hardly dates. Says he goes on the apps a lot, but he doesn't often meet up with matches because he's 'busy with work' and 'doesn't usually click with that many people', as though he and I have some sort of profound connection.

I smile, before biting into another crisp. I wonder if any of this is true. Julian doesn't look like someone who's avoiding female attention. He works out, a lot. In fact, his first picture on Tinder was a gym selfie. For a moment, I couldn't figure out where I knew him from, and I was into it. Looks-wise, he's definitely my type, with his ripped, imposing physique. He's hot. And he was charming to chat to as well, disturbingly so, given what I knew about him. He seemed sweet, unsure of himself almost. He seemed to be really trying to impress me. He claimed that, like me, he was into fashion and reading, although when I dug a little deeper, his love of fashion didn't amount to much more than being a regular customer at Topman, and the last book he seemed to have read was *Of Mice and Men* at school.

I glance at his beer. He's two-thirds down. He'll be feeling fuzzy soon. I reach for another crisp.

'So, what makes me the lucky girl then?' I ask, playing along with his I-never-date story. I eat another crisp.

Julian makes a comment about how I 'just seemed special'. I resist the urge to smirk. Puh-lease. It's because I'm pretty, I live alone, and he thought I'd be rapeable. This sentiment is confirmed by the way that even in his increasingly wasted state, he keeps glancing eagerly at my wine, as though urging me to drink it. I'm a bit worried that soon he might start noticing it's barely gone down in volume. I need to get him more fucked up before he senses something's wrong. Not that he seems particularly on it.

I suggest another round. Julian nods.

I head to the bar and order tequilas.

Taking the tray from the bar, I carry the shots back to Julian.

He smiles, grabbing one and tossing it down his neck, not bothering with salt or lime. He starts telling me about some night out he had recently, going on about some club. Some DJ.

'Cool!' I act interested as I tip a small amount of salt on to my hand and lick it off.

Julian watches my tongue. I knock my shot back.

He's talking about the set. I'm not really listening. Instead, I take in his unfocused eyes, his paling complexion. He's talking shit. Laughing at nothing. His mouth is slack. He doesn't look attractive like this at all. That would have been me.

I keep listening, making the odd comment here and there, eating crisps, watching him. He's looking more and more out of it. I need to get him out of here before the bar staff notice.

'Julian,' I interrupt, slipping my foot back between his ankles, stroking with my toes. 'Let's go back to mine.' I reach across the table and take his hand.

He smiles, eyes black, keen.

'Yeah, yeah let's do that,' he slurs. He blinks, his eyes roll.

He's beginning to lose it, but seems pleased that we're going back to mine, as though his plan is coming together after all.

Julian attempts to stand, but staggers and clutches the table for support so heavily that his near-empty pint rattles against the shot glasses.

'Come on.' I head over to his side of the table and place my arm around his back, offering him some support. He slings his strong, heavy arm around my shoulders, gratefully. 'Let's go,' I say before moving towards the door. We walk slowly, our bodies locked together, moving like an arthritic beetle.

I pull the door open. I glance over my shoulder towards the bar. The staff aren't paying any attention. Julian and I scuttle on to the street.

'Where y'place?' Julian slurs.

'This way,' I reply, steering him down the street towards the park where I want to deposit him. It's not far, just around the corner, a little way past my flat.

Hobbling along, it's hard to walk. Julian must be thirteen stone, maybe fourteen, built like a brick shithouse, yet despite him nearly crushing me I know I'm the one in control right now. If I let go, he'll collapse to the ground like Bambi on ice.

I did this to him. Julian is putty in my hands. The feeling is strange: I feel powerful, knowing he's at my mercy. And as we shuffle along like drunks, I wonder: is this why men use date rape drugs? I'd always thought it was about getting a guaranteed fuck, but now I see it's about having a sense of complete control. It's about being godlike. Perpetrators wanting to reduce women to toys. Play things. Real-life blow-up dolls. It could be the fucked-up reason why good-looking men like Julian, who wouldn't have any trouble getting women into bed, would bother.

My heart jumps. Further down the street, I spot someone I recognise: my lover, Abay. He works at my local gym. *Fuck.* He's wearing his gym hoodie; he must be on his way home. He's got his head down, probably with earphones in, lost in his own world. He doesn't look like he's seen me yet, but I can't have that happening.

Cursing, I turn Julian around.

'Come on.'

I lead him back down the road, towards my flat, my heart hammering in my chest. I'm half expecting Abay to call out my name. What would he make of seeing me with a drugged man?

We reach my building. I punch in the door code, my hand clammy with sweat. Julian leans against me, his weight piling into me. I glance over my shoulder: Abay's getting closer. His head is still down though.

I push the door open and pull Julian inside. We cross the foyer and slip out of sight.

I breathe a sigh of relief and press the button for the lift. I'll take him upstairs for five minutes, make sure Abay is long gone before we head back out.

The lift arrives and we get in. Julian glances around. I feel a tremor of unease. I didn't intend to bring him here. I don't want this creep anywhere near my home. But it's not like he'll remember where I live in the morning. I bought the roofies that guarantee complete amnesia.

Nine floors up, we emerge. The hallway smells fresh: jasmine with a hint of rose. I've lived here for five years now, and I still don't know where that smell comes from. There's no air freshener plugged into a socket, no potpourri, but it always hits me when I step out of the lift: home. I reach into my handbag for my key. Julian paws at my waist, groping, his breath heavy on my neck as I unlock my front door, shiver out of his grasp and step into my flat.

Julian follows me in. Even in his drugged state, he pauses – stupefied, impressed. It's hard not to be by a massive Mayfair penthouse – pristine-clean, decorated with the highest-end, most luxurious furnishings around. I can't help feeling smug. Seeing people gawp over my beautiful flat never gets old.

I head to the open-plan kitchen to pour us glasses of wine. I need to gather myself. Plus, I may as well put half a roofie into Julian's to send him over the edge. He's still a little too alert for my liking. I open the kitchen cupboard and retrieve two wine glasses. Baccarat crystal for me. A cheap glass I never use for Julian. I'm not having him dropping my crystal. I glance over my shoulder at him. He's leaning against an armchair for support, blinking at the paintings on the wall: some contemporary pieces I picked up from an independent gallery down the road. I reach for a bottle of Antinori Tignanello Toscana. A great wine. Too good for Julian, but I only have good wine. I uncork it and pour a small glass for him – just enough to take away the taste of the roofie I crumble in – before pouring a bigger glass for myself.

I pick it up and take a sip. Notes of plum, cherry and dark chocolate burst over my tongue. Delicious. I place my glass back down, stuff the cork into the bottle and turn to put it back on the counter, when Julian's voice distracts me.

'What's this?' he says.

I look round to see him staggering towards my British Fashion Industry Awards trophy: a glass orb on the mantelpiece, engraved with the words 'Camilla Black, Editor of the Year, *Couture* Magazine' and the British Fashion Industry Awards logo. Julian grabs it, peering at the engraving.

'Don't touch that,' I hiss, swooping over and snatching it out of his hands, cradling it like a baby. If he'd dropped it, I would have killed him right here. Right fucking here.

'Camilla?' Julian says, raising an eyebrow.

I roll my eyes.

He knows me as Rachel. Rachel off Tinder. I never use my real name on that site. If Julian googled my real name, he'd realise within seconds that I'm not your average Tinder girl. The thing is, I'm kind of famous. Not stop-you-in-the-street-and-ask-for-a-selfie famous, or paparazzi famous. I'm a fashion magazine editor – not exactly Taylor Swift, but people do know me. My face appears from time to time in the *Evening Standard*. I'm always at Fashion Week: London, Paris, New York, Milan. I have a big social media presence. And the magazine has a decent following. I'm the sort of person who can walk into a restaurant in Mayfair and get a table – the best table – without having to give my name, because the staff instantly know who I am. Shop assistants will lavish me with glasses of champagne and comment on the latest issue while I try on expensive shoes. My new dermatologist asked about our recent feature on probiotic skincare before I'd even mentioned where I work. That kind of thing.

'Camilla's my flatmate,' I lie. 'You shouldn't just grab other people's stuff.'

'Chill out,' Julian says. Or at least attempts to say. It comes out more like 'shallot'.

Ignoring him, I go to stash the award in my bedroom where it will be safe. I love that award. When I found *Couture* magazine, I found a home. A luxury style guide with a modest but affluent readership, we feature nothing but the highest-end labels, the most exclusive of designers. I adore my job there. Ever since I came into money, fashion has been my thing. Getting good clothes was life-changing, and if you think that sounds stupid, then you've probably never experienced the magic that comes with a designer wardrobe. Sprinkle the fairy dust of Gucci, Prada, Valentino, Givenchy or Lanvin over yourself and watch as people change the way they behave around you. Watch as they treat you differently. Do favours for you. Respect you. They don't even realise they're doing it. Fashion elevates you from the shadows. Good clothes change the shape and tone of your day. They can make an invisible girl an empress. Transform a monster into a queen. I wrap my award in an Hermès scarf and stash it in my wardrobe.

When I come back, Julian is lying on my brand-new Amode Minerale corner sofa. Handmade in Italy. Feather and foam cushions. Reverse stitching. The softest calf leather money can buy. I can't blame him, really. I'd probably want to collapse on to a huge, sumptuous sofa after consuming a roofie, two tequilas and a few beers too, but I still feel a prickle of irritation. He'd better not leave a big man-shaped dent in the cushions.

I walk over to the kitchen counter to get the wine. I take a sip as I head back to Julian, handing him his glass, before sitting down in my favourite armchair. I kick off my heels and throw my legs over the armrest. The armchair is much older than my Amode sofa and nowhere near as expensive. I'll probably be replacing it soon, so I let myself get comfortable. I take another sip of wine and eye Julian over the rim of my glass. He looks totally relaxed, as though melting into the leather.

He blinks slowly, eyes drifting over my flat. 'You don't have much stuff,' he says, slurring.

'Yes, I do,' I insist, huffily.

What's he talking about? I have a ton of stuff: an Artemide Demetra floor lamp in anthracite grey, a Verona oak coffee table with a polished marble top, an Elie Saab Brushstrokes rug crafted from silk and Tibetan wool, a Cattelan Italia Taxedo Magnum mirror, a genuine 1920s art deco marble sculpture by Enrique Molins-Balleste, a vintage opalescent Ceylan vase by René Lalique. And that's just in this part of the flat. I mean, what more does he want? I even have framed photos of friends on the walls. And pictures of my family. Or at least, the strangers I call my family.

The Bryces are a random family with lax privacy settings, whose profiles I found on Facebook. I liked the look of them in all their wide-smiled, rosy-cheeked, wholesome glory, so I saved a few of their pictures and had them printed. They live in Ohio, but you can't tell from their photos. I've invented a whole backstory for them. Hilary Bryce – who I tell my friends is my mum, Anne Black – teaches English at a private school. She's into gardening, baking, and country walks with the dogs . . . She loves reading, mostly romances, and she's a bit of a homebody. Prone to anxiety in the city, actually, which is why she never comes to London to visit. It's a bit much for her. My fictional dad (real name John Bryce, but I've renamed him Robert) is a mortgage advisor. A quiet, understated man, but diligent and kind. A loving father. I'm an only child and I was brought up in the quaint village of Somerleyton in Suffolk. I attended a private school locally and had an idyllic childhood – fishing for newts in the nearby lake, long dusky walks on Sunday afternoons with our old golden retriever, Sadie, playing with dolls in my bedroom in the evenings.

All my colleagues and friends buy the stories. I don't think they care enough to question, but I still go to Suffolk a few times a year to keep up appearances. I take larky pictures of myself on bike rides, me having picnics, me reading on the porch, which I post to my social media with captions like 'Countryside air and strolls! The ultimate medicine for the soul' or simply 'Home sweet home' with a string of heart emojis. The people viewing these pictures don't realise I'm alone in all of them, that I use a tripod with a camera on timer, taking fifty shots until I get one that looks sufficiently natural. They don't know that the gorgeous five-bedroom country house in all the pictures is one I rent every year from Airbnb. Costs a fortune. The owner must think I'm nuts staying there all alone.

Sometimes I find myself wondering what my life might have been like if I had been raised by a family like the Bryces. Maybe I'd feel safe, happy, at peace.

'You don't have *stuff*,' Julian reiterates, interrupting my thoughts.

I roll my eyes. 'I have loads of stuff,' I scoff. 'What do you call this?' I gesture towards my Molins-Balleste cold-painted sculpture of a nude woman holding a glass globe.

Julian doesn't respond.

Why are people so obsessed with stuff? I don't get it. I hate clutter. Minimalism is my thing. If I could live in an empty room, with just a bed, a few books and maybe a pot plant, I would. As long as it had a walk-in wardrobe, of course. That's the only part of my home that I like to be full, that I like to be *stuffed*. Otherwise, I prefer clean lines and open spaces, the purity of emptiness.

Except, apparently, that's not socially acceptable. It's not just Julian who's piped up about it. One of my friends, Annika, came over for brunch once and asked, with a look of concern in her eyes, if I was 'struggling to furnish the flat' as though I didn't have the money to. That hurt. That's when I went all out with the furnishings. I may have gone overboard with my choices: my art deco sculpture set me back £16,000 alone, but I was smarting from Annika's comment when I bought it. I'm still smarting from it now if I'm totally honest.

''S'nice flat, babe. Come here,' Julian says, beckoning me towards him.

I raise an eyebrow. Surely he doesn't still think we're going to fuck?

'Give me your phone,' I say, placing my wine glass on the coffee table. I feel like getting to know Julian a bit better.

'What? Why?' he says, although it's so slurred that it comes out more like 'wally'. Fitting.

'I need to make a call. Mine's run out of battery,' I tell him.

Hmmm. Not my finest lie. I am at home after all, with easy access to both a charger and socket.

''kay,' he says, reaching into his jeans pocket and pulling out his iPhone. He hands it to me.

I smirk. Can you imagine getting a fuckboy to hand over his phone under normal circumstances? As fucking if. That's the thing about Rohypnol, it makes you completely trusting. Utterly compliant.

'What's your PIN?' I ask.

'One, three, zero, seven,' he tells me, without quibbling. His eyes roll into the back of his head. He's losing it.

Probably his date of birth. I wouldn't put it past someone like him to be born on the 13th. It was probably a Friday too.

'Thanks, babe,' I say, before wandering over to the opposite side of my living room, where I have a grand piano. A Yamaha GC2 in polished mahogany. Told you I went all out with the furnishings.

I can't even read music, although I can play a few bars of 'Moonlight Sonata', having memorised the way one of my more musical friends' hands moved across the keys at a party once. I sit on the stool and type Julian's PIN into his phone. The screensaver is of a fluffy white dog – a bichon frise or something. Seriously?

The first thing I do is put his phone into airplane mode so it can't be tracked from here on out. I click into his emails. There are a few from work colleagues – Julian's a financial controller at a foreign bank – but they're boring: formal, to-the-point, profes-sional. He placed an order on ASOS recently, which happens to include the shirt he's wearing tonight. There are dozens of unread finance newsletters. I scroll down. He's been making a complaint about a protein shake he claims never arrived; the company insists it was signed for. Dull. There are a few other fitness-related things: emails from his gym about new hot yoga classes, spam about energy supplements and activity trackers, blah-blah-blah. An email from mattyboy92@hotmail.com catches my eye. Could be more inter-esting. I click into it, but it's just a message from a friend about booking tickets to see Ed Sheeran at the O2. Fuck me, he's basic.

I catch Julian looking over. He seems pretty far gone, but maybe I should fake a call just to be on the safe side. I pretend to be dialling. I hold the phone up to my ear.

'Hey, Becky! How's it going?' I ask, before shrinking behind the piano so Julian can't see me.

I click out of his emails and scroll through his gallery instead. There are a few pictures of him with what I can only assume is his brother – same nose, same eyes, same mouth. They're both in pink shirts; Julian's is baby pink, his brother's salmon. They've got matching black unbranded sunglasses hooked to the top of their button plackets and they're both smiling into the camera on a balcony somewhere. Probably Marbella or something. So nouveau riche. So try-hard. There are more pictures of the fluffy dog. The dog lying on its back. Julian cuddling the dog. The dog in a jumper. The dog with its tongue out, Julian posing next to it, also sticking his tongue out. Fucking hell. There are a few taken at some kind of street festival. Julian posing with friends around a bonfire. He looks stoned, eyes bloodshot, puffy.

I keep scrolling. It's just friends, the dog, a few gym selfies – quite a lot of gym selfies, actually – the dog and then, oh shit, what's this . . . ? A woman, naked in bed, with a split lip, eyes swollen shut, huge reddish-purple bruises all over her thighs. She looks unconscious. Beaten unconscious. Fuck. My heart hammers in my chest. My fingertips prickle with sweat. I scroll to the next picture. Julian's cock in her mouth. Her mouth bleeding on to his cock. She's lost teeth. He's grinning into the camera. My hairs stand on end. I glance over at him; the back of his head protrudes over the armrest.

I remember that I need to maintain my fake phone call.

'What are you up to?' I ask 'Becky' as I scroll on, my hand shaking.

Julian's fucking the same girl from behind now, there are scratches and bruises all over her back. I feel like I'm going to be sick, but I keep scrolling. It's the bichon-fucking-frise again.

Friends. A joint. A bowl of noodles. The gym. A sunset and then bam. Another one. An unconscious redhead with purple eyes, lying on a bed, legs spread, bite marks on her breasts and thighs. Smears of blood on her skin. Cunt. Fucking cunt. I want to scream. I want to charge to the kitchen, grab a knife and plunge it into Julian's neck. I scroll to the next shot. It's another blow job selfie. Perhaps it's Julian's signature move: stuffing his cock into the mouths of unconscious girls, grinning into the camera. In the next shot his dick is rammed so far down the girl's throat that he looks like he's suffocating her. Maybe she died that night. I realise I'm crying and flick the tears from my cheeks. I thought my date rape experience was bad. It was bad, but at least I got out in one piece. The only scars I had were emotional. God knows what these girls are going through now.

I don't want to see any more, but I need to know exactly what I'm dealing with. I knew Julian was bad – a rapist, a woman-beater – but this is a whole different league. I was going to drug him, mess him up a bit, abandon him in the park, but I'm not sure that's enough. He deserves harsher punishment.

I wade through more normal life pictures until I find shots of a petite, battered and bruised girl lying in an alleyway, her skirt hitched up around her waist. Jizz all over her pussy, covering her thighs. He's sick. He's so fucking sick. My skin is prickling. I'm scared. This monster is in my flat. I know he's drugged and disorientated, and I could take him down in a second, but I'm still freaked out. I keep scrolling. Dog. Gym. Dog. Friends. Brother. Food. Car. Girl. This one looks barely eighteen. Out cold on a bed, make-up smeared all over her face, her mouth hanging open. I scroll onto another shot. Her skin is covered in red slap marks. Julian's fucking her from behind. I can't take any more.

I slam the phone down on the piano, forgetting it's a fucking piano. Jangled notes ring out. For fuck's sake.

Julian turns his head and blinks groggily, stupidly, curiously towards me. I look back at him, my heart pounding. Can he see the fear, the tears in my eyes, the fact that I'm shaking? I force a smile and push it all down.

I need to be strong. I need to be tough. I need to be powerful. I need to be a huntress. Because tonight, Julian *has* to die.

Chapter Two

I feel like a kid before Christmas as I think of the kill I've got lined up for Julian.

I know I should probably be more morose after the pictures I've just seen, but I can't help smiling to myself as I look out of the window of the minicab, lost in thought, London passing blankly over my irises. It's a slaughter I've been imagining for a while. A fantasy that's been building in my mind. It's going to be spectacular. I knew I'd find the right person to bring it to life with eventually. Or death, in my case. Maybe this date was written in the stars.

'Stop it!' I grumble as Julian attempts to slide his hand over my thigh, groping up towards my crotch.

He's out of it, his eyes barely open. The second roofie tipped him over the edge, but it's still not enough to stop him being a gropey perverted prick. I keep batting his hand away, but within seconds, he's at it again. Bat. Grope. Bat. Grope. Bat. Grope. Is he going to keep this up all the way to Hayes?

The driver glances up at the rear-view mirror. He works for a dodgy minicab company down the road. They have terrible reviews. One of the drivers was in the local paper recently, arrested for stealing from elderly passengers. I'd never dream of using them usually, but they're a good choice for tonight since it seems they give the authorities a wide berth. I don't want anyone talking to the police about having seen me. I avoid the driver's gaze, even though I'm already in disguise, wearing a new wig: a long, wavy blonde ombré one I bought off Amazon called 'The Ciara'. I'll be Ciara tonight. Her hair is the complete opposite of my naturally dark, neat, shoulder-length bob. Julian hasn't even noticed. I've teamed my wig with a denim cap I bought from H&M during my lunch break a few weeks ago. I wouldn't be seen dead in such a thing usually, but it was a good addition to my disguise wardrobe. I gave Julian a cap to wear, too, and a hooded coat. Told him it was cold out. He was too out of it to question anything. I wanted to keep his face covered, not that I really need to. He can barely hold his head up as it is.

Tonight will be my last kill. I have to stop, I really do, but sometimes I just can't help myself. Besides, I can't let someone like Julian walk the streets. I simply can't. It's not like I'm going to report him to the police. What's the point when the entire system is stacked in favour of men like him?

Less than 2 per cent of reported rapes even result in a charge or conviction. Even if the police got hold of the photos on Julian's phone, they'd probably still go easy on him. He'd probably get a slap on the wrist, maybe a few years behind bars. Then he'd get out having served half his sentence, and he'd be back to smoking pot with his friends and taking selfies with his dog, like nothing ever happened.

No, I can't let that happen. I won't tolerate that kind of bullshit. Laughable sentences, suspended sentences, community orders, blind eyes turned to people like him. I can't pretend it's okay. No, sometimes I fight back. Sometimes I snap.

Death is what Julian deserves, and death is what I'm going to give him.

But it's risky. After all, I didn't exactly plan to kill Julian tonight. If I had, I'd have been a hell of a lot stealthier about it. I wouldn't have met him at a bar for one thing. But I think I can get away with it, just about. We didn't particularly stand out in the bar. No one was paying us much attention. And I'm pretty sure Abay didn't see us. I can get away with it. The police aren't too hard to outsmart.

I sigh, peering out of the window. We're far out of central London now and I scan the streets, trying to get my bearings. We're getting nearer to Julian's resting place. I recognise an old police station, converted into cheap flats. This part of London feels darker than Mayfair. It's as though the streetlights don't shine as brightly. Cheaper models, not as many. I like it. Every time I come here, on a certain level, I relax. It almost feels more like home than Mayfair. Mayfair is who I want to be, Hayes is who I am. My veins are the dark streets, pulsing with traffic. There's wreckage all around: craterous potholes, crumpled railings, abandoned cars, derelict homes. Nothing's ever repaired. It's all broken. The poverty's inescapable. The air perpetually stinks.

Julian's hand creeps over my thigh again. Fucking hell. I bat it away. Although, can I blame him for feeling frisky? I've told him we're on our way to a sex party at my friend's house. I said that's what I was talking about when I borrowed his phone. Still laughing to myself about that one.

I ask the taxi driver to pull into a lay-by, where Julian and I disembark. Julian looks around at the dull A-road lined with bushes.

'Where's your friend's place?' he asks, although it comes out more like 'woplice'. I'm surprised he's still talking. That shouldn't last much longer.

'This way,' I reply, slipping my arm through his for support.

Julian nearly crushes me as we walk down the road towards my garage. I'm small, and he feels even heavier now than he felt before, his body a dead weight, but it's not like I could get the taxi driver to drop us off right next to my deepest, darkest, most secret place, even if I did choose to use a dodgy minicab firm.

Julian and I shuffle along, one step at a time, until finally we arrive at a row of garages. The ninth one along, with the peeling burgundy door, is mine. Julian looks around, perplexed. He mumbles something but I ignore it. We walk towards my garage. I reach into my jacket pocket and retrieve my key. I changed my outfit during our date, swapping the Chloé dress I was wearing for a pair of leggings, a hoodie, a puffer jacket – all black, all from H&M. I'll dispose of them later. Julian didn't notice my outfit change either. He was probably too busy picturing me naked to have even remembered what I was wearing in the first place.

'Wha . . . ?' he slurs as I insert the key into the garage door and unlock it.

'Just sit down. I need to get something. Some sex toys,' I explain, trying not to smile.

Julian flops down on to the tarmac as I pull up the creaking garage door.

This garage is where the real me lives. It's where I keep everything I need for my dark pastimes: a wide selection of the sharpest knives and cleavers, a few choice tools I keep as torture implements (a screwdriver, a pair of pliers, a mini saw, rusty nails, a corkscrew), an axe, a vat of acid, latex gloves, cable ties, a hammer, rope, drugs, bin bags, a few more wigs, a few more hats. Stuff like that. I have a bunch of ill-fitting men's shoes I picked up in Primark and a load of socks that I layer on when I wear them. Better that the footprints I leave at crime scenes resemble those of a size ten or eleven man than a size six woman.

I've also got a bin bag full of bits and pieces I've stolen from various rapists, wife beaters and paedophiles who've been on my radar for a while. According to forensic science theory – Locard's exchange principle – the perpetrator of a crime will always bring something to a crime scene and leave with something from it, and both can be used as evidence. But what if the perpetrator leaves a ton of red herrings? What if the perpetrator leaves five people's DNA? Then what? Then who's the perpetrator? I like thinking of the police, following a million different pointless leads, spinning their wheels, getting nowhere. Or, best-case scenario, they bang up a paedophile rapist piece of shit for my crimes, while I slip through the net, undetected. It makes me smile.

I like fucking with people, if you hadn't guessed already.

The only furniture in my garage is an old armchair that smells of damp, and a cheap, nasty chest of drawers. The top drawer contains my burner phones. Ones with pay-as-you-go SIMs that I use for getting up to no good, like ordering roofies online or going Tinder-hunting. The middle drawer's full of random crap – crime novels, newspaper clippings, a few notebooks where I jot down thoughts and add to my hit list.

The bottom drawer is my favourite. Like every serial killer, it's where I keep a box of trinkets, souvenirs from my kills. I know, I'm that clichéd. Like something from a movie. I always thought I'd be tough enough to resist that particular trope – after all, I do hate clutter – but I couldn't help myself. I guess I'm just a sentimental old schmuck like all the rest. I wanted tokens too. Mementoes. I keep them inside an old aluminium box sealed with a padlock, the combination of which is the one I used for my bike lock back when I was eleven. Imagine if that girl could see me now. God no, she'd have nightmares.

I look over at Julian, passed out on the ground. Perfect. I hook my forearms under his armpits and pull him inside. He slumps on to the floor. I yank the garage door shut and flick on a camping lamp.

I feel like having a little meander down memory lane. I find my box of mementoes and kick off my trainers before settling, cross-legged, in my skanky old armchair. I place it on my lap and click through the dials of the lock, entering the combination: three, eight, two, four. The padlock springs open. I slide it off and open the box.

The first item I pick out is a silver cock ring I pulled off the corpse of a 'sugar daddy' who went by the name of David online. His real name was Edmond Wyatt.

I had noticed some sex workers sharing pictures of his ugly mug on forums, warning each other that he was using sugar daddy sites to sweet-talk women, convincing them to meet him in hotel rooms. He'd promise £500 for a fuck, but then beat them unconscious the second the door closed. Then, he'd rape them, steal their stuff and leave them with nothing. I couldn't resist. I posed as a hooker and reeled him in.

We met at a hotel in Bond Street. 'David' was mid-sixties and looked even worse than his pictures had suggested, with dark rings around his eyes and sallow, pasty skin. It made my heart hurt thinking how desperate these girls must have been to be willing to fuck him. I get that £500 is a lot when you're broke, but he was so rank even £5,000 would have felt low. His eyes were bright blue – wolf-like, cold, blazing. We went up to the hotel room. My hand was clamped around the knife in my trench-coat pocket. The door clicked closed. We were alone. He placed an envelope of cash on the bed. I looked into his wolf eyes and waited for a blow, but he lunged towards me and kissed me instead. It took everything in my power not to vomit into his mouth. I pulled away. His hands were shaking with anticipation. He started trying to remove my clothes, his fingers fluttering around the lapels of my coat. I excused myself and nipped into the bathroom, in shock.

Closing the door, I wondered what if these girls were talking shit? What if David was just a regular punter and someone had a vendetta against him? What if he wasn't planning to hurt me at all and only wanted sex? I don't approve of crusty old fucks paying vulnerable women for sex, but it's not exactly a murderable offence.

I couldn't knife him for that. When I came out of the loo again, he was naked. Standing there in all his skinny, wrinkly, flaky, shrivelled, repulsive glory, with a silver cock ring on his dick.

I gripped the knife in my pocket, not knowing what to do. I'd never prayed for someone to punch me before, but I did then. I walked up to him, and he came to me again, clearly wanting to kiss, his hands quivering with excitement, rattling around my tits. Then, all of a sudden, our eyes met and his pupils exploded like volcanos, his eyes dilating, eclipsed by blackness, and I knew it was coming. His quivering hand hardened into a fist, and he swung at me. I ducked, pulled out my knife and plunged it into his stomach. Pulled it out of him. Plunged it in. In and out, in and out, piercing him like a pin cushion. I was crying tears of joy, overexcited. I couldn't contain myself. I was gasping with relief.

After, I went into the bathroom, cleaned up a bit, changed my clothes and left. I was wearing a blonde wig that day, dark sunglasses. I even added a fedora. The papers were all over that story for weeks. A grainy CCTV image of me leaving the hotel ended up everywhere. At the time, the papers dubbed me the 'Sugar Daddy Slayer'.

I liked that, although I was paranoid for a few weeks. Some detective – DCI Wheelan, I think his name was – really hawked the image to the press, begging for someone who recognised me to come forward. No one did though. I don't think anyone really cared that Edmond had been murdered. He hadn't exactly been a sympathetic character. It turned out that he had convictions for rape, GBH and sexual assault. Not particularly surprising. He didn't have any close friends, no family. It's not like he had relatives pleading with the media to help find his killer. The only person who really seemed to care about bringing me to justice was Wheelan.

It's funny – you can get away with murder far more easily if you choose your victims right. The city was able to breathe a sigh of relief once Edmond was gone: one less piece of trash to worry about. People were retweeting my picture, a few were even thanking me, calling me a hero, using praying emojis. It was great. I even hit 'like' on a few of the tweets. Didn't dare retweet them though.

I drop the cock ring back into the box and wipe my hands on my leggings. Just the memory of Edmond makes me feel dirty.

I pick up a decaying pink rose, a token from a paedophile I met online. I posed as an eleven-year-old girl called Emily in a chat room for kids and waited for the nonces to come. The messages were buzzing through in seconds. Dick pics, wanking videos, bored 'Hey, how are you?' messages, but it was @justaguy78 who caught my eye.

I could tell he was the real deal. His opening messages were sweet and gentle; he started softly, softly, going for the long game. Always the way for the most manipulative, committed and dangerous groomers. Conversation was friendly to begin with – light, peppered with 'lols', as he tried to build my trust. He told me his name was Darren and asked questions about my family. Like Julian, he wanted to make sure I was an easy target, with few people around who cared about me. I told him daddy wasn't in the picture, mummy drinks – poor lil' Emily. 'That sucks, babe, I'm here for you. You got me to talk to now lol,' he said. A few days later, the messages intensified. 'What you up to? Feeling a bit lonely tonight, babe xxx Wish you were here' and 'I'd love a cuddle. Bet you smell so good!'

'Wish I could cuddle u n make u feel better!!! xxx,' I replied. The stream of delighted kisses he responded with felt like it was going on forever. Darren was over the moon.

It wasn't long before he started telling me how he 'can't talk to anyone like I can talk to you'. He said I was 'a smart, special, beautiful girl'. He opened up about some ex of his, saying she'd broken his heart, as a segue to ask me about boys. He wanted to know if

I'd ever kissed anyone. Ever seen a cock. Ever touched one. I said no. He said 'a mature girl like you needs a mature man' then he started sending sickening selfies of himself doing kiss-faces. Then a dick pic. 'This is what they look like lol! xxx'.

'Omg!!! Lol!' I replied with a string of monkey-covering-its-eyes emojis.

A few days later, he suggested we meet, saying how he'd been feeling 'really lonely' lately. Poor thing.

We arranged to meet in Darren's hometown of Hull. I suggested a park, the kind of place an eleven-year-old like Emily would want to meet. Darren seemed keen on that idea. I went up to Hull a few days earlier to scout out the parks, found one with an alleyway, no CCTV. I suggested we meet there and asked Darren to bring me pink roses – my favourite – so I'd know for sure it was him. I saw him standing at the end of the alleyway on the day we were meant to meet, greasy-haired and pale, wearing a childlike T-shirt with a pattern of dinosaurs under a black fleece jacket. He was holding the roses. He looked shifty. His eyes slid towards me, slid away. He coughed. I walked down the alleyway, purposefully, casually, like I was going somewhere, then I reached into my bag for the knife.

'Fucking nonce,' I growled as I spun round and slashed him.

The look in his eyes was priceless.

I stood, watching, as he dropped to the tarmac, blood oozing out of him, glistening red, staining his pathetic T-shirt. The roses fell from his grip. I pulled out a stem and fled.

I disappeared. The police thought a bloke killed @justaguy78, real name Alfie Morgan. Tripped them up with the size ten footprints in the mud. I wore men's clothes that day; I looked like any other grainy hooded criminal in the CCTV images that caught me fleeing the scene a few streets away. The local cops never saw through it. The case certainly never made its way to the Met. No one would ever have suspected I was behind it: Camilla Black, editor of *Couture*. As if.

There's a Casio watch from a rapist in my box too. A condom from another paedophile. A wedding ring from an abuser. The list goes on, but I can't sit here reminiscing all night. Julian's waiting for me. We're late for our sex party.

I grab a duffel bag from a hook on the wall and fill it with the things I'll need for his kill: rope, duct tape, cable ties, a spanner, a crowbar, a few other bits and pieces. Then I pick up my pièce de résistance – the one item I've been waiting to use for months: my crossbow. An Excalibur Crossbow Matrix Mega 405. Sharp arrows. Fast speed. Silent release. Maximum penetration. I've been gagging to use it and I feel a thrill of anticipation as I sling the case on to my back, before reaching down to turn off the lamp.

Julian lies drooping against the wall of my garage, eyes shut, mouth hanging open. I pull him out on to the tarmac outside.

'Come on you, we've got a sex party to get to,' I tell him as I pull down the garage door. It rattles into place.

Julian doesn't stir. I lock the door, checking a few times to make sure it's definitely locked. I always get a bit paranoid about that.

'Earth to Julian!' I trill, giving him a kick. 'Wakey-wakey!' He doesn't move a muscle.

For a terrible moment, I fear he might be dead. What if he's choked on his own vomit or something and I didn't notice? I'm meant to kill him. He's *my* kill. That would be such a fucking drag.

I crouch down to his level. 'Oi! Julian!' I poke his chest. 'You fucking asshole, wake up!'

I poke him again, harder, harder, until finally he stirs, blinking groggily, mumbling something.

'Get up!' I order him, tugging his arm.

It's not easy pulling a thirteen-stone man up from the ground, especially not while carrying a crossbow. But eventually I manage it.

'We need to get to the party. It's in full swing. We're late.'

Julian stands, swaying a little, leaning against me for support. 'Okay, okay,' he mumbles.

We stagger along. Arms linked, we're like a Victorian gentleman and lady having a promenade in a garden. Kind of. Okay, not quite. Julian keeps falling and I have to haul him up every five steps. We pass the garages and walk down the street towards the building where I'm taking him. Council flats in dark brick practically blend into the night sky. A few shoddy, crumbling terraced houses sit behind overflowing bins. The slabs of the pavement are cracked, uneven. We pass a wall that caved in during a car crash a few months ago. It still hasn't been repaired. Bricks have tumbled on to the street. No one's bothered to remove them. A man in an imitation Adidas tracksuit walks past us. He reeks of fags. He glances our way, but it doesn't bother me. Julian and I just look wasted. And for that reason, we fit in around here. Everyone looks a bit odd in this part of London; it's the bin of the city, full of lost souls – addicts, criminals, the homeless, waifs and strays. Julian and I blend in perfectly.

I wait until the man's out of sight, then steer Julian down a narrow path towards an old council block. I noticed it one day when I was on my way to Poundland to replenish my duct tape supply. All the tenants had been evicted, and the building was empty, boarded up. It lingered in my mind and I thought it might come in handy later.

'Here we are!' I declare, once we reach our destination.

The windows and doors are covered in plywood. The walls have been spray-painted with nonsensical graffiti. I look up and take in the building's twelve-storey expanse. It doesn't look like an ideal venue for a saucy sex party but Julian's too out of it to care at this point. I let go of his arm. He hobbles forward a few steps before slumping to the ground.

I walk to the entrance and set to work removing the plywood boarding so I can jimmy the door open.

This is the part of the night I've been the most worried about. It's usually quiet around here, but the last thing I need is someone spotting me breaking in, and pissing all over my parade before I've had a chance to have any fun. Fortunately, the plywood boarding has been shoddily installed, and I manage to wrench it off easily with my crowbar.

I glance over my shoulder at Julian. He's staring at the ground; he doesn't have a clue what's going on.

Right, now I have to pick the lock. I check no one's around and get to work. I reach into my bag for my tension wrench and slide it into the keyhole, before retrieving a paperclip from my bra. I twist the tension wrench and insert the paperclip, feeling for the pins in the lock. It takes all of my concentration and coordination to pick it and I'm regretting the wine and tequila. I twist the tension wrench again, feeling around with the paperclip but the lock's not budging. My heart hammers in my chest and I'm starting to sweat. What if I can't get the damn thing open? What if all this is for nothing? Just as I'm beginning to lose it and panic, my tension wrench glides clockwise, the door clicking open. Beautiful. I'm in.

I push the door open and gaze into the darkness inside: cobwebs, damp-stained walls, graffiti, dust, dereliction. I smile, before turning to drag Julian off the floor.

'Come on, you,' I say as I pull him inside.

I deposit him on the dirty linoleum, littered with sharps, bailiff letters, flyers, rubbish. A mouse darts across the corridor, making me jump. Julian doesn't react.

I close the door behind us and fasten it shut, slipping my crowbar through the two pull handles. I don't want to be disturbed.

Taking a deep breath to steady myself, I breathe in the dank, pungent air, feeling the emptiness of the building sink into me. The silence.

I turn to Julian, prostrate on the floor. 'Get up.'

He doesn't respond. I grab him and pull him to his feet. 'Get up!' I spit.

He hobbles up, confused, compliant.

'This way.' I lead him towards the staircase.

I scoped this building out a while ago, prized off one of the boards from a window, smashed it and snuck through.

The site was empty. I was surprised no one had moved in. No scagheads, no drunks, no homeless people. But when I thought about it, it made perfect sense. There aren't many homeless people in this part of town since they know they won't get a penny begging from anyone. And every third person is a scaghead around here; they're already settled. They don't need to take refuge in an abandoned council block.

I wandered through the dirty corridors, checking the building out. Drifting through its ghostly empty flats, littered with the debris of past tenants: discarded kids' toys, crack pipes, newspapers, broken electricals, ratty old unwanted clothes. I walked up to the very top of the building and had a poke around. That's when I discovered a door that opened on to a narrow external staircase leading to an asphalt roof. I climbed up and looked around, stunned. The roof was the best part of the whole place. I was towering over everything. It felt calm, peaceful, serene. I was out of sight. Above everyone else. Away from prying eyes. Away from CCTV. Invisible. Invincible.

That was when the seed was planted. This roof could be my playground, but how would I like to play? It wasn't long before an idea took hold. A certain painting had been stuck in my mind for a long time: *Saint Sebastian* by Andrea Mantegna. I first saw the small, narrow painting on a trip to Vienna for my friend Priya's thirtieth birthday. In between sipping champagne in Café Central and enjoying our hotel's five-star spa facilities, we took a trip to the Kunsthistorisches Museum to take in the Klimts, the Caravaggios and the Rembrandts, but it was Mantegna's work that caught my eye. I felt my heart swell when I saw the picture. Saint Sebastian's muscular body had been bound with rope to a marble pillar, amidst Roman ruins. Arrows littered his flesh, piercing his chest, ribs, stomach, waist, thighs. A giant one had impaled his head, slicing through his chin and emerging from his forehead. Blood seeped from his wounds. His dark eyes gazed towards heaven, pleadingly, full of pain.

I knew I had to bring it to life.

I bought my crossbow when I got home: a modern-day archer. And then I waited for my victim.

'Keep walking,' I urge Julian.

He's clutching the stairway banister, staggering, heavy-footed, but he does what I say. He keeps walking up the stairs, floor after floor. Maybe he thinks the sex party's taking place at the top. Or maybe he just doesn't know what the hell's going on. The latter's more likely.

Finally, we reach the top floor. I steer Julian down the corridor towards the roof door. I yank it open and push him on to the stone steps outside that lead up to the asphalt expanse. Julian spills on to the roof, collapsing on the ground. Dragging his drugged feet up twelve flights of stairs has clearly taken it out of him. I lower my crossbow, drop my duffel bag and stand back, hands on my hips, catching my breath. I look out over the city, at the smog, the glimmering lights scattered over the darkness, the moon, round and full, the stars obscured by clouds. I look down at Julian, lying on the asphalt. His eyes are wide open with the empty, unseeing stare of a date rape victim. I wonder what's going through his head; if he realises the tables have been turned. How does he feel to be the helpless one? The abused?

'Oh Julian . . .' I say, crouching down next to him.

I place my hand on his cheek, my fingers cold against his warm skin. His mouth is agape, but I can't help admiring his perfect, strong-boned features; such symmetry, such fine proportions, with that beauty spot setting the whole thing off, like the final expert stroke of an artist's brush that brings the painting together. He's so gorgeous. Why did he have to be so rotten?

I straddle him and begin unbuttoning his shirt. Even though I know he's a rapist piece of shit, I still find myself getting turned on as I expose his body, button by button. His chest is stunning, his muscles sculpted and strong. He's a wonder. I reach up and touch my breasts through my top; my nipples are hard. Urghh. If only he hadn't been such a creep. I'd have fucked his brains out if he'd been normal.

I edge backwards and reach down to Julian's jeans. Black skinnies. High street. I unzip his fly and peel them off. He really does have a great body: lean, muscular legs. I tug his jeans free from his ankles and toss them to the side, where I chucked his shirt. His boxers leave a lot to be desired: bobbling cotton with a scrolling Next logo. *Eww.* Why on earth would you want that logo on show? I peel them off, revealing his flaccid cock. I shudder as I think about where it's been, as the images of what he did to those girls flash through my mind. I toss his boxers aside and climb off his body.

Right, now for the tricky bit: binding Julian to the steel phone mast in the middle of the roof. I rummage in my bag for my rope. Once again, I hook my arms under his, and pull him over to the post. I can't be bothered to try to get him to walk. I'm pretty sure he's past walking at this point. He's barely conscious, dead weight. It takes all of my strength and coordination to pull him up and wrap the rope around his arms, shoulders, hands and feet, binding him to the mast.

I breathe a sigh of relief once I'm done and stand back to admire him. His head lolls against his chest. I take in his body. Those muscles. His slumped, defeated frame. I expected this to be good, but Julian's everything I could have wanted and more. My very own Saint Sebastian from Mantegna's painting. *Saint Sebastian* 2.0.

Saint Sebastian was sentenced to death by the Roman emperor Diocletian when it was discovered he was Christian. But despite being shot with arrows, he was nursed back to health by Saint Irene of Rome. Diocletian got him in the end though. He was clubbed to death eventually, and subsequently venerated throughout history as a Christian martyr. Unlike Diocletian, I'm going to get Julian the first time round. No one will be coming to save him. And he won't be martyred. Julian's death will be no great loss to the world. There's nothing holy about this cunt.

I unzip my crossbow bag and take it out, reverentially, stroking its strings like a harp. I load an arrow and stand back. I peer through the viewfinder, tracing it over Julian's body, as I decide where to fire my first shot. I linger over his heart, but I don't want his death to be quick and easy, so I lower the viewfinder down towards his thigh and pull the trigger. The arrow releases from the bow with a soft satisfying click. It glides through the night sky and thuds into Julian's thigh. He gasps, suddenly springing to life, sucking in air. He looks down at his thigh, sees the arrow piercing his flesh, the blood trickling down his leg, and he starts to whimper in fear. He begins to writhe, wrestling against his rope bindings. He looks up at me, and for a few seconds, it's like he hasn't been drugged at all. Adrenaline cuts through his stupor. His eyes are sharp and alert, full of pure, unadulterated terror. I smile. A delicious smile. One that spreads slowly over my face.

'W-w-wha' ya doin'? Sto'. Le' m' go!' Julian pleads, his speech slurred.

I laugh as I load another arrow into my bow. I lift it up and peer through the viewfinder.

'Nice six-pack,' I say, taking aim at one of his abs. I pull the trigger. The arrow releases: click, thud. Into his flesh.

Julian cries out and starts screaming. It's annoying.

I load another arrow. 'Oh, shut up!' I hiss, heaving the crossbow up and peering through the viewfinder.

'St-st—' Julian attempts to plead.

'Do you mean "stop"?' I ask. 'Hmmm . . .' I peer over the top of the crossbow and do a thoughtful face. 'Let me think about that for a second . . . Nope!'

I lower my crossbow and take aim at his neck. 'Le' m' go! Lemmo!' Julian begs.

I aim at his vocal cords and pull the trigger. Click. Thud.

He starts crying. His eyes are wide, stunned, leaking with tears. Blood pours from his neck. A thick stream cascades down his body.

Now that I've shut him up, it's time to really get going.

I load another arrow and shoot, piercing his other leg. Thud. Blood flows from his wound. I load, I shoot. Load, shoot. Load, shoot. Click, thud. Click, thud. I'm getting into the swing of things now. Hopping around the roof, loading my crossbow, firing my crossbow, shoot, shoot, shoot, click, click, click, thud, thud, thud, the moon glowing as I rain arrows into Julian's broken body.

With no arrows left, I drop my crossbow and stand in front of him like I stood in front of Mantegna's painting, yet this time, I'm admiring *my* handiwork. I watch the blood leaking from Julian's wounds, his neck decimated, his head hanging low like the bud of a drooping flower. I drink it all in. The black sky behind him, his blood shining in the moonlight, the arrows casting criss-cross shadows over his body, his skin almost translucent as the blood stills in his veins. Tears leak from my eyes, my soul overcome. My skin is covered in goosebumps. Julian looks so beautiful, I want to cry, I want to take a picture, I don't know what to do, I just stare, stare, stare. Walking around him, taking him in from all angles, taking a step closer, a step back. Observing, as his blood drips in the moonlight and he withers before my eyes. Something rotten turned pure. Something vile turned beautiful. Something evil turned sacrificial.

I gaze, I look, I marvel, I take it all in, until my heart can't take any more. Until I've memorised as much of it as I can. Finally, knowing I'll remember this forever, I gather my stuff, tamper with the crime scene, wrench an arrow from Julian's corpse as a trophy, and leave, my heart bursting, my eyes full of tears, my soul ablaze.

Chapter Three

I gaze at my reflection in the mirror of my face powder compact and top up my lipstick. I threw out Dangerous Liaison when I got home last night. I knew I'd never be able to wear it again without thinking of Julian trying to drug me.

Today's shade is a playful pink called Pretty Persuasive by Tom Ford. I press my lips together, admiring my pout, before clicking the lipstick closed and popping it in my desk drawer. I preen my hair, ruffling my fingers through it, and once satisfied, I snap my mirror shut, slip it into my drawer too, and pick up my phone.

'Hi, Jess. You can send Rayna up now,' I tell my assistant.

'Sure. I'll go and get her,' Jess replies.

'Thanks.' I hang up.

Jess is my sidekick. The yin to my yang. The good cop to my bad cop. She's everything I'm not: bubbly, sweet, warm. I'm known at work for being formal, analytical and decisive. I keep my cards close to my chest, only speaking up when I have something to say, whereas Jess is just *chatty*. I think my colleagues assume my aloofness is a seniority thing, a work persona, but it's just the way I am. I can turn on the charm if I have to, but I'd rather not. I hired Jess because she takes the edge off. She makes up for the things I lack. And I like her. Despite our being polar opposites, I genuinely like her. I wish I could be more like her, but you can't force a square peg into a round hole.

There's a knock at my office door: Jess. 'Yes,' I call out, rising to my feet.

Jess opens the door. She's wearing an eye-popping cobalt-blue dress with a red berry floral print and balloon sleeves. She's teamed it with a cropped, checked Gucci jacket. Only Jess could pull off an outfit like that. Even our dress sense is juxtaposed. Jess likes flowing Isabel Marant dresses and quirky Marni designs – bold prints, asymmetry, florals, polka dots, ruffles. Her clothes suit her, but I wouldn't be seen dead in that stuff. I prefer a more muted look – block colours, sharp tailoring, clean lines – Alexander Wang, Givenchy, Lanvin. That sort of thing.

Jess leads Rayna Mikhailova into my office. Rayna is the niece of Andrei Mikhailov – the Russian oligarch who owns *Couture* magazine. I met Rayna at a party years ago, but we don't really know each other. She's wearing a double-breasted, black, tweed Balmain jacket with a matching mini-skirt. Under her jacket, she's got on a blouse that looks like something from Joseph or Valentino. It bothers me a little that I'm not sure which. It's a smart outfit – respectful, reverential. She didn't have to. With a click of her fingers, Rayna could get me fired. I've had meetings with heiresses before, who know their power and come to see me in between yoga classes and brunch, wearing sportswear, their hair bundled into a ponytail. But Rayna's made an effort. Her hair is slicked back, her make-up on point. She's wearing a pair of Oscar de la Renta gold drop earrings that I've had my eye on for a while. I glance down at her feet – Micky 85 pumps by Jimmy Choo. Nice.

'Rayna, so happy to see you!' I gush, leaning in to kiss her on the cheek. I mouth 'thanks' at Jess as she ducks out of my office, discreetly closing the door.

'So good to see you, too!' Rayna enthuses, smiling broadly.

'Please, take a seat.' I gesture at one of the chairs surrounding the oval-shaped oak table in the centre of my light-filled office.

'It's such an honour to be featured in *Couture*! Thanks for inviting me in,' Rayna says, draping a garment bag containing samples from her new swimwear range over the table, before sitting down.

I narrow my eyes at her for a microsecond, trying to read her. An *honour*? Rayna's being featured because I received an email from Andrei with a link to her website and the curt message: 'My niece wants a feature.' It's not like I chose to feature her or decided to invite her in. It was an order from above. Usually, these heiresses know that. These rich, well-connected fashion girls with jewellery lines or accessories labels tend to have enough nous to realise they're not being featured because I'm enamoured with their design flair. Their lines aren't much more than an excuse to call themselves a designer at parties or pep up their Instagram bios. A status symbol. They know they haven't gained coverage because they worked for it, but that doesn't bother them, they feel entitled to it anyway. There's normally a tacit understanding that we're cooperating to create a myth around them, hyping them up as the kind of designer they're not. It's my least favourite part of my job – it makes what I do feel cheap – but I've come to realise I can't escape it. Yet unlike those calculating, uncaring heiresses, Rayna looks genuinely invested in this meeting. She seems nervous, keen. She keeps smiling. She crosses and re-crosses her legs.

'So, tell me about your line. How did it come about?' I ask, opening my notebook and unscrewing the cap of my Montblanc pen. If Rayna's taking this seriously, that means I need to as well.

'Well . . .' Rayna clears her throat and begins telling me about a fashion master's she did in Moscow.

I nod, throwing in the odd 'Wow, that's so interesting', 'Sounds fabulous' and 'Absolutely' as I make a few notes. I don't actually need to make any. I'm pretty sure I'll remember the necessary details, but I want to look engaged. Rayna clearly holds me in high esteem, and I have to live up to that.

I'm good at my job – surprisingly good, actually. I never set out to work in fashion or become an editor, but when you don't have much going on inside, good clothes are essential. If people knew the depravity underneath my designer wardrobe, they'd have nothing to do with me, but clothes give me camouflage. They make me look and feel almost normal. Better than normal. Clothes are a language I understand. I observe what people wear; I'm hooked on it. There are other people who'd love to be in my shoes, to edit like me, but they don't have what I have. They don't have the same obsession, the attention to detail that stems from emptiness and a desperation to conceal. I'm hooked on fashion; it's a lifeline to me.

As Rayna goes on, I absently check out her earrings, admiring their layered hoop design, their smooth finish. I decide I'll buy myself a pair this afternoon. My thoughts then wander to last night's kill. I still feel twitchy, unsatiated. I may have satisfied my bloodlust, for now, but ever since I crawled on top of Julian on that roof last night, I've been thinking about the curve of his pecs, the swell of his biceps, his thickly muscled thighs. If only he hadn't been an abuser, a rapist . . . I need release. Sometimes overpowering men does this to me. It makes me desperate to be dominated as though my subconscious is trying to give me some kind of penance, settle the score. Tit for tat. I'll have to call one of my lovers later.

I ask a few questions, fuelling Rayna's ego, conscious of what she'll say to her uncle afterwards. A 'Camilla was so lovely' or 'Camilla was such a sweetheart' could prove beneficial down the line.

After what feels like a sufficient amount of ego-stroking, I say with aplomb, 'Now you must show me your designs! I can't wait.'

Rayna grins and reaches for the bag draped over the table. She unzips it and places a swimsuit in front of me. It's nice. Black, strapless, with a bustier style and a belted waist.

'The range is about being sexy, without compromising on sophistication,' Rayna says.

I nod appreciatively, fingering the fabric, examining the swimsuit's careful construction.

Rayna presents a bikini with strapless cups and high-waisted bottoms. It's nicely designed, and no doubt flattering. I check out a few other pieces. I can't help wondering if Rayna really designed them or if she had assistance. But, of course, I can't ask.

'They're gorgeous. You should be so proud,' I tell her. I stiffen a little, wondering if I've taken the flattery too far, but Rayna beams back at me.

'Thank you! I'm so thrilled you like them. What a compliment!' she enthuses.

We discuss the feature – a four-page spread. I tell her I'll get one of my writers to do a more in-depth interview. We'll arrange for a photographer to take pictures of her in her studio. I stifle the urge to yawn. Last night has taken it out of me and I need coffee.

I glance at my watch – a Cartier Baignoire in rhodium-finish white gold with diamonds – taking a beat longer than necessary in the hope that Rayna notices it. I feel a swell of satisfaction when she clocks it, raising an eyebrow, impressed.

'I'm sorry, Rayna. I have another meeting coming up,' I tell her. She won't care. In fact, it's better if I look like I'm in demand.

'Absolutely, thank you so much for your time,' Rayna says.

She's sweet. Naive, but sweet. Perhaps the two go hand in hand, I ponder, as I screw the cap back on to my pen, close my notebook and stand up.

We talk a little more about the feature and I wish her well as I lead her out of my office, promising we'll 'chat soon'. Jess gets up from her desk to show Rayna out.

'Camilla, sorry,' Rayna pipes up as I turn back to my office.

I pause. 'Yes?'

Rayna smiles awkwardly, looking a little sheepish. 'I hope you don't mind me asking, but who's your facialist? You're glowing.'

'Oh!' I reach up to touch my face. 'That's so sweet!'

The truth is I haven't had a facial for weeks, but I'm used to this. People always think I've had a facial after a kill. Sometimes my friends think I've got laid. Nothing like a good murder to get the blood pumping.

'Erm, actually, I just bought a new La Mer face mask. I'll email you the link,' I tell her.

'Wonderful, thanks, Camilla,' Rayna replies gratefully.

'No problem!'

I close my office door and let out a sigh of relief. I arch my spine, feeling it click, and then sit down at my desk. I reply to a few emails and scan my diary to see what I've got on for the rest of the day. Another meeting with a designer. A phone call with one of the board of directors. A meeting with production. I definitely need coffee. I pick up my Givenchy Antigona tote and slip on my new Burberry coat. It's made from Italian cashmere. I've had it for a few weeks now, but I still can't get over the way it feels – the fabric's unbelievably soft and smooth. I stroke the lapel before sweeping my hair from underneath it. I head out of my office.

Jess is back at her desk. She looks up, perplexed. 'Going somewhere?' she asks.

'Just heading to Starbucks,' I tell her. 'Want anything?'

'Oh, err . . .' Jess frowns. 'I'll go. Don't worry about it!' She rises to her feet.

'No really, Jess, it's fine,' I insist, gesturing for her to sit back down. 'I want a little walk, get some fresh air.'

It's true. I really do. It's a bright, cool day. Crisp winter sunshine with a chilled breeze: my favourite kind of weather.

'Oh . . . Okay,' Jess says, sitting slowly back down. She still looks uncomfortable.

I understand why. Some of the other editors working for titles owned by Mikhailov wouldn't be seen dead in Starbucks. Public spaces are beneath them. They're the type of people who spend their whole lives in private schools, private members' clubs, private resorts, private jets and private cars. They'd probably have a panic attack at the thought of entering somewhere like Starbucks, where *anyone* could just wander in, but I'm tougher than that. My colleagues know my Suffolk upbringing was more normal, they know I can handle Starbucks, but I think it still makes Jess feel like a bit of a slacker when I do things like coffee runs myself.

'Could you do me a favour? One sec.' I nip back into my office and grab the notebook on my desk.

I close my office door and hand it to her. 'Could you type these notes up? From my meeting with Rayna.'

Jess's face lights up as she takes the notebook. At least now she'll feel useful.

'Sure!' she says.

'Thanks, Jess,' I reply with a smile.

'Oh, how was your date?' she pipes up, just as I'm about to leave. Told you she loves chit-chat.

I don't usually divulge my personal life to colleagues, but Jess walked in on me the other day while I was on the phone to Julian arranging our date, and I didn't think there was too much harm in admitting I was meeting up with a new guy. Drip-feeding details of my life here and there helps me seem normal.

'It was okay,' I tell her, shrugging. 'He was good-looking, but we didn't really have much of a connection.'

'Oh, that's a shame.' Jess's face falls. 'You could have a second date, just to see if things develop?' she suggests.

I picture Julian across the city, bound to the mast, blood pooling, congealing at his feet. His beautiful body decomposing on that rooftop, birds landing on the arrows sticking out of him, pecking hungrily at his eyeballs.

'I don't think so . . .' I murmur.

'Really? I reckon you might like him more than you're letting on,' she says, eyeing me with playful suspicion.

'No, honestly,' I insist. Jess must have mistaken the wistful look in my eyes as I pictured Julian's corpse for infatuation.

'Are you sure?' Jess presses.

'Yes, definitely. He was a bit dull. A bit *lifeless*,' I tell her, smiling to myself.

'Oh . . .' she replies glumly.

'He was a one-date wonder. That's all!' I give her a pointed look, like I really mean it.

'Fine!' Jess trills, before opening my notebook.

Jess is married. I know she wants me to find Mr Right and have my own happily ever after, but she'll have to wait a bit longer for that.

As I emerge on to the street, I'm struck once more by how glorious the weather is. I put on my Chanel sunglasses and walk towards Starbucks, pretending I'm oblivious to the eyes that turn to me, magnet-like, as I make my way down the road. I can never tell if the people around here recognise me, or if they just like my designer clothes, my face. I head into Starbucks. It smells cloying, of coffee beans, cleaning products and the stale breath of the freelancers who sit here for hours tapping away on their laptops. Someone needs to open a window. I try to ignore the smell and join the queue.

The staff are taking forever making coffees, the baristas shouting out orders over the rumble of the coffee machines.

They're reiterating orders, clarifying if drinks are grande, venti or tall, shuffling between coffee machines, depositing extra shots, flavoured syrup, soya milk, hot milk, cold milk, almond milk, coconut milk, putting together coffees with a meticulous, fastidious degree of precision, as though coordinating a trip to Mars. I tap my foot against the linoleum floor, irritated, itching for caffeine.

Bored, my gaze drifts to a girl three or four people ahead in the queue. Her dyed-black hair is tied into a scruffy bun. It has the brittle, leaden, frizzy look of hair that's been coloured over and over again using cheap five-quid dyes from Boots. I know because I used to have hair like that. She's wearing a hooded top with a faux-fur trim underneath a quilted Barbour jacket that's seen better days. Bobbles of fluff have attached themselves to the stitching and a few of the quilted diamonds are beginning to unravel. She has a boho bag in faux leather with fringed detailing slung over her shoulder. Her jeans are too tight, as though she's in denial that she's put on weight and wants to squeeze into size twelves for as long as possible even though size fourteen would probably be more comfortable. Her shoes are cheap. Imitation Chloé Susanna boots – one of the most copied shoes in history. They're creased, scruffy-looking, the heels done in. Although her clothes are all wrong, she looks like someone with aspirations. Someone confused. A poor girl who wants to be the sort of rich girl who wears Barbour and Chloé, but rich girls don't wear their jackets until they're falling apart. Rich girls don't mismatch Barbour jackets with boho bags.

The man in front of her takes his receipt and walks to the opposite end of the counter, where the coffees are being dispensed. The girl steps forward. She places her order, turning to talk to the barista. I catch sight of her face. She looks tired: shadows under her eyes, sallow skin, a breakout of spots on her chin. But despite that, her features aren't bad. She has large eyes, a straight nose, full lips. It's like her features are cloaked in a veil of stress. She could be really pretty if the veil were lifted. Sensing my eyes on her, she looks my way. I fail to divert my gaze in time, and she shoots me a defensive, accusatory look as though she doesn't appreciate being stared at. As though she knows she doesn't look her best and doesn't need my judgement. I smile weakly, apologetically, but she just scowls and turns back to the barista, pulling a card out of a battered wallet crammed with receipts.

I wonder what this girl's life is like. I feel like I want to help her. I want to reach out to her. I want to write her a cheque so she can buy some real Chloé boots or a new jacket. I wish I could do something, but of course, I can't. At least I'm doing one good thing for girls like her: I'm cleaning out the rubbish. Now that Julian's dead, there's one less fucker out there to prey on her. She takes her receipt from the barista, and glances anxiously at me before going to collect her coffee. I smile. She doesn't return it.

She reminds me of how I used to be, before I reinvented myself, before I became Camilla Black. Maybe I'm just so narcissistic that I'm projecting myself on to everyone, but I see my old self in this girl's tired, haunted eyes, in her poor-girl dress sense. She looks how I once looked, before I took control of my life, before I killed. Although I didn't realise at the time that murder would set me free.

My first victim was my old boss, Martin Summers. I never meant to kill him, but it turned out to be one of the best things I'd ever done.

I was working for a newspaper back then, trying to get ahead in journalism. I'd wanted to be a court reporter since I was sixteen. Ever since the time I plucked up the courage to take my dad to court for the things he did to me and it felt like the only person who believed me in the entire courtroom was a local reporter – Hannah Jones – who'd show up each day and sit in the gallery, head down, hair wound into a bun, making notes in sloping shorthand. Everyone – the jury, my lawyer, even my social worker – had written me off as a wild teenager making stuff up, but I could see in Hannah's sympathetic eyes that she knew I was telling the truth. I could see her conviction in the stories she was writing, in the way she'd always go for the most damning angle she could get away with – casting my dad in the worst possible light. She came up to me at the end of the trial, after the not guilty verdict had been read out, and gave me a hug with tears in her eyes. She told me how sorry she was and urged me to be strong, insisting that I mustn't let him ruin my life. That was the only time during the trial that I broke down. Hannah's compassion was so foreign to me, and it changed everything.

From that moment on, I wanted to be just like her. I dreamt of covering trials, shaming perpetrators, sympathising with the under-dog. I'd be the outsider who relied on gut feeling and facts, and showed sympathy and understanding, rather than being swept up with the herd. I wanted to make notes like Hannah, write stories and hold everyone to account. In spite of everything I had gone through, I managed to get good grades at school, but my dream turned out to be harder to bring to life than it should have been when Martin got in the way. I sometimes wonder whether Hannah ever had to deal with a boss like mine, or if she had someone decent, someone reasonable. I've googled her a few times over the years, but with a name like Hannah Jones, she disappeared into the ether long ago. It's strange to think that if Martin had never come along, I might have ended up like her. Would I be sitting in a courtroom right now, my hand dashing across a notepad?

Martin was in his late thirties, privately educated, loud, brash, not as smart as he thought he was, yet pumped full of self-importance nonetheless. He treated the *Cambridge Gazette* as though it were the *Sun* and he was Rupert Murdoch. Three other graduates and I worked under him. We all thought he was a fool, but we were ambitious enough to support his self-delusion – treating him like the big boss – in our efforts to get ahead and move on to greater things. I could handle Martin's delusional nature, but I couldn't handle the way he groped my arse in the staff kitchen, stroking his fingers over me, ignoring my shudders, knowing I'd be too stunned to say anything. I couldn't bear the way he'd wrap his hand around my knee as he told me which stories he wanted me to cover. I hated the way he always sat too close, or crouched over me, breathing on to my neck. I couldn't handle his invasive questions about my personal life, the texts at the weekend, the phone calls – his constant aggressive interest.

He made my life hell, and I didn't know what to do about it. Our paper was such a low-budget operation that we didn't have an HR person. And I knew anyway that if I tried to report Martin, it would be his word against mine, and that had never worked out well for me in the past. All that would happen would be that he'd find a way to fire me, I'd lose my job, get a reputation for being a troublemaker and struggle to find work. The only person who'd suffer would be me. And I wasn't able to simply leave my job. I didn't have anyone to support me. It's not like I had warm understanding parents to take me in and help me get my life back on track. I was terrified that if I quit, I'd become unemployable and I'd fall back into the life I was trying to run away from: a life of poverty, struggle and misery. I'd applied for dozens of jobs, but no one was getting back to me. I guess it didn't look great that six months into my first position, I already wanted to leave. Meanwhile, I felt I had to keep taking Martin's abuse without complaint, out of fear he'd give me a bad reference.

I was miserable. Utterly miserable. Between covering court cases and dealing with Martin's abuse, my days were characterised by trials for rape, battery, theft, sexual assaults and the odd murder. I'd spend my time sitting in the courtroom, trying to maintain a thick skin, before heading back to the office to endure Martin's bullshit. My colleagues weren't really on my side. They hadn't taken to me; I've never exactly been the popular girl. And they were from different worlds: they had nice families, most of whom were supplementing their low salaries. They could afford to do fun things and go out at the weekends, while I couldn't. I was a loner with no family and no money – pitiful, a drag. I spent my weekends alone, reading, wondering if this was all life had in store for me. At least at university, hope had got me through, it had driven me forward, but now I was a fully fledged adult and all I could do was ask myself, was this it? I went on a few dates with random guys I met online, looking for company, fun, but I only got preyed upon. I sank into despair, falling into an abyss-like rut, until one day, I couldn't take it any more.

Martin went too far. I was making tea in the office kitchen, and he let himself in as the kettle was boiling. I smiled and turned to pick it up, pouring steaming water into my mug. Martin approached from behind and reached over me to get something out of the cupboard. He was too close, and I shrank away, recoiling, but he moved closer and then I felt something hard against my lower back. I spun around to see his dick tenting his trousers, pressing into me. I shrieked and jumped away, splashing hot water all over the counter, but Martin just laughed, smirking, as though the whole thing was a funny accident. I ran to the loo, although I didn't even feel safe there. I was shaking, my heart pounding in my chest. I felt dirty, disgusting, despairing. Why me? Why had Martin chosen me? There were other pretty girls at the paper, but he'd targeted me. Would I always be fair game for abusers? Was there something about me?

I needed a way out. Over the next few days, I came up with a plan. Rumour had it that Martin had money. His father had died a few years earlier from a stroke, leaving him thousands of pounds. I didn't know exactly how much, but I'd heard it was a lot. Apparently, his dad had been dealing in some black-market trades, not declaring income, flying under the radar by storing stacks of money in his home. Wads of cash were supposedly found in shoeboxes under his bed when he died. Paranoid about his bank or HMRC asking questions, Martin was said to have followed his father's lead, keeping the money close by. A few colleagues said he'd been bragging about it after his dad's death. I hadn't paid the rumours much attention, writing them off as nonsense, office gossip, but after the incident in the kitchen, I began to wonder. If the rumours were true, then I was going to use Martin's money as my ticket to freedom.

I'd rob him. I'd wait until a time when I knew he'd be out, then I'd break into his house and root around for that money. I'd take it, stash it away somewhere, carry on like nothing had happened for a while, and then take flight. I'd leave my job and use Martin's cash to start afresh somewhere new. It's not like I'd have any guilt about stealing from him, when his behaviour had driven me to it.

My plan gave me a feeling of hope that I hadn't felt for months – a sense of purpose. I stopped wallowing in self-pity and planned my break-in instead.

I carefully researched Martin's home – a little bungalow in the countryside on the outskirts of Cambridge – using Google Maps, and when I knew he was heading to London to see a band in Shepherd's Bush with a friend (a rare highlight on his pretty much non-existent social calendar that he'd been talking about for days), I headed to his house in person. I scoped out his bungalow, examining doors, locks, windows, analysing points of entry, checking for security, neighbours, dogs. I found a loose brick falling off a garden wall and I was half tempted to just chuck it through Martin's bedroom window there and then and get the whole thing over and done with, but I resisted. I had to do this right; there was too much at stake if it went wrong.

I installed encryption software on my laptop to hide my internet activity and began researching lock-picking techniques and tools, tricks for jimmying doors open, clueing myself up on all things breaking-and-entering. I was browsing lock-picking sets when I had an idea.

I'd been covering a spate of break-ins across Cambridge. As a reporter, I was one of the first to know when three or four salubrious family homes had been broken into during half-term while the occupants were on holiday. I even interviewed an investigating officer about the burglaries. I knew a lot about the incidents, from the burglar's description (a slim white male, around six foot) to his preferred method of entry (lock picking), the type of thing he was prone to pinching (jewellery, cash, designer goods), how he got away (on foot) and even his shoe size (eleven). With his practised lock-picking skills and ruthlessly methodical approach, combined with similar incidents having taken place in nearby towns, the police believed the culprit to be some kind of prolific, experienced criminal passing through. I didn't get the impression they were particularly optimistic about their chances of catching him. I decided I'd carry out a copycat break-in, in the hope that the police would link it to the profile of the burglar they already had. I'd hardly be a likely suspect – a quiet unassuming reporter – but my plan still gave me peace of mind. I needed to get away with this so I could start my new life.

I got ready. I bought lock-picking tools, watched dozens of how-to videos, practised on my own front door and any other lock I could get my hands on. I bought a pair of size eleven trainers, leather gloves, a black beanie, a black hoodie, a dark backpack. Then I waited patiently, day after day, week after week, until Martin finally mentioned in office chit-chat that he was going away at the weekend for a cousin's wedding. My moment had arrived, and I was raring to go.

On Saturday evening, I tweeted about how I was heading to the local cinema, and I really did go. I cycled there, bought a ticket, and chatted for far longer than necessary to the cashier in a bid to leave an impression (in the highly unlikely event that I might need an alibi). I even went inside the theatre, before sneaking out the fire exit, hopping back on my bike and pedalling to Martin's place. I left my bike a few roads away from his bungalow, pulled on my hoodie and hat and crept through the surrounding fields to Martin's house, adrenaline surging through me – more excitement than nerves. I was confident I was going to get away with it, and after all this time being put down by Martin, I couldn't wait to finally get one over on him.

His bungalow looked strangely vulnerable as I approached it in the darkness. I scanned for neighbours and passers-by, but the street was silent. I rang the doorbell, just to be on the safe side. I waited, rang it again. Nothing.

I looked over my shoulder, slipped my lock-picking tools from my pocket and began picking Martin's lock. In less than a minute, I'd got it open. I was in. I stepped into the hallway, closing the door behind me. Martin's place smelt stale. It was messy. He'd left his worn leather shoes discarded in a pile by the front door. A couple of pegs were loaded with old jackets, scarves, blazers. The hallway was dirty and unswept, not particularly surprising since Martin was a bit of a slob in the office, but I noticed I was leaving good, solid, size eleven footprints in the dust from the men's shoes I was wearing. I crept straight to his bedroom, having figured out the layout of his bungalow from my previous visit.

Martin's bedroom was a depressing sight. Dirty clothes had been slung all over the floor, amongst discarded scuzzy tissues, a grubby laptop, even McDonald's wrappers. Gross.

I quickly drew the curtains, before rushing over to his bed and kneeling on the floor, peering under it. I found a few files, some old bills and letters, but no cash. None. My heart was hammering in my chest. I needed the money. There was nothing else worth taking. I turned to Martin's chest of drawers, briefly noting the dead cactus on top of them. So useless he couldn't even keep a cactus alive – what a man. I began pulling the drawers open, starting from the bottom, praying I'd find the cash hidden away, while wondering if I'd got all this wrong. What if the rumours were just rumours? Was this whole thing a bust? Was I going to have to go back to my old life, dealing with Martin, day in, day out? Putting up with my shitty job and miserable existence, only to be even worse off than before, because on top of everything else, I'd have the additional stress and worry of potentially getting caught for this pointless crime?

I ransacked every drawer and found the square root of fuck all. Just boxers and T-shirts and jumpers and jeans. Despairing, I ran over to the wardrobe, but there was nothing in there either, apart from familiar suits and shirts. A car drove past outside, my heart was pounding, and I was close to giving up when I spotted a bedside table I'd completely overlooked with a small tarnished lock on the front, and I wondered, could it really be there? Could Martin really be keeping thousands of pounds in his bedside table, behind a lock that I could probably jimmy open in a few seconds?

I walked over to the table, with a strong inkling that the money would be there: right by his bed so he could sleep next to it. So stupid, and yet I wouldn't have put it past him. I wrenched the door open with a screwdriver. It swung on its hinges and the first thing I saw was a shoebox. I pulled it out and lifted the lid, only to find it full of cash.

Time stilled as I took in the contents of the box. There it was: *money*. Stacks and stacks of money. I pulled out another shoebox, prized it open. More money! I pulled out another, and another. The rumours were true. I grinned to myself, my heart pounding with excitement now as I crouched over the bed and emptied the boxes into my backpack. I was going to be free. Free! It was all going to work out after all. But then, all of a sudden, I felt a chill sweep over me, and it was like the air pressure had shifted. In my excitement, I hadn't noticed that someone else had entered the room, but now I could hear their breathing.

I turned around and there he was: Martin. Standing there, watching me, eyes wide.

'What the fuck are you doing?' he asked, his voice ominously low.

I stood up, staring at him, my mind racing as I tried to figure out my next move. What was he doing here? He wasn't meant to be back until tomorrow.

'You crazy bitch. I'm calling the police.' He reached into his trouser pocket for his phone.

'No!' I shrieked as he swept his thumb over the screen, lighting up the darkness between us.

I reached over and slapped his phone out of his hand before he could dial. It landed on the floor.

'What the fuck?' Martin scowled, before plunging to retrieve the phone.

I shot down and tried to grab it first. There was no way I was letting Martin call the police. No way. He managed to grab the phone, but I gripped his hand, desperately trying to seize the handset, pleading with him.

'I'm sorry, Martin. I'm sorry. Please don't call the police, please. It was just a mistake. I'm so sorry.'

But it wasn't working. Martin was hell-bent on calling. He wasn't going to let me off the hook.

'Get off me,' he hissed, yanking his hand away.

'Please, I'll do anything,' I begged, meaning it. I'd have fucked him at that point if that's what it took. Anything to stop him calling the cops. But he wasn't listening. He was looking at his screen, he was about to dial. It wouldn't take long before the police would be here, and it would be game over. I needed to do something.

I spotted an empty bottle of lager on his bedside table and decided I'd knock him out and make a run for it. Then it would be his word against mine that I'd ever been here. I was wearing gloves; it wasn't like I'd left fingerprints anywhere. Hopefully, there wouldn't be any traces of my DNA. And I had my cinema ticket after all – there was a chance I could get away with it. I grabbed the bottle and, in one swift motion, I swung it, smashing it hard against Martin's lowered head, still illuminated by the light from his phone. Smack. But the blow didn't knock him out like on TV; instead, the bottle just smashed against his head, causing blood to pour from his temple. Martin stared at me, in horror, bringing his fingers up to the deep gash, blinking in shock at the droplets of blood.

'You crazy cunt!' he yelled.

Anger flooded his eyes, and not just regular anger, but rage. It's a look I recognised instantly. There's a switch that goes off in a person when rage takes over, and they become unstoppable. I used to see it in my dad's eyes when he'd beat and abuse me, and I saw it in Martin's now too. I knew it was him versus me.

'You psycho bitch,' he screamed, lunging at me, fists raised.

I dodged his fists, brandishing my broken bottle in defence. I had to get him before he got me. There was still a chance I could get away with this, that it could be Martin's word against mine, if I could get out of here without leaving blood, DNA. He swung at me, but I ducked, then he pushed me hard. I fell on to my back, and just before he climbed on top of me to strangle me, punch me, rape me, God knows what, I shoved the half-smashed bottle into his neck. I don't know if it was self-defence, self-preservation or just pure rage, but I rammed the bottle in deep, as far as it would go. Blood began pouring out of him. I wriggled out from underneath, and scooted back as he collapsed on to the floor, blood gushing from his neck, soaking the carpet.

Fuck.

I wanted to run. But the money was still on the bed. I grabbed it, my hands violently shaking as I shoved it into the bag, shoebox by shoebox, stack by stack, getting as much in as I could, while keeping an eye on Martin over my shoulder as he bled all over the floor. I felt like I was being watched. It was as though his soul was leaving his body and watching me from the corner of the room as I pocketed each wad.

I zipped up my bag and paused for a moment to take in Martin's lifeless form. The blood was still oozing from his neck, shining darkly in the grey light seeping through the window. I peered down at him. His eyes were half-open, but there was nothing behind his irises any more. He was gone. And yet, I was coursing with adrenaline – shock, fear, rage, excitement, surprise, awe – and I felt more alive than ever.

I snuck out of the back door of Martin's bungalow and raced in the darkness through the fields until I arrived at the side road where I'd left my bike. Then I cycled home, a cool, steady wind blowing over my face, strong and sharp – refreshing – like the rush of triumph flowing through me.

The police ended up putting Martin's murder down to a burglary gone wrong, pinning it on their original suspect profile just like I'd hoped. According to Martin's cousin, he'd got into a fight at the wedding and had left in a mood, driving back after one too many drinks. The police suspected he'd confronted the burglar and things had got out of hand, which I guess in a way was true.

I got away with it, and it was almost too easy.

'Excuse me. Madam? Madam?'

I blink. 'What?'

I realise a barista is staring at me. A coffee machine churns in the background.

'What can I get you?' he asks a little wearily, as though it's the second or third time he's had to ask.

'Err . . . a venti Americano, black,' I say, clearing my throat. 'And a venti chai latte, please,' I add, ordering for Jess too. She loves chai lattes.

The barista punches my order into the till. He's wearing a branded cap, looks mid-twenties, Spanish.

'Daydreaming, huh?' He smiles indulgently, his eyes flickering with flirtation.

'Yeah.' I laugh. 'Something like that.'

'Thought so,' he says, holding my gaze.

I pay for my order, swiping my card against the reader. 'What's your name?' he asks.

I raise an eyebrow. Is he really going to chat me up? Right here? In the middle of Starbucks?

'Err . . . Camilla,' I tell him hesitantly.

'Great,' he says, pulling a marker from a pocket on his apron. 'It's for the cups.' He winks, before scrawling my name down.

'Right!' I laugh, shaking my head as I walk to the end of the counter to wait for my drinks.

Chapter Four

By the time I get home, I'm dying for sex.

I cross the jasmine-and-rose-scented hallway and slide my key into my front door. My flat is pristine, as always. I was barely home last night, apart from the brief interlude between the bar and Julian's death, and all Julian and I did then was share a bottle of wine. I left our glasses in the sink when I got back from killing him, had a shower and went to bed. But my cleaner has vacuumed, anyway. She's tidied away the glasses, spritzed the surfaces of near-imperceptible dust, plumped up the cushions on the sofa, and made my flat exactly the way I like it: immaculate, spotless, as clean as a luxury hotel.

I walk over to the kitchen and place my handbag on the breakfast bar. I open the fridge and retrieve a bottle of sparkling lemon and spirulina water and pour myself a large glass. The bottle of half-drunk Antinori Tignanello Toscana is still on the counter, but I can't face more alcohol today. The tequila shots and wine I had last night were a lot for me, particularly when coupled with the adrenaline rush I got from using my Excalibur crossbow. After that excess, I need something healthy, cleansing, calming. I need to replenish and get my endorphins back up, and that's where sex comes in.

I take my sparkling water and walk over to the sofa, kicking off my Dolce & Gabbana pumps before lying back into the soft leather. I picture Julian lying in this exact spot last night, how he made himself at home, slumping into the cushions. I turn my head and sniff the leather, wondering if I might be able to smell him on it. He smelt of washing powder, deodorant and sweat, but now I can't detect his scent. All I can smell is the skin of a dead calf, more present than Julian at this point. I sit up a bit straighter and take a sip of my drink, wondering who to call.

I have a few lovers on the go at the moment. The longest-standing is an actor I refer to as Mr USA to my friends. His real name's Alexander Müller and he's not actually American; he's German with the kind of striking looks that mean he's constantly being cast in war films. He used to be based in London, but he's in LA these days, trying to crack Hollywood. We were introduced at a party a few years ago and the attraction was instant, the chemistry magnetic. He's gorgeous, but alas, he's in Hollywood at the moment, playing a detective in a spy thriller.

Who else? There's Vanessa. An incredibly beautiful academic I met in a gay bar in Soho one Friday night. She appealed to me not only because she looks like something from a Pre-Raphaelite painting but because she's totally clueless about popular culture. She barely knows what *Couture* magazine is, let alone that I'm the editor. And for that reason, we can be discreet. She thinks I'm a fashion designer, and since she's not even remotely interested in fashion, she's asked about as many questions as I'd ask an insurance broker. She's doing a PhD on 'metaphysical modality' – whatever the fuck that is – and she reads Aristotle and Kierkegaard for fun. Although, Aristotle's her favourite. She likes to go on about achieving eudemonia – living well through virtuous and moral deeds. It almost makes me feel a little bad for her that she's fucking a serial killer. Her fashion sense, which mostly consists of hoodies and leggings, is horrific, but I prefer her with her clothes off. It's Vanessa's body that gets me. Her round, pert breasts with their pretty pink nipples like cherries on a cupcake. But I'm not in the mood for Vanessa tonight. I want Abay.

Body-wise, my other lover Abay, whose full name is Abayomi, isn't wholly dissimilar to Julian, although he's even more ripped. Fifteen stone of muscle and six foot two, he's huge. Unlike Mr USA and Vanessa, he's not even good-looking. One of his front teeth is chipped from a fight he got into years ago, and he couldn't care less about getting it fixed. He's only twenty-seven, but he already has a deep frown line permanently etched into his forehead. He has the most aggressive resting bitch face I've ever seen. In fact, it's a resting don't-fuck-with-me-or-I'll-fucking-kill-you face, and yet I find him weirdly attractive. I like how little he cares about being charming. He's not interested in what anyone thinks of him and that makes him insanely appealing. And he fucks like an absolute animal. He throws me around, uses me, reduces me to a piece of meat to be toyed with, manipulated into whatever position he likes.

Abay is what I need tonight. I want to be used, like I used Julian. I'm dying for someone to overpower me.

I click into WhatsApp and send him a message.

Me: Hey, what are you up to?

This is my way of saying, do you want to come over for sex, and Abayomi knows it. I take a sip of my drink and stare at the screen, urging him to come online. I haven't seen him for a week now.

He's usually quite freely available since he works at my local gym, five minutes down the road. Fitting hook-ups in between personal training sessions is handy for both of us. Abay gets to release all the pent-up sexual tension he experiences from being in an environment packed full of pheromones and sweat and sexy people in Lycra, and I get my very own cardio sessions. We manage to see each other once or twice a week. In fact, it occurred to me recently that I probably see Abay more than I see anyone else outside work. I see him more regularly than my friends.

And we have a strange rapport. As well as sex, we chat, share day-to-day problems and give each other advice. But we both know where to draw the line. We don't get too personal. Abay knows nothing about my family, my hopes, my dreams or my secrets, and he doesn't want to know. Our chats are like water cooler conversations you'd have with an office confidante – close but not too close. I know Abay keeps his distance on purpose. He's a skilled Casanova and he thinks that, by keeping conversation light, he'll stop feelings from developing. But he doesn't realise I'd never open up anyway. That the place where my feelings are meant to be is a void. That our water cooler sex chats are as close as I'll ever get to anyone.

I stare at his name on my phone. Abayomi. It's Nigerian. I googled it once – it means 'born to bring me joy'. That made me laugh. I stare at my phone, willing him to reply. He appears online, but then disappears. Urghh.

I think back to when I spotted him down the road as I was staggering along with Julian. What if he did see us after all? What if he thinks I'm with another guy? Could he be jealous? We're not exclusive, but maybe it's wound him up. Or rattled him in some way. I'm probably overthinking.

If he'd only just reply. I chuck my phone on to the cushion beside me and let out a groan, pondering my vibrator collection. Even a session with my new Satisfyer wouldn't come close to sex with Abayomi. It's just not the same.

I roll my eyes, cursing my fate, when suddenly my phone buzzes. I grab it. It's him!

Abayomi: Busy with a client. Free from 9. Shall I come over?

I grin, clutching my phone to my chest.

Me: Sounds good. See you soon x

Perfect.

'Hey,' Abay says as I open the door.

'Hey,' I reply as he steps into my flat.

He's wearing a branded gym T-shirt under a zip-up hoodie with black tracksuit bottoms. Clothes always look strange on Abay, like shrink wrapping. He's like one of those superheroes: the Incredible Hulk. It feels as though with one deep breath, one roar, his chest could burst right through the flimsy fabric.

Unlike Abay, I'm delicately dressed, in a black, embroidered Fleur du Mal Lily bra with matching knickers. I've thrown on my new pearlescent-pink Gilda & Pearl Mia silk robe with ostrich-feather cuffs. The feather cuffs tickle my wrists, but the silk is light and smooth against my skin. It's a beautiful robe and I've been dying to wear it. The whole outfit is gorgeous, but it's the kind of thing Mr USA would appreciate more than Abay.

Abay doesn't care what kind of underwear I've got on. He wouldn't know Agent Provocateur from Asda.

I'm so accustomed to using fashion to get ahead, to project the right kind of image. But to Abay, it doesn't matter what I wear. I don't have to worry about how I come across when I'm around him. Trying to pass as the kind of person I'm not requires a constant, sustained effort, and it can grow wearying. Sometimes, I simply can't be bothered, and I want to be around people like Abay – unpretentious, normal people. When I'm around him, I can let my guard down, just a bit. It doesn't matter if I trip up, if I let my roots show. Abay doesn't even notice. He takes me as I am. To him, I'm just Camilla – the hot woman from the gym. And that's enough.

Abay looks me up and down, taking in my robe and my underwear, but he doesn't even smile. Although, despite his permanent scowl, I can see from his wide eyes that he's somewhat impressed.

He leans in for a kiss. Quick. Gruff. His hands trace over my hips, lightly, fleetingly, electrifyingly. His smell is immediate. It always hits me. A musty smell, sharp, unapologetic and incredibly sexy. Abay dumps his sports bag by the door and shrugs off his hoodie. He hangs it on a peg, next to my Burberry coat, which I've draped over a hanger that dangles from one of the hooks. I keep all my coats on hangers, naturally – a habit that Abay finds ridiculous, claiming only an English person would 'hang a hanger on a hanger'. Whatever. My Burberry coat is hung up next to my new, incredibly cool PVC Fendi trench, my chic, beige, camel-hair coat from Max Mara, and my unashamedly ostentatious, panelled, mink Zen jacket by Liska, which is concealed in a plastic sheath. I keep the rest in my wardrobe, but these are my current favourites. As if I'm just going to hang them straight on the pegs! Unlike Abay with his cheap hoodies, my coats cost thousands. But of course, he doesn't understand, so I let him poke fun.

'What's up?' he asks as he heads to the kitchen. He retrieves a glass from the cupboard and fills it with water straight from the tap. That's another thing Abay laughs at me for: he finds my refusal to drink tap water hilarious. As well as preferring the taste of Evian, I admitted to him once that I worry the high levels of oestrogen in London water could make me fat. Abay cried with laughter, before coaxing me into taking a sip of his water. Then he led me to the bedroom to burn it off.

I reflect on his question. *What's up?* Nothing much. Killed a rapist last night. The usual.

Instead, I make a glib remark about being busy at work. Abay responds by offloading about his boss, Rebecca, who he's always giving off about. His latest grievance is that she's changed his shift pattern from starting early in the morning to midday.

'It's much harder to get clients then. I swear she has it in for me,' he insists, glowering as he sips his water.

I laugh. One thing about Abay is he's an overthinker. A bit paranoid, like me in that respect. He's not your usual personal trainer: all muscle, charm and chat. He's actually quite smart. He got a place to study maths at Newcastle but dropped out in his second year. From the sound of it he couldn't keep up and moved back to south London, where he'd grown up, where he felt at home. Except I think the whole experience has made him feel like an outsider ever since. Abay knows he's a bit too good to be a personal trainer and yet he's never quite felt good enough to aim higher. That's probably the reason behind his permanent scowl and his insatiable sexual appetite, like a druggie constantly looking for a fix, an escape.

'I'm sure Rebecca doesn't have it in for you,' I say, sidling up behind him as he refills his glass.

I place my hands on his taut hips, solid underneath the creased cotton of his jogging bottoms. I slide my fingers under his top and roam over his body, feeling his abs rippling under my fingertips, his hard pecs.

'I'll help you feel better,' I purr into his ear. 'I don't have it in for you.'

I start tracing the hem of his jogging bottoms, before slowly sliding my hand inside. His dick is already hard.

He doesn't react, taking another sip from his glass of water instead.

I hold his dick, feeling his warm skin, the familiar bulge of his cock. It's taut, tightening against my touch.

'What are you doing?' Abay spins around so fast that my hand slips away. He gives me his signature scowl, but I respond with a playful smirk.

'Excited, are we?' I ask, raising an eyebrow.

Abay glares at me, but his eyes flicker mischievously. He places his glass down on the counter and holds my gaze.

If I was that twat in *Fifty Shades of Grey* right now, my inner goddess would be doing somersaults or some shit, but instead I just stand facing him, my Mia robe gaping open, my nipples straining against the soft lace of my bra, a throbbing heat between my legs.

'Come here,' Abay says, and in one swift motion he slips his hands around my thighs and lifts me like I'm an origami bird, placing me on my marble kitchen counter. That's another reason I adore Abay – he makes me feel so light, so insubstantial, so powerless. When I'm around him, I have no menace, it's all his.

I sit at the edge of the counter. Abay stands in front of me. I open my legs to let him closer. He looks me up and down, taking in my eyes, my lips, my smooth stomach, my pretty underwear. His dick is bulging under his tracksuit bottoms. He's not kissing me yet, preferring to tease me instead. I'm wet already, begging for his touch. I shrug off my robe, letting it fall on to the marble worktop behind me, then I reach behind my back and undo my bra, lowering it slowly from my shoulders, watching Abay's eyes cloud over with desire as I do so.

'Mmmm . . .' Abay takes a step closer and plunges his lips to my neck, vampire-like.

He bites me gently, sucks, licks my skin, his hands on my waist, reaching up, pinching my bullet-like nipples. I let out a moan, unable to suppress my desire any longer. Abay responds by kissing me, plunging his tongue into my mouth. We kiss passionately, hungrily, ravenously. He lowers his lips to my breasts and sucks hard on my nipples, flicking his tongue expertly over them. I groan, throwing my head back, my hair falling over my shoulder blades. I open my legs wider, inviting him to touch me, but he keeps teasing me instead. I grab his top and pull it off him, revealing his body, his magnificent chest. His body never ceases to amaze me. I love his large muscles and his soft, dark skin. Abay has a natural glow, a radiant luminosity that I know isn't achieved through high-end products. His skin's like polished wood – buffed, smooth, reflective. His body catches the light, the contours of his muscles like the work of a skilled carpenter. He's a marvel. I drape myself over him, winding my legs around his back, pulling him closer. He presses his lips to mine, his kisses hungry and deep, betraying his desire. The need and want his scowling face would never admit to.

Abay likes to kiss, but I prefer it when his tongue is on other parts of me. I pull away, sighing 'Fuck me' into his ear. He half smiles and picks me up, feather-light. He carries me into my bedroom and drops me on to my pink silk La Perla sheets. I land indelicately, like a bag of bones. I make an effort to recover my composure and recline sexily. Abay stands over me, staring at me with those hot menacing eyes, as he pulls off his jogging bottoms and boxers in one swift motion. He drops them to the floor and slowly crawls on top of me. I feel tiny underneath him. His massive body makes my bed dip. He plants kisses on my neck, my breasts, my stomach, and finally, he pulls off my knickers, chucking them aside.

'Mmmm . . .' he moans. 'I love your neat little pussy.'

I smile.

He slips his fingers between my legs and slides one, then two inside me.

'You're so wet,' he groans, moving his fingers back and forth. The feel of his thick fingers inside me makes me even wetter.

My pussy's so slick, so soft and warm, that it feels like it's melting. I let out a sigh of pleasure. I could come right now. The sight of Abay's body, his rock-hard cock, his powerful physique, his fingers drilling into me, the mean look in his eyes, laced with lust – it's enough to send me over the edge.

'Do that harder,' I tell him.

He slams his fingers into me, pointed like a revolver. He pounds me, smacking into me, making my whole body jolt with each movement. I moan. He bites down on his lip, scowls at me; he loves what he sees. His cock is bulging, the tip glistening with pre-cum.

'Choke me,' I plead.

He knows what I like. His hand is already raised. He presses his palm down on to my neck, as he simultaneously lowers his lips to my nipple. He sucks my breast while restricting the blood supply to my brain. He slams his fingers into me, over and over, while slowly tightening his chokehold. It's intoxicating. When Abay and I first started sleeping together, he was surprised by some of the things I was into. He was worried about being too rough and hurting me, but I assured him that as long as it's on my terms, then sometimes I like to be hurt. Sometimes that's exactly what I want. Then he relaxed. He got into it. He started enjoying it.

The pressure inside me grows as his hand grips my throat, building and swelling, until I can't contain it any more, until it's all too much, and all the tension I've been holding in since Julian overwhelms me and I break, free-falling, cascading, spiralling, collapsing into an abyss of pleasure. My mind is obliterated, blank, owned by sensation alone. Tears leak from my eyes, cries pour from my mouth as I convulse against Abay's fingers. My body beads with sweat, glistening. Glowing. Beating. Shaking.

The release is incredible. I lie there, blinking at the ceiling, as reality seeps slowly back.

I look over at Abay. He's smiling – a smug, self-satisfied smile. He loves the power he has over me. His dick is still rock solid, standing to attention. I catch my breath, then roll on to my side. I move towards him and take him in my mouth. He fills me – his generous girth and length bulging inside my small mouth, making me sputter and drool. It's degrading – his dick is so far into my throat that my eyes are watering; I'm choking, my face straining – but I love it. I'm not Camilla in moments like this, I'm just a giver of pleasure, a means to an end. I feel servile. Less lethal.

Abay holds my head and pulls my mouth further down his shaft. His hands are in my hair, gripping me. I sputter as his dick slides down my throat. I look up at him. He smiles that self-satis-fied smile before gyrating into me and tipping his head back.

Once my gag reflex subsides, I let my eyes wander over his body, taking in his glorious abs, his pecs, the groove between them, the dips under his collarbones. He really is stunning. If I were a painter, I'd paint him. If I were a sculptor, I'd sculpt him. If I were a photographer, I'd photograph him. But I'm just me, so I fuck him. I feel myself getting aroused all over again, even though my last orgasm was so intense that I'd expected it had finished me off for the night. I take his dick right back into my throat. He moans, sighing, as his cock disappears down my neck.

Finally, Abay pulls my head back, sliding his dick out of my mouth. It's shiny with my spit, swelling.

'Turn over,' he hisses.

I dutifully get on to my hands and knees, tilting my ass up towards him, presenting my wet pussy to him. He slips two fingers inside, feeling my renewed wetness and warmth. I watch him over my shoulder as he gets behind me. He places his large hands on my hips and slowly slides into me, observing intently as he enters me. I groan as he pushes himself deeper. We've fucked dozens of times before, but my body never tires of Abay's huge, impressive cock. It always startles me, fills me, satisfies me on a primal level that I can't even explain.

'Oh God,' I moan as he slides in and out of me, picking up a rhythm, getting into it.

I could fuck Abay forever. I could die happy fucking him, I think to myself as he plunges into me, pounding me, reducing me to a quivering, shaking mess with each strong impactful thrust.

'You like that, don't you?' he hisses as he slams into me.

'I love it,' I answer as he lands a heavy slap across my ass, mak-ing me cry out, making my whole body flinch, tightening around his cock. He does it again, and again, until my ass is raw. His slaps are almost like lashings, a penance for my sins.

He buries his hand in my hair, rubbing the back of my head, before pushing me down into the soft sheets. His fingers dig into my scalp and slide across the side of my face, pinning my head against the bed. With his other hand, he takes hold of my thin wrists and clutches them behind my back, gripping me tightly before slamming into me again. I groan into the silk as he thrusts. I can barely breathe against the sheets. My mind is blank. Abay slides his fingers into my mouth. They smell of rubber from the gym, they taste salty like sweat. He slams into me as I suck his fingers and I come again, my pussy convulsing over his dick. He comes too. Spasming into me. He lets out a primal groan of pleasure, a raw cry of satisfaction. It's so uninhibited, so ecstatic, so wild, that it's like music to my animal ears. It sets me off even more, like his dick that bursts into me, feeling even more beautiful as it jolts and erupts, out of control.

Eventually, our orgasms subside. Abay pulls his hand from my mouth and traces his fingers over my back, slick with sweat. We pull apart and fall side by side on to the sheets, panting. I roll over and reach for a tissue from the bedside table, dabbing at the moisture between my legs.

I chuck the tissue into the bin and blink at the ceiling. We lie in silence for a few moments, catching our breath, basking in the afterglow of our orgasms, but a few minutes later, I'm wondering, what next? I want a shower, or a bath. A long, luxurious bath with a slug of my favourite Jo Malone Pomegranate Noir bath oil. And Netflix. Even better. Now I just need to get rid of Abay.

I turn to look at him. He's lying, eyes closed, a blissed-out expression on his face.

'That was amazing,' I say, reaching over, affectionately stroking his abs.

'Mmm . . .' Abay responds, without opening his eyes.

Sometimes he sticks around for a bit, but often he has to get back to work. He'll say he has a training session with a client or he's on a shift or something. I'm not sure if his excuses are genuine or just a way to see himself out, and I don't really care either way, as long as he goes. Once he's gone, I'll often lie on the sweaty sheets for hours, sometimes I sleep in them, breathing in our sex smell, basking in the musky, raw, masculine scent of him. Then I wake up reeking of us, of him. I love that, but that's as close as I ever need to get to sleeping with Abay. I certainly wouldn't want him staying over.

'Come here,' he says, reaching out to me, opening his eyes a crack.

Come here?

We've already fucked, what more does he want from me? I eye his open arms. His eyes are blissed out in a puppy-dog gaze. I raise an eyebrow. I'm half expecting him to burst into laughter, having wound me up.

'Really?' I ask.

'Yeah, come on!' he insists, reaching out for me.

'Okay!' I say in a high-pitched voice that doesn't sound quite my own as I edge into his embrace.

He pulls me close in a sort of bear hug, sweeping me into him until I'm flush against his body. What's he doing? We don't cuddle. What is this? I lie, stiff in his arms, wondering what he's playing at. I glance up at him. His eyes are closed. He's *cradling* me.

Okay, this has to stop.

'Do you want a drink?' I ask, prising myself free from his grip. He sighs.

'I don't drink,' he reminds me, eyes still closed.

'I know.'

Abay's teetotal, low-carb, paleo. He likes to remind people as often as possible, joking that his body is a temple. As if we can't already see that.

'I meant juice,' I clarify.

'Okay,' he replies.

I get up and grab my knickers from the carpet, pulling them on. My body's still damp with sweat. I glance at my reflection in the mirror. My hair's a mess. My cheeks are rosy. I look *fucked*. I smile and head to the kitchen, where I pour two glasses of apple and elderflower juice, cool from the fridge. I mix mine half with water. I don't need the calories of pure juice.

I slip on my bra and Mia robe, which I left on the worktop, and carry the glasses back to my bedroom. Fortunately, Abay seems a bit more alert now. He sits up, leaning against my padded headboard.

I hand him a glass.

'Thanks,' he mutters.

I walk around to the other side of the bed and perch, taking a sip of the cool, sharp juice, before placing my glass down on a coaster and swinging my legs on to the bed. We can drink this juice together, then I'll pretend I have to call my mum or something.

Abay leans forward and grabs his jogging bottoms from the floor. Promising. But instead of putting them on, he just pulls his iPhone out of the pocket and drops the bottoms back on the floor, before checking his messages.

God.

I sip my juice and listen to the distant sound of the cars passing by on the street below.

'There's been a shooting in a market in Amsterdam,' Abay says. 'Two dead. Possible terror attack.'

I don't respond. These things are becoming so commonplace that they barely even feel like news any more.

'Did you hear about that guy?' Abay asks after two or three cars trace their way down the street.

'Huh?' I place my juice on the bedside table and reach for my hairbrush.

'That guy they found. On some rooftop in Hayes. Murdered. Someone shot him with a ton of arrows,' Abay says, looking up from his phone.

'What?' I utter.

'The police found this guy's body. Not just any murder though, he got shot with a crossbow. It was on the news. Didn't you see?'

'No . . .' I reply, my voice small.

'Yeah, it was crazy.' Abay shakes his head. 'Some mad attack.'

'Hmmm . . . Sounds weird!' I comment, pulling my brush through my tangled hair before reaching once more for my juice.

I take a sip. I don't even register the taste this time. *Fuck. Fuck. Fuck.* Julian's been found. No one was meant to find him. I imagined him rotting up on that roof, like everything rots in that part of London. I imagined him being reduced to bones. Being slowly parched in the sunlight, pecked at by birds. I pictured his flimsy remains, scattering amongst the rubble when the demolition team finally stepped in with a wrecking ball and the block was knocked down. Yet he's been discovered. Even more intense than panic is the horrible, vulnerable feeling of exposure. My handiwork, my spectacle, my private homage to Mantegna, has been found. Officers will have taken pictures. Inspected the scene. Pulled it all apart. I feel tainted, trampled upon, violated. This was not how it was meant to go. I liked the idea of Julian bound to that mast, fading to nothing, getting what he deserved. I liked the thought of his family and friends not knowing what had happened to him, forgetting about him quicker than they knew they should. I wanted him to just disappear.

But he hasn't disappeared. He's being talked about in the news. He's being talked about by my lover, in my bed. This is fucking awful.

'Let me see,' I ask, reaching for Abay's phone. Mine's still on the sofa next door.

He closes a message from someone. Probably already arranging his next hook-up. Not that I give a shit. I'd probably do the same.

'One second,' Abay says.

He goes on Google and looks up the story, pulling up an article. He hands his phone to me.

Man killed in 'savage' crossbow murder

The body of a man shot dead with arrows fired from a crossbow has been discovered on the roof of a derelict council block in west London.

The victim, believed to be in his twenties, was found in the Willow Tree Lane estate in Hayes by two teenagers on Monday 18 January. It is estimated that the victim died less than 24 hours earlier.

The male had been shot with thirty arrows in an attack investigating officer Detective Chief Inspector Glen Wheelan describes as 'savage and evil'.

'This was an appalling and unimaginably violent attack,' Det Ch Insp Wheelan said. 'Officers, including myself, are shocked by the extreme nature of this deeply callous and calculated crime.

'This is one of the most disturbing crime scenes I've seen, and our force will leave no stone unturned in our efforts to bring the killer to justice.

'We are appealing to the public and those in the local area to get in touch if they have witnessed anything suspicious or seen anything unusual. It is vital that any information, however minor it may seem, is reported to the police.'

Efforts are being made to contact the victim's family.

No arrests have yet been made.

Hmm. DCI Wheelan, the detective who wanted the public to identify me from the CCTV footage after my sugar daddy slaying, is back on my case. He's still scouring London's streets for murderers. And he's clearly taken aback by my latest work. Savage and evil. Deeply callous. One of the most shocking crimes he's ever seen. Wow. Go me!

Suddenly, I feel Abay's eyes on me. He's giving me a strange look, frowning.

Shit. I'm meant to react, like a normal person would.

'That's terrible!' I exclaim. 'Crazy. Who would do that?' I feign a look of disgust as I hand his phone back.

'Some madman,' Abay comments, sighing, as he takes his phone.

'Yeah,' I sigh, mirroring him.

I lapse into a pensive silence as I go over the crime scene, assessing whether I left anything that could possibly incriminate me. I don't think so. I never do.

They won't catch me. They never do.

Abay yawns loudly. He arches his spine, making it click. He gets up.

'I should probably go,' he says, scooping his tracksuit bottoms from the floor. 'Need to be getting back to the gym.'

'Cool,' I reply.

Chapter Five

Fucking Julian. That prick is everywhere.

He's even made it on to the front page of fucking *Metro*. Some guy handing out copies thrusts one into my hand as I come out of my flat. The vendor, in his cringey *Metro*-branded cap, is always there, trying to foist the paper on me. I usually ignore him, but today I glance at it and spot Julian on the front page. I take a copy, unfolding it as I walk to the waiting car parked on the street.

I take in Julian's face. Fuck me, he really was gorgeous. Why didn't he use this picture on his Tinder profile, for God's sake! His profile on there was just gym selfies. Unsmiling shots of him sitting on a weight bench in front of a mirror, a barbell at his feet, leaning forward with his elbows on his knees, the muscles in his arms bulging. The same thing standing. He undersold himself. I knew he was handsome, but he really was striking. This picture shows him in his best light. That perfect strong-boned face. That beauty spot. Christ.

My driver opens the car door for me.

'Thanks,' I mutter, from behind my sunglasses, my eyes still fixed on Julian's picture.

'Awful story, isn't it?' he says.

I look up. It's a driver I haven't had before. Middle-aged. A friendly face.

'Yeah, awful,' I agree as I step into the car.

I'm not in the mood for small talk. I want to look at those pictures of Julian. The driver closes the door. It's one of the perks of my job that I have a chauffeured car to take me to work.

I properly take in Julian's photo. He has the kind of face that makes your soul melt. That turns your eyes into love-heart emojis. He's smiling in the picture, a wide, radiant smile that shows off his perfect teeth. He looks totally happy, beaming, content. His head is tilted to the side a bit, as if he was posing with someone else, leaning into them, but that person has been cropped out.

The headline reads: *Promising financier killed in brutal slaying.*

Promising financier? I got the impression Julian was pretty much an office dogsbody. But 'brutal slaying'? I like that. *Brutal slaying.* I roll the words over in my mind, smiling to myself.

I gaze out the window as the car pulls away from the kerb. It's a bright day, with a crisp blue sky. People are walking with their heads held high, a spring in their step. They grab copies of *Metro* from the vendor. They look at the cover. My brutal slaying is going to be the talk of the town.

I catch the driver looking at me in the rear-view mirror, frowning slightly. Shit. He's probably wondering why I'm smiling. Why did I have to get a fucking nosy driver on a day like today?

'Thought I saw someone I know,' I tell him, gesturing out of the window. 'Wasn't them though.'

'Ah, happens,' the driver responds, with a polite laugh, before pulling out into the traffic.

I look down at the paper, feigning an expression of sombre focus.

Julian's boss has described him as 'an ambitious and focused member of the team', calling his death 'deeply disturbing', 'a tragic loss'. Whatever. The article goes on to state that 'Julian lived in his family home in west Dulwich with his parents and brother, Richard'. Ha. He told me he had his own flat. Liar.

There's a quote from his mum, Alison Taylor. 'Julian was a loving, caring, helpful person. He always put his family first. He was a sweet, devoted son and a loyal brother. Words cannot describe the shock and loss our family is feeling right now. We cannot comprehend why someone would inflict such a horrific attack on our beloved boy.'

That pisses me off. Loving? Caring? Helpful? Does Julian's mother not care about his court case? Is she simply lying about his true nature or is she in denial? Does she not realise she gave birth to a piece of human shit? The fucking asshole's being treated like a fallen fucking hero, a poor, tragic victim, when he was the worst kind of perpetrator of them all. I wonder if his victims will come forward, but they probably won't. They might feel too scared or ashamed. Or they might just want to move on from what they went through. They'll probably just be glad he's dead.

Everything else in the article is pretty much the same as the stuff I read during the night. It doesn't even mention Julian's recent conviction. It's practically a tribute piece. I shake my head, disgusted. Men really do get a free pass in this world.

I know I shouldn't give a shit about Julian; I know I'll never get found out. But I can't help feeling a little bit rattled. Usually my kills go to plan, but this one hasn't. It was too spontaneous. Too ambitious. Firing at Julian with my crossbow. What was I thinking? I should have resisted my urges. Killed him in a way that was more controlled.

I keep wondering how Julian's body was discovered. Did someone hear me? Did someone see me? It's freaking me out. But if someone did see anything, they'll have seen a scruffy girl with long wavy hair. Someone who looks nothing like me.

And it's not like they can trace Julian's Tinder messages back to me, or his texts. Not only did I delete his entire messaging history and destroy his phone, but I was using one of my pay-as-you-go numbers when we contacted each other. I had encryption software installed too. But still, the whole thing's a bit unsettling. I kept waking last night, flicking through articles on my iPad, scanning for updates.

At around 2 a.m., Julian's body was identified, but the details were sparse: his name, age, where he was from. No pictures of him had been shared at that point. I kept an eye on Twitter, waiting for more information to come through. I scrolled and scrolled, but it seemed to plateau, and after a while, I fell asleep.

But this latest article has the addition of a picture. A picture that speaks a thousand words. Everyone's going to care way more about Julian's brutal slaying now that they realise he was hot. Such a loss to the world when someone sexy dies.

I turn a few other pages of the paper to see if anyone's added anything else, but there's nothing relevant, just tiresome – a plane crash, Kate Middleton 'wowing' in an ugly Gucci blouse and Jigsaw trousers. I fold the paper and toss it on to the seat next to me, before gazing out of the window for the rest of the journey.

A little while later, I arrive at work and walk through the open-plan newsroom towards my private office at the back. A hush follows me as I cross the room, but that's nothing new. I get it every day. Everyone goes a little bit quiet when I arrive at work. I like to tell myself it's out of respect and possibly due to a degree of fear, but deep down, I know it's because all my staff are as fashion-obsessed as I am, and they'll literally stop whatever they're doing just to check out what I'm wearing. Today's outfit is a particularly good one: a high-waisted silk-blend Lanvin skirt teamed with a Haider Ackermann satin tie-neck blouse, finished off with a belted

Maison Margiela leather coat and pointed Malone Souliers Bly pumps.

'Morning, Jess,' I say as I walk past her desk.

Jess is wearing a wrap-front patterned blue dress from IRO with tortoiseshell Oliver Peoples Gregory Peck glasses. I know she has 20/20 vision, but they really do suit her.

'Morning, Camilla,' Jess replies, glancing over from her monitor.

I head into my office and close the door behind me. I take off my coat and sit down at my desk. I'm about to get started on my emails when there's a knock at my door.

'Yes,' I answer.

Jess comes in, carrying some post and a few international editions of our magazine that I like to keep an eye on.

'Forgot to give you these,' she says as she places them on my table. 'Paris has a great feature on Cosima Bosch. Maybe we should feature her too?' Jess suggests.

Cosima Bosch is an up-and-coming French designer known for her use of studs, ruffles and endless embroidery. Jess loves her. I'm not so keen.

'Yeah, maybe,' I reply, reaching for *Couture Russia* instead.

I get on well with the editor – a sharp, decisive, forward-thinking woman. I always appreciate the fresh tone she brings to the magazine. I flick through a spread of models posing against a dark backdrop in seventies-inspired clothes: bright Balenciaga dresses, romantic Valentino flares and chic Marc Jacobs coats.

Jess goes next door and comes back with more magazines and papers.

'Westminster is an absolute joke, really,' she comments, rolling her eyes as she dumps *The Times* and the *Telegraph* down on the table.

I murmur in agreement, although I'm more interested in checking out the price of an Alexander McQueen choker worn by a model in the spread.

'Did you hear about that guy?' Jess asks.

'What?' I look up.

Jess places the *Financial Times* down on my office table, followed by the *Sun* and the *Mirror*, which both have Julian's face on their covers. I try not to flinch.

'What guy?' I ask, silently urging her to be talking about a fashion designer. Perhaps she's referring to Ben Hao, a designer from Taiwan who's just released his spring/summer collection full of playful yet monochrome styles. His designs are up Jess's street, but I like them too.

'That guy who was killed,' Jess says nonchalantly, gesturing towards the *Sun* as she leans against the table.

'Oh, yeah. The "brutal slaying",' I comment. 'Awful.'

'Yeah, it sounds intense. Shot with arrows. It's, like, biblical,' Jess says, her eyes wide. She clearly knows nothing about Saint Sebastian.

'I know, it's so weird,' I note.

Jess stands there, looking at me, as though expecting something more. But what more does she want? Julian's death was weird. There. I have nothing to add.

'Thanks for the papers,' I say, getting up and retrieving the *FT* from the table. I bring it back to my desk and let its salmon pages fall open across my lap.

Jess is still leaning against the table, not taking the hint. I turn over a page.

'Wasn't the guy you went on a date with called Julian?' she says eventually, her words bursting into the air between us, finally freed, as though she's been gearing up to them.

The page I turned falls flat – an ad for an airline.

'Huh?' I utter, wracking my brains for how on earth Jess knows Julian's name.

'You were on the phone to him last week, remember? I came in and you hung up. You said you'd been talking to a guy you were going on a date with. You said, "Bye Julian",' Jess explains.

Bye Julian. Fucking hell, she's right. I was sitting here chatting to Julian on the phone last week when we arranged to meet.

Then Jess entered the room, and in my desperate bid to come across as normal and chummy, I told her I had a date lined up. I thought I could get away with telling her that bit, but I didn't realise I'd said his name out loud. For fuck's sake. For fuck's sake! What is wrong with me? How on earth could I have been so stupid? I hesitate, desperately trying to come up with a way out of this, but I draw a blank.

'Oh yeah, he was. Why?' I respond, looking up.

Jess stares at me from behind her fucking Oliver Peoples glasses.

'That's the name of that guy,' she says, eyeing me coolly, blinking. 'The one who was killed.'

'Okay . . . !' I laugh. 'Oh yeah, I forgot to mention, I killed my date!'

Jess laughs, her face relaxing a bit.

'Odd coincidence, isn't it?' I murmur, looking down at the paper, flicking over another page. Another ad. I don't take it in, I'm concentrating too hard on pretending to be normal. On getting through this moment.

'Yeah, definitely! Especially since you don't really meet many Julians,' Jess comments.

Are her eyes boring into me, or am I just imagining it? I pray she can't see the sweat patches that must be starting to appear under the arms of my satin blouse.

'I guess.' I shrug. 'I've met a few though. I think the name's getting more popular.'

I turn another page.

'Hmmm . . . Want a coffee?' Jess says, standing upright, seemingly forgetting it. Putting the weird coincidence behind us.

'Starbucks or canteen?' I ask.

'What do you want?'

'Starbucks would be good,' I say.

'Cool. BRB,' Jess says, before turning to leave.

'Thanks, Jess,' I murmur, flicking over another page of the *FT* as though I'm engrossed. I swivel my chair back around to face my desk as I hear the door snap shut. She's gone.

I let out a sigh of relief.

I think I just about styled that one out, but fuck me, how could I have been so careless? Blabbing Julian's name like that and then killing him. For God's sake. I need to read fucking *Serial Killing for Dummies* because I am clearly out of my depth.

My palms are sweating. My heart is hammering.

I close my eyes. Cursing myself. Cursing myself. Cursing myself. Jess is right, there are hardly any Julians. I may have shrugged her off for now, but what if something else connects Julian to me? What if the police figure out he'd been in Mayfair? What if Jess starts putting other bits and pieces together?

Oh my God. My heart's pounding, but I force myself to draw in a deep, shaky breath. I need to pull myself together, for appearance's sake, if nothing else.

I pull open my desk drawer and retrieve my face powder compact. I click it open and check out my reflection. Thank God for Botox. My face looks smooth: stress- and blemish-free. Most women I know get Botox to avoid ageing. I use it to maintain a poker face. By freezing my muscles, Botox prevents my thoughts from reaching my face. It also prevents the flicker of micro-expressions, the tiny frowns, the raised eyebrows, the giveaways. It keeps me impassive. My thoughts remain my own. The real me is a crying, wailing bag of rot, like Dorian Gray's painting, festering and filthy in an attic somewhere, lined with rage, pitted with sin, washed out with angst. But the face that looks back at me is pretty. My cheeks have a nice pink glow thanks to Abay's attentions last night. I smile at my reflection, taking in my blue eyes, the curve of my cheekbones, my neat nose. I finger my hair, silky smooth from the conditioning treatment I put on in the bath yesterday. I couldn't look less like a killer if I tried. I laugh, snapping my compact closed. Jess was merely commenting on a funny coincidence. She couldn't possibly suspect me.

I flick through the *FT* a bit more and finish looking through *Couture Russia* before turning my attention to my inbox. Eventually, there's a tap at my door. Jess.

'Come in,' I say, not bothering to look round. Jess walks up to my desk.

'Venti Americano, black,' she says, placing the coffee down by my keyboard.

'Perfect. Thanks, Jess!' I reply, trying to sound chirpy.

'No worries,' Jess replies breezily, before heading back to her desk.

The door snaps shut. I prise the lid off my cup and breathe in the coffee smell, watching the spiral of steam emerge. I reply to an email from Advertising, delete some spam. I should get in touch with Ben Hao, find out what he's up to. Arrange a feature. But I can't quite bring myself to. I still feel a bit unsettled. The Jess encounter has rattled me, even though I know it's nothing. But still, I can't help wondering, what if I were to get caught? How many years would I go down for if the police figured out what I've done? Would they realise who they were dealing with? Connect my other kills to me? It's been a while since a thought like that has even occurred to me. For so long, I've felt like I've been operating outside the law, like an animal. Wild. Prowling through London, striking when I need to strike.

I need to clear my head. I grab a notebook from my desk drawer and start trying to make a list of all the men I've killed. I write Martin's name in shorthand. I haven't had to use shorthand since back when I actually knew Martin, when I was a reporter, but it comes in handy sometimes, especially when I'm trying to be discreet.

Martin.

It all started with Martin. It was meant to end with Martin. I never set out to be a serial killer. Never in a million years did I expect I'd make a habit of it.

After pocketing Martin's cash, I lay low while the police failed to make an arrest for his murder, and then moved to London with a mission: to become someone. That kept me occupied for a while. I rented a cheap studio flat near Chelsea and decided to fake it till I made it. I got a capsule wardrobe of decent clothes, a gym membership, a decent haircut, and I made sure I looked the part. Then I went to the right bars, the right parties, mixed with the right people. I got a part-time job working in PR for a designer, spent my evenings at press events, shows and launches, but far too quickly, my money started running out. I'd managed to take around £30,000 from Martin, but that only lasts so long when you're living it up on the King's Road. And my job was only a gesture at a job – the same kind of thing my friends had. The girls I'd befriended were gallery assistants, interior designers, PAs. Their LinkedIn profiles looked nice, and they had nice offices to get dressed up to go and potter about in occasionally, but they didn't actually work. Their trust funds covered their bills and kept them in Chanel and Chloé. Their jobs were just pocket money. I didn't want to leave their world, but I could only fake it for so long, so I did what I had to do – I set about finding myself a rich boyfriend.

Along came *Gerard*. I write his name down in my notebook too. Gerard wasn't exactly the type of guy I'd had in mind when I went looking for love, but you're not meant to judge a book by its cover, are you? And honestly, who did I think I was going to find? I was never going to end up with a nice Chelsea boy. They wanted the Hatties and Millies of the world – the rich, adoring simpletons who'd look up to them and hang on their every word. That kind of guy has never taken to me. I was deemed fuck-worthy, but I wasn't considered girlfriend material. While the girls of Chelsea were happy enough to be friends, the boys sensed my wild side. They couldn't handle my sexual proclivities, my kinks, my bisexuality. Not to mention my personality. I'm not take-home-to-meet-the-mother material. Far easier to date a sweet girl.

Older men, on the other hand, were game. Like my ex-husband, Gerard.

I met him in a stuffy old bar off the King's Road where I used to go sometimes to read. It was the kind of place that was fusty and uncool enough that I was confident I wouldn't bump into anyone I knew, and I'd go there and devour books to plug the gaps in my state school education. I clued up on British history, royalty, theology, philosophy and art. I learnt the rules of sports I'd never played, like lacrosse, fencing, netball and polo. I studied languages, gaining basic fluency in German, French and Spanish. I even taught myself some Latin. I'd sit for hours on end, just poring over my books, making notes, drinking nothing but coffee.

I knew my presence amused some of the regulars; they must have found me quite an odd sight amongst their usual older gentlemen clientele. One day, a man in his sixties who always wore a suit with a silk pocket square, whatever day it was, asked if he could join me. He was short and unremarkable-looking, with thinning hair and crumpled skin, but his eyes had life – they were humorous, interested and engaging – and I warmed to him immediately. He noticed that I was reading a biography of Churchill and commented on it, offering to buy me a drink. I'd been reading alone for a few hours and didn't see the harm in accepting and sharing a bit of light conversation.

Gerard bought me a Martini and we talked about World War Two – sparring, testing each other – before moving on to easier topics like London life, Chelsea, our backgrounds: he came from a long lineage of wealth and privilege. I trotted out my usual Suffolk spiel – my parents, Anne and Robert Black, our gorgeous old farmhouse, private education, after-school clubs, Sadie the dog – the works. If Gerard questioned why a supposedly well-educated girl like myself was spending Saturday afternoons reading books like *Latin for Beginners*, he was too polite to ask.

We chatted away and I laughed at his jokes. I could tell how much it meant to him to share a drink with me. He couldn't take his eyes off me – they'd pass over my lips, my teeth and my hands as I reached for my drink, as though I were the most beautiful thing in the world. Weirdly, I liked how Gerard's admiration made me feel. I wasn't attracted to him; he was twice my age and then some, but he made me feel so beautiful, like an exotic flower, hyper-aware of my own youth and charm. And he wasn't boring either. He didn't just drink and shop and gossip about who was dating who, like most of the people I knew. He could hold a conversation; he was reflective and shrewd. We started running into each other regularly, and although I knew it was desperately uncool to while away my afternoons chatting to an old guy in a fusty bar, I couldn't deny that I secretly enjoyed our conversations. I liked the way he made me feel protected, taken care of, safe. Daddy issues, eat your heart out.

After a few months of dating, Gerard surprised me by proposing. And I surprised myself by agreeing, thinking we might be able, in our own weird way, to make it work. I wasn't exactly thrilled at the prospect of becoming Gerard's wife, but he let me do my thing. He didn't mind me working. He didn't stop me going out with my friends. He turned a blind eye to my occasional affairs. He bankrolled everything. I figured life could be way, way worse than marrying an old guy who doesn't really bother you that much and puts you up in his luxurious Chelsea mansion. I couldn't think of a reason not to marry him. But married life turned out to be very different to what I'd expected. Something about putting a ring on my finger, and me changing my name to his, made Gerard think he owned me. Over a few months, he went from being easy-going and charming to controlling and toxic. I stopped being the pretty young woman he admired and adored and became his property – a piece of meat to use for sex whenever he wanted, not to mention an unpaid cook and cleaner.

One night, Gerard pinned me down on the bed. I had a headache; I wasn't up to it. I said no. I tried to push him away, but he kept grabbing at me, pressed his crotch against me like Martin had done, and I snapped. I flipped. How dare he? I pushed him off so hard that he smashed his head on the bedside table and tumbled to the ground. He lay still. Collapsed, like a discarded puppet. A pool of blood slowly began to form around his head. I watched, intrigued, wondering if his injury would be fatal or not. His chest was softly rising and falling, he was still breathing.

What if he got up, enraged, wanting to rape me or hurt me? I couldn't risk it.

I crept over to him, my eyes not leaving him for a second as I crouched down and gently enclosed my thumb and forefinger over his nostrils. I pressed one hand over his mouth and squeezed his nostrils hard, holding my own breath, tense, watching, waiting, willing his chest to stop moving. He started squirming, his body putting up a last-ditch fight even though he was unconscious. Fear flooded through me, but I maintained my grip and then, finally, his breathing stopped, and he lay still. Gone.

It was like snuffing out a candle.

I was shit-scared the police would nail me for Gerard's murder, but they didn't. Idiots. Amongst a long list of health issues, he had breathing difficulties, emphysema, and the police bought my story that he must have fallen out of bed, knocked his head hard and stopped breathing. I took sleeping pills straight after I killed him, and woke up six or seven hours later next to his cold corpse. I called the ambulance, claiming I must have been too sedated to have heard him fall. The paramedics and the cops bought my story, just about. They didn't test my blood but, if they had done, everything would have added up. There was one officer – a woman around my age – who I could tell didn't trust me, but she couldn't prove anything. Gerard's autopsy ruled that he'd died from a concussion and breathing difficulties. And I was free.

Gerard didn't have any next of kin. Like I'd marry someone who did. And so naturally, all his wealth passed down to me. He was even richer than he'd let on. A retired oil tycoon, I thought he was worth two or three million, but it turned out he was worth way, way more than that. Crazy amounts. All mine, now. Not only had I gotten away with murder, wiping out an awful rapist creep, but I'd become rich. Filthy, filthy rich.

I thought my new-found wealth would make me happy and it sort of did, for a while, but then the buzz of it passed and I felt strangely alone. I was living in Gerard's house, full of memories of what he'd become, and I felt rotten. The initial triumph I'd experienced at having gotten away with killing him faded and I slid into grief. Not for Gerard but for the dream I'd had.

I'd genuinely believed I might be able to be married. I thought I could possibly lead a relatively normal life, and yet I'd ended up alone again, in a house full of horrible memories. I'd ended up more broken than before, burdened with even more traumas. Two dead men behind me. I tried to distract myself by doing the things I used to do before Gerard. I went to the bars I used to go to, but the people who'd once included me in rounds, the people who'd invited me on the holidays and nights out I used to struggle to afford, no longer wanted me around. They saw me as a gold-digger; they knew I wasn't like them. London stopped feeling like a place where I could reinvent myself, it felt tainted. I craved a sense of belonging, home.

But being me, home has always been hard to come by. I tried my luck though. I contacted my cousin, Rita. She's a few years younger than me and we used to hang out when we were teenagers, getting drunk together at the weekends, back when I was a mess, a waster. We'd get dressed up in the skimpiest, ugliest dresses, plaster on make-up and false lashes, spritz ourselves in cheap perfume and listen to the latest hits on the radio while knocking back whatever booze we could get our hands on. We'd get the bus to town and go to clubs where we'd flirt with guys, both of us damaged and desperate for attention. Sometimes we'd take them home, screw them. Pretend it was cool. Wake up the next morning, wondering if we'd remembered to use a condom. Alone.

Rita still lives in the town where we grew up, she still drinks in the same bars, still dates the same loser guys. She has a job in retail and drinks her weekends away. She's never had the ambition I have. She had a rough childhood too, but she's not interested in changing her life. She's not like me, and yet, in my lowest moments, I missed her. I wanted to be with her. I wanted to be drowning my sorrows, having a laugh. I called Rita and told her my husband had died. I asked if I could come and stay with her for a few days. She agreed and I jumped on a train out of London feeling almost normal: a girl who had family to turn to in times of crisis.

When I got there, things were okay at first. I'd forgotten Rita's smell: Daisy by Marc Jacobs mixed with apple shampoo. I'd forgotten the way she always wore baggy men's jumpers around the house and put her head in a side plait when she got home from work. I'd forgotten how she'd always sing in the shower or when she was cooking, and how nice and note-perfect her voice actually was. I'd forgotten the way she'd compulsively draw on things: receipts, bus tickets, flyers – doodling, like a graffiti artist. I liked reacquainting with these things, realising that somewhere within me was a reserve of details like this. Memories. Memories that didn't cause pain. A neglected sense of familiarity.

I began to settle into Rita's small terraced house, sleeping in her tiny spare room. I'd watch TV while Rita was out at work. I'd tidy her place, go to the supermarket. I went for walks around the local park, visited the cinema. I started to feel okay, like I was healing. I began appreciating sunny days, a good song on the radio, a nice lunch at the local pub. I even latched on to the storyline of a soap opera. I didn't give too much thought to how long I'd been at Rita's, I figured I'd be there for as long as it took to feel better, because that's what family's about, right? Supporting each other through the hard times.

But then one night, Rita came home late. She must have gone out after her shift.

I was curled up on the sofa watching TV when I heard a man's voice, loud, from outside. I thought it must be a dodgy neighbour and I wanted it to look like no one was in, so I lowered the volume.

'Let me come back, baby, please,' the man begged.

'I can't. My cousin's here,' Rita replied, her voice heavy, slurring. They'd clearly been out drinking.

'Oh, come on, who cares?' he protested.

'I can't. Just leave it. Next time,' Rita replied.

I felt like jumping up off the couch, opening the front door, telling them I didn't mind, that they could do their own thing. I'd go for a walk for a bit. I felt bad for getting in the way, and yet I was also touched that Rita was being so considerate.

'Come on, baby. Your cousin won't care. She's probably in bed,' Rita's man suggested.

I'd moved to get up and put my shoes on, when Rita spoke up again.

'She won't be in bed. She waits up for me. It's fucking annoying,' she said.

'Why?' her companion asked.

'I don't know. She's just kind of desperate,' Rita replied.

'She can't be that bad,' the man insisted.

Rita laughed. 'She is. If you met her, you'd understand,' she joked.

'Well I would, if you'd let me,' the man teased.

Rita laughed again. 'Seriously. She's just weird. She's a fucking drag. She always has been.'

'I thought you said you guys used to hang out?' the man commented.

Rita scoffed. 'Yeah, only because she had no friends. No one else would hang out with her. My dad felt bad for her because her dad hated her, and her mum topped herself. He'd give me twenty quid to go out with her. I'd just take the money and get drunk,' Rita explained.

'Fuck!' The guy laughed. 'Why did you let her come back?'

'Felt sorry for her.'

'Well, it's been ages. Get rid of her. I miss touching you. I miss being with you.'

I imagined him cuddling her, kissing her neck.

'Move out of your dad's then, and we can go to your place,' Rita teased.

I pictured her joke-punching his chest. Him grinning. A kiss. 'Or just get rid of your freak cousin,' he suggested.

'Don't worry, I'm on it,' Rita groaned.

I pointed the remote at the TV, turned it off and dashed upstairs to bed.

The next day, I was gone. I never spoke to Rita again. She never tried to contact me. She was probably relieved I'd disappeared – probably still is.

I have no family. No one. Not one person. It's strange how that makes you feel. I'm alone. Truly alone. Sometimes I feel liberated. There's no one to impress. No pressure. No expectations. I have no relatives asking why I haven't settled down yet. No birthdays to remember. No taxing family gatherings to attend. I'm free of all that and I'm free to be me. People think family is everything. Families give them a sense of identity and belonging, but with that come limitations. Consciously or subconsciously, people define themselves based on what their relatives have achieved. They aspire to similar ideals. They frame their dreams within the framework of their family's dreams, but when you have no one, you can be anything.

I left Rita's and arrived back in London with a mission to reinvent myself. I changed my name. Revamped my looks. Got a fancy new haircut. Got Botox, lip fillers, implants. Bought a shit ton of new clothes. I sold Gerard's old house and bought a flat in Mayfair. Hung out with new people. Got a job at *Couture*. The part of me that had been craving support went cold. It simply froze over. I was empty, alone, held back by nothing.

Yet even though it's freeing, in a way, not to have family or anyone to disappoint, the flip side is that there's no reason not to be terrible. I sometimes wonder if I'd have snapped the way I did if Rita had loved me. Despite everything I've been through – my mum's suicide, the abuse I endured as a child, Martin, Gerard – I think I might still have been able to draw a line under things and move on, if Rita had just loved me. But when I realised that no one did and no one cared, then there was no point trying to be good any more. I had nothing to lose.

I tried to date, like a normal twenty-something, but it didn't work out. There's something off about you when you've been abused, when you're damaged, broken. You're different. Men can sniff out the pain in you, like dogs picking up on a scent. I'd put my make-up on, wear my nicest dresses, go on dates and try to be on my best behaviour, but they never bought it. They could see the cracks in my eyes, the holes in my soul, the emptiness waiting to be filled. Men aren't knights in shining armour – that's fairy-tale bullshit. They're not looking for someone to save. Men like simple girls. Off-the-shelf girls. Ready to go. Easy company. Decent hearts. They're not there to heal you or rescue you.

I thought my looks would help. A bat of my lashes will make a man do a favour for me, but it won't make a good guy fall for me. My pretty face isn't valuable enough currency to make up for the scars. The men I dated picked up on the trauma, the voids, the hurt, and they didn't want it in their lives. They didn't want it in their homes. They didn't want its legacy in their children.

I tried not to let it hurt me, but it did. I realised I could never move on from my past. Every man who fucked me and disappeared reminded me of home. I'd lie in bed, texting some idiot, wondering if he'd want to see me again, and I'd get ignored, unmatched, ghosted, and I'd think of my dad. I'd think about the way he used to creep into my room, use me, and then creep out again like it was nothing. I'd think of Rita, laughing about what a drag I was. And I'd feel pain. Pure pain. Pain, pain, pain. Pain no amount of money could take away. Why did I have to end up like this? Broken beyond repair. Irredeemable. Every man an incarnation of my father. Why had fate decided I was trash, the kind of girl who could be used and discarded? And why couldn't I recover from it? I wanted to. I tried different tactics. I tried not drinking on dates, suggesting wholesome things to do, dating men I met through friends, men I'd heard were decent. I tried holding out – not having sex – but it made no difference. It always amounted to the same. It was like the moment the men were inside me, there was no pretence any more. They could just sense I was nothing. A void. They always left when they'd had their fill. I've stopped trying now. I don't look for love. I don't pretend to be something I'm not. I like what I've always known. I like to be dominated. I like to be hurt. I like to be slapped. Choked. Used. That's sex to me now. That's it. That's all I've got.

With each rejection, I felt more and more broken inside, but I didn't think about killing. I had no intention of killing again. It's not like I ever set out to be a killer; I'd just crossed paths with a few unsavoury men and survival instinct had kicked in. I never imagined I'd prowl the streets as a murderess, but somehow that's what happened. At first, I dedicated myself to my role at *Couture*, determined to rise from features writer to assistant editor. At the weekends, I partied, networking and schmoozing.

But then, one Saturday night, things took a strange turn. I'd been at a club with friends, but I ducked out in the early hours when I couldn't stand the rubbish music and sticky floors any longer. I was walking home when I spotted a stacked guy in his twenties trying to chat up a girl who was slumped, close to passing out, down a side street next to a club. He sounded stone-cold sober. His tone was too measured, too determined, too forceful for me to walk away. He offered to walk the girl home, but I knew he had other intentions. He took her by the hand and led her deeper down the side street.

Curious, I followed, watching as he pulled the girl out of sight, towards a CCTV blind spot near some wheelie bins. Hardly walking her home. I lingered in the shadows and looked on as he groped the girl's slumping body through her cheap dress, his hands roaming under her biker jacket, before he reached down to his fly, unzipped it and got his cock out. He pushed the girl on to her knees and began stroking his dick in front of her drooping face. He grabbed her hair, yanked her head up and was about to shove his cock into her mouth when a switch flipped inside me and rage coursed through my veins, injustice swelled in my heart, and I stepped forward.

'Get the fuck off her,' I hissed, expecting him to be so shocked at being caught that he'd spring away from the girl and scarper, but he didn't even flinch. Instead, his cold eyes met mine and a slow smirk spread over his lips.

'What are you going to do about it?' he snarled. He looked me up and down, leering. 'You could join in if you want?'

I stood there, speechless, as he pushed his dick into the drunk girl's mouth, holding her limp head in his hands.

'You fucking creep,' I spat. 'Get away from her.'

His eyes darkened. He let the girl go and she wilted instantly to the ground. But then he turned and lunged towards me, throwing me up against the wall.

'I said, what are you going to do about it?' he asked, holding me against the bricks, his hand cupped tightly around my throat. The same hand that had been wrapped around his dick.

I tried to push him off, but he was too strong. I was struggling to breathe. He smiled as I scrabbled to break free. Then he shoved his hands between my legs and squeezed my crotch. Bad move. I reached into my coat pocket, thinking I'd find my keys, hoping I could gash him with them, but instead, my hand wound around a long, pointed nail file, and my heart leapt. I gripped it tightly and in one swift motion plunged it into his neck, piercing his thick, bulging jugular. His eyes widened with shock as blood began pouring from his neck. It spurted on to my face. Warm and fresh. Shock replaced the anger in his eyes as he attempted to pull the nail file free and defend himself, only to find me twisting it.

Killing viciously like this, turning my weapon, feeling his blood drip down my face, was so much more intense than the quick, impulsive ways in which I'd killed Martin and Gerard. It was *so* much better. It was wilder, hotter, more thrilling. He tried to push me away, but he was disintegrating before my eyes. He fell to his knees. I watched, as though in slow motion, taking in each second as blood pumped out of him. Soaking his cotton shirt and jeans. Filling his hands. I gasped as he stared into my eyes, helplessly, his whole being falling into submission, the fight in his eyes disappearing. Drifting. Dissolving. My own eyes misting with tears at the beauty of it.

He collapsed, and it took me a few moments to come back to reality and look beyond his wasted, blood-drenched body towards the girl, who was lying, passed out by a bag of rubbish, oblivious to the world and the rapist dying next to her.

I tiptoed over to the rapist and pulled the nail file from his neck. Folding it into a discarded wrapper I found on top of the bin,

I stashed it in my bag, before tearing off my blood-spattered coat and top. I spat on the hem of my top and wiped the blood from my face, soaking up spots on my leather skirt.

I lifted the girl off the ground. She was unsteady on her feet, couldn't keep her head up. She didn't have a clue what was going on. I asked for her jacket, but she didn't respond so I pulled it off her. I slipped it on, zipping it up over my bra. The girl was slightly bigger than me, but it fit fine. Then I put my arm through hers, clamping her to my side, propping her up as I led her through a series of shadowy backstreets, before emerging on a main road, where I flagged down a taxi. Stuffing a couple of twenties into the girl's hand, I bundled her in, hoping she got home safe. Then I ducked back into the darkness and weaved my way back to my flat, dropping the nail file into a gutter along the way. When I got home, I burnt my clothes.

The man I killed turned out to be called Ahmed Iqbal, a call centre worker from Croydon. His mother claimed he was 'a kind, good-natured, loyal son'. As if. His death was yet another unsolved stabbing on London's streets. His family buried him and he rotted in the ground, forgotten, a pest eliminated. It felt good. I couldn't deny it. It felt like the score was being evened. Me versus the world. Me versus men, versus abusers, finally getting justice. I felt better than I'd felt for a long time. Calmer. I felt justified in what I'd done. I'd saved a girl from rape. I'd removed a predator from the streets. I wasn't just a damaged victim anymore; I was a vigilante, of sorts. I was making the world a better place. And underneath all the logic, all the justification, all the words, I couldn't deny that I simply got off on the raw, visceral, electrifying thrill of watching the life drain out of that low-life creep. I craved the power surge I got from killing. I craved the vivid, shimmering adrenaline rush, the smug swell of satisfaction and warm afterglow of accomplishment that comes with getting away with it. I tried to ignore my desires, but they were like an itch I had to scratch, I couldn't keep pretending they weren't there. Eventually, I gave in. I went hunting.

It wasn't like I was going to kill just anyone though. I'm not a total monster. I figured I'd kill people who deserved it. I'd prey on predators. Wipe out men like Martin, Gerard and Ahmed, men who had one thing in common: a predilection for abusing women. I decided I'd stand up for the vulnerable. Girls like me. I'd kill abusers. Predators. People who prey on the weak. I wouldn't just expose them in a newspaper like I'd dreamt of doing years ago, I'd wipe them off the face of the earth. I'd be performing a public service, satisfying my own bloodlust, while making the world a better place, one kill at a time.

I decided to start with paedophiles, figuring such low-life perverts would be easy targets. Plus, the idea of killing paedophile scum excited me the most. I joined Chat World, an online chat room. That's when I posed as eleven-year-old Emily and met @justaguy78 – the paedo I knifed to death in Hull. Watching him bleed to death, relishing in his pain and confusion and knowing it was the total opposite of the excitement and gratification he'd been expecting, was incredible. There was something so satisfying and empowering about causing someone so depraved to die and then slipping quietly away, knowing I was free and that victims had been spared, while his wretched soul had been condemned.

I got into murder after that, I can't deny it. I bought my garage, amassed a collection of knives and tools and weapons. I began skipping nights out with friends to stay home and trawl the net, looking for my next victim. I browsed chat rooms, message boards on the dark web and forums on fetish sites looking for targets: someone who gave me a buzz, someone who felt right. When I heard about sugar daddy Edmond Wyatt in a sex-worker forum, I knew he was the one. It would be a more daring kill than my last few since he wasn't just a pervert, he was violent too. I knew I'd have to play it right if it was going to work. The danger was greater, but that only made it all the more exciting.

After that kill, I really got into my stride. I wanted to take down someone even more threatening, someone even more toxic. I browsed and scrolled, until I found *Kevin Symes.*

He made my heart beat faster as I swiped right on Tinder. There was something truly nasty-looking about him. Something that set me on edge. We got chatting and eventually swapped numbers. I entered his number into the search bar on Facebook and found his profile. Got his surname. Googled it. Found out that he was a rapist and a wife beater. Only recently out of prison for having battered his ex-wife, breaking her jaw, stabbing her with a corkscrew in the neck and raping her. We got talking about our favourite films and he invited me over to watch *Reservoir Dogs.*

He lived in a shitty flat in a rundown block in Elephant and Castle. It was dirty, sleazy, dingy. Just a mattress on the floor and a bench press, but I pretended not to be repulsed. I asked him where his TV was and he laughed in my face, a cold, sneering laugh. He told me it was too late for that, there would be no movie-watching. He pushed me on to the mattress, crawled on top of me. I pretended to be overwhelmed, frightened, but I reached into my pocket, pulled out a can of pepper spray and doused his eyes with it. He flailed around, unable to see, punching the air, trying to get me. But I knew I had the upper hand. I retrieved a syringe from my pocket, rammed it into his neck and pressed on the plunger, injecting him with a high dose of ketamine. He passed out instantly. He was heavy, really heavy, but I managed to haul his body on to a chair and bind him to it with cable ties and rope. I waited a while until he came around. He was drugged and disorientated, but he started putting up a fight, twisting and turning and screaming and shouting, trying to wrench himself free. I held a knife to his neck and warned him I'd slash his throat if he made one more sudden movement, or dared scream one more time. I meant it and he could tell.

I ordered him to confess to every single one of his rapes or I'd slaughter him. He pleaded innocence at first, until I stuffed a ball gag in his mouth and tried out my brand-new nail gun on one of his hands, shooting through it like stigmata. That got him talking.

Panting with fear, delirious with shock and the drugs, he began his story. *The Life and Times of a Rapist*. His offences began way earlier than the one he'd been banged up for. I knew they would have done. They started when he was just twelve years old, when he raped a little girl behind the bike sheds at school. He went on and on.

After rape seven or eight, I couldn't take any more. I put the ball gag back on him and emptied my nail gun into his flesh, before slashing his throat for good measure. Then I sat back and watched him die.

It was way better than any movie.

I felt satiated for a while after that. I didn't strike again for quite some time. I landed the promotion I'd been craving and became the assistant editor at *Couture*, and I was too busy getting to grips with my new role to even think about killing, but eventually, the hunger crept back, and I decided to go paedo-hunting again. I re-joined the chat room where I met @justaguy78 and posed as a twelve-year-old girl called Lexie.

Within a few minutes, I got talking to @birdwoody. He asked what I was up to. I told him I was in care, that I'd had an argument with my foster parents, said I was feeling down. Like most predators, @birdwoody took my vulnerability as a green light to prey on me, and rapidly moved the conversation on to sex. He asked what I was wearing, what my underwear was like. He wanted me to send him pictures, and when I shyly refused, he asked if I'd like to meet instead. I told him I lived in Hayes, but even though he was in Leeds, he wasn't deterred. He was so stupid that he even agreed to send a selfie at the petrol station on the drive down. He was a weedy, tiny, little man. I knew it wouldn't be hard to take him down. It was dark by the time he arrived, and I asked him to meet me in a subway where I knew there was no CCTV, telling him I'd sneak out of bed once my foster parents were asleep so we could spend the night chatting in his car.

I waited in the shadows until he appeared, barely breathing. He didn't notice me until I ran towards him and swung at him with a baseball bat. He gasped in shock and pain, buckling to the ground. Then I grabbed his scraggly hair, yanked his face up, and stared into his fearful, beady, erratic eyes before jamming a screwdriver through his left eyeball. I thought stabbing someone through the eye would be a badass way to kill, but even serial killers have a gore threshold and the sight of @birdwoody's eyeball bursting and dripping down his face like a bloody egg yolk was too much for me, coupled with the gruesome squelch of his brain against the screwdriver. I had to swallow vomit back to avoid leaving DNA all over the scene. My throat was burning from stomach acid for what felt like days, and every time I thought of the kill, I felt the bile rising again. I couldn't bring myself to kill again for a while, but then I saw Mantegna's painting in Vienna, and I knew it was only a matter of time.

I jot the names down and scan the list.

Martin

Gerard

Ahmed

@justaguy

Edmond

Kevin

@birdwoody

Julian

God. Eight men. Hard to believe it's that many. I'd go down for life if the police ever found out. I've managed to avoid justice so far, but what if they trace Julian's murder back to me? What if they were to unmask me, uncover everything? I'd get multiple life sentences. I'd never see the light of day again.

There's a knock at my office door. Jess.

I flip my notepad closed. 'Yep.'

She peers around. 'Just letting you know you have a meeting with Poppy about the kitten heels feature.'

'I'd completely forgotten,' I reply, genuinely startled. I'd been so focused on writing my list that my meeting with our features director about kitten heels was the last thing on my mind. 'Thanks, Jess.'

'No worries,' she says.

'Can't believe kitten heels are making a comeback,' I add.

'Yeah, those things *need* to die.' Jess laughs, rolling her eyes as she closes the door behind her.

Jess and I may have totally different fashion sense, but one thing we do agree on is that you should either go hard or go home when it comes to pumps. Flats or six-inch, no in between.

I reach for my handbag and take out the Tiffany pill box I keep in there containing emergency Valium. I bite off half a pill and swallow it with a sip of my cold untouched coffee. I tear the page of names out of my notebook and feed it into my shredder. It may be in shorthand, but I'm not taking any more chances. Paranoia is eating away at me, although the Valium should take the edge off. Not to mention get me through an hour of going on about kitten heels.

Chapter Six

I get that he was hot and everything, but surely there are better things to talk about on a Friday night than some knobhead who's been murdered?

But no, my friends are insisting on picking apart every detail of Julian's death.

'It's just so intense,' Annika comments, stirring her straw through the ice cubes of her Negroni cocktail. 'It must have been a crime of passion. You don't shoot someone with arrows like that unless you *really* hate them.'

Of all my friends, Annika is the most likely to have spent her week poring over the papers. A former model with pale blonde hair, she now lives with her financier boyfriend in a sprawling estate in Surrey, where she has a perfume studio. She claims to spend her days making bespoke scents for private clients, and while she is indeed a master at what she does, she also has the kind of salacious knowledge of current affairs and celebrity gossip that can only really be gleaned from a lot of time spent reading the papers, listening to the radio and watching chat shows.

Annika's probably my least interesting friend, but if it weren't for her, our little group might not even exist. She's the glue that binds us all together. The one who texts everyone and organises drinks and spa days, and books tables at the nicest restaurants. She's like our group's administrator, and for that, I'm so grateful.

'Yeah,' Briony murmurs, taking a sip of her cocktail. 'It's horrific. Poor guy.'

Like Annika, Briony also spends a lot of time at home. She's an actress, although she hasn't worked for quite a while. She hasn't really needed to; the dust has only just settled on her second divorce – an acrimonious split that left her several million richer but with an air of exhaustion that she's still trying to shake. A lot of people wouldn't believe it, looking at how rich Briony's got from both her messy divorces, but she's only ever wanted a simple family life. She's actually an incredibly sweet and caring person. But when you look like her, with her Debbie Harry style, rock star temperament and neurosis to match, happily ever after is harder than you'd think to come by. Even Briony is exhausted by her own drama at this point, although she's trying to straighten her life out. She devotes herself to her kids – Spencer and Eugene. Her life revolves around them these days.

'It's really sad. He was so young too. Only twenty-eight. Younger than us,' Priya points out, sighing.

Priya is the most academically smart in our group, but she does have a slightly annoying tendency to see the world in black-and-white and point out the obvious. She's an Oxford-educated lawyer who works in-house as a solicitor for a global investment bank. She's an absolute force to be reckoned with – incisive, clever, strong-minded, while also being impeccably glamorous and put together. She's a little less creative than the sort of people I usually spend time with, but I have a lot of respect for her strength and success.

Like me, Priya grew up on a council estate and managed to get ahead through sheer grit and determination, although unlike me, she got to the top through merit rather than murder. Priya doesn't realise I'm from a similar background to her though. Like everyone else in my life, she thinks I had a cushy childhood in Suffolk.

'It's so sad. What a loss,' Briony agrees, shaking her head morosely.

She's probably imagining how she'd feel if a similar fate befell Spencer or Eugene. I roll my eyes.

'Guys, you know, this Julian bloke might have been a real asshole, right? If someone went to the effort of killing him like that, maybe he did something really fucked up to deserve it,' I suggest.

Annika scoffs, raising an eyebrow. 'So you're saying if someone does something fucked up, it's justifiable to string them up to a post and shoot them with arrows?'

Eva, the only one of my friends who's yet to voice an opinion on Julian, smiles wryly. Of all my friends, Eva is probably my favourite. Not that I do best friends. And not that Eva would either. She's an antiques dealer and tends to keep herself to herself, despite being effortlessly smart, interesting and cool. She dresses solely in black, vapes whenever possible and never wears make-up. She has a tendency to go off the radar a few times a year, holing herself up in a second home she owns in Venice. Rumour has it she has depression and likes to escape there, wandering along the dreamy canals – resetting – before coming back to London for round two.

I shrug. 'I'm just saying that just because he was young and good-looking, it doesn't make him a saint. He might have been a real dick.'

'Honestly, even if he was a "dick",' Annika mocks, doing air quotes, 'he still didn't deserve to die like that, Camilla. No one does.'

I shrug, reaching for my Montepulciano. I take a sip as my friends continue to lament Julian's death. The only person who's not joining in is Eva, who puffs on her e-cigarette. As much as I like Annika, Briony and Priya, it's moments like this that I realise I'll never fully relate to them. Julian did deserve the death he got. If anything, I went easy on him. Cunts like him deserve brutal slayings. If my friends had seen the pictures on his phone, then maybe they'd agree.

'Did you hear he was on a date?' Briony comments.

The news reports released this detail a few days ago. Julian had apparently told a friend he was heading out to meet a girl called Rachel. He'd texted a few hours earlier and said he was going to 'get some'. Asshole. He got some all right. Got some arrows to the chest.

But his friend started blabbing about this and reporters have been going crazy, dubbing Julian's fateful night his 'deadly date'. It's kind of annoying, but still, Julian having been on a date with a girl called Rachel hardly incriminates me. It's not like they can trace his phone records back to me. Naturally, I destroyed his SIM.

'Yeah, I heard that. Do you think she did it?' Annika asks, her eyes glowing with excitement.

I suppress the urge to laugh, exchanging a sly smile with Eva instead. This is the thing about my nice law-abiding friends. They pretend to be holier than thou, all high and mighty, and yet I haven't seen them this animated for weeks. They love a good murder. They and the rest of London are one hundred per cent getting off on this.

'No, a woman could never have done that,' Briony comments, sipping her cocktail, her black fingernails cupping the glass.

Briony doesn't only have the looks of Debbie Harry, she has the style too. She wears the kind of clothes that would make most women want to hide from reflective surfaces, but she can get away with it. She manages to look cool in ratty old T-shirts, skinny jeans, crumpled leather jackets and shapeless floral smocks. Even now, she's wearing a worn, grey chiffon dress with a daisy print that looks like something she picked up in a charity shop, yet with her face, it somehow seems cool.

'He looked huge. As if a woman could have overpowered him,' Briony scoffs.

She said something similar when my 'Sugar Daddy Slayer' kill was in the papers. That was a hair-raising night. We were sitting in this bar, and someone had brought a copy of the *Evening Standard* with them, with the grainy image of me leaving the hotel in a blonde wig and fedora. There was this odd, unnerving moment when Briony looked up from the picture and kind of squinted at me. It was as though she had seen right through my mask, seeing the real me. At the time, I pretended I didn't see her look, I acted blasé, brushed it aside. I worried for a moment she might go to the police, but I guess she let it go. We carried on drinking that night, had fun. Things were fine. She must have figured she was being paranoid.

'But according to his friend, he was heading out to see her,' Priya points out. 'It could have been her.'

'I just find it hard to believe that some girl would kill her date like that,' Briony remarks, pulling a face. 'I mean, seriously!'

'It would explain why she's single,' Eva interjects, and everyone falls about laughing.

Bitches.

I laugh along with them. Even though I'm laughing at myself. They keep chatting away about my kill, gossiping, occasionally interrupting their salacious speculation with interjections about what a 'tragedy' the murder is. I sip my wine, trying not to smirk as I look around the bar, at all the other young people out on a Friday night. I feel almost like a normal woman.

To an outsider, I fit in, but inside, it's a constant effort. An act. It's easier to pass as normal in a group, like this. One-to-one, however, tends to be suicide. The coldness and aloofness I conduct myself with at work, that some people even revere me for, doesn't fly when your friend's just been dumped or is trying to have a sentimental girly 'moment'. The social cues of friendship are easier to pick up on in a pack. I simply mirror. There's a lag sometimes, a blank gaze on my face where an emotion should be, but I vibe off my friends, quickly correct it, join in.

I didn't mean to end up like this. Dead inside. But I remember when it happened. I was about twelve or thirteen. Before then, I was in pain. Loads of pain. I yearned for love, kindness, compassion, I craved it constantly. It was exhausting. I wanted to be free from my dad, I wanted peace and happiness, and then one weekend, he went out on a Friday night and left me naked and bound in the garage, unable to break free, starving, and by Sunday, when he came home and let me out, my feelings had gone. From that moment onwards, I never felt crushing lows or occasional highs again. I just felt drained, hollow.

The only real emotions I experience these days are fairly consistent low-level sadness, anger, greed and desire, and frustration if I can't get what I want. I don't feel happiness or love or contentment. Or joy or hurt or shame. There's something almost childish about those kinds of emotions to me because, in a way, I grew out of them. But I can fake them when I have to. Alcohol helps. My fake backstory helps too: the Bryces. My friends might think I'm a bit cold, but they'd never suspect I've been through the things I've been through.

I take another sip of wine. Briony looks across the room, eyes wide, mouth dropping open.

'Oh my God, he's back . . .' she mutters, shrinking into her seat.

'Who? What?'

'Back?'

'Huh?'

We turn to look, following her gaze across the bar.

'Stop it,' Briony hisses, flapping her hand around, gesturing for us to turn back. 'Stop looking. Seriously.' Her voice is sharp and insistent, so we do.

'Who is it?' I ask quietly, my interest piqued. Briony's face looks like she's seen a ghost and we don't get many of them in this bar on a Friday night.

'Don't look,' Briony implores. 'Really don't.'

'Okay, okay.' We all agree.

'Miles Brady just walked in,' she whispers.

'Miles who?' Priya asks.

'Miles Brady. I can't believe he's showing his face after what he did.' Briony shakes her head, looking over at him, not even trying to conceal her disgust. 'The audacity.'

The urge to look is overwhelming but I manage to resist.

I take a sip of wine. 'So what did Miles Brady do then?' I ask.

I expect I already know what Miles Brady, whoever he is, has done. It will be the same kind of thing that all of the men around this part of town have done. Cheating on their girlfriends or spouses, getting caught with the nanny, being busted having had some drunken threesome, spunking the couple's savings on an escort, or even, in the case of one acquaintance, getting found hooking up with the neighbour's husband. What surprises me more than anything is why these men's antics are even considered gossip-worthy anymore. Infidelity is so commonplace, it's barely even worth mentioning.

'He . . .' Briony leans in, and gestures for us all to lean closer too. She fixes us with her kohl-lined eyes. 'He molested children,' she says.

What?

'He was working as a piano teacher, offering private tuition to kids around Mayfair,' Briony continues. 'One of Spencer's friends' mums hired him. He'd had a really impressive career as a concert pianist. Played all over the world. He even performed for the Queen. All these parents were clamouring to sign up when they heard he was offering lessons. Anyway, one little boy went to his mum after a lesson and said Brady had exposed himself.'

Briony pauses, wincing at the words. 'His mum freaked out and reported him to the police. Word got around. Then a few other parents got paranoid and asked their kids if anything had happened during their lessons. A couple of other kids spoke up. It turns out Miles had been abusing them,' Briony says, her jaw tightening with anger.

'How come we haven't heard about this?' I croak.

'It was a few years ago now. I didn't know Cynthia, Spencer's friend's mum, back then,' Briony comments. 'She'd be livid if she knew he was out.'

'Out?' I echo.

'He was in jail. Got five years for child abuse – rape, molestation, exposing himself. Apparently, the police found loads of child porn on his computer,' Briony explains, glancing down, before taking a hungry sip of her cocktail.

'How long was he in for?' Priya asks.

'Can't have been more than two years, maybe even less,' Briony says, glancing across the bar, a scathing look in her eyes.

Two years. I want to spit out my drink. What a fucking joke.

'Why did he get let out so early?' I sneer.

'Think he had some health problems. A heart murmur or something. They went easy on him during his trial because of that.

Maybe that's why, but I honestly don't know,' Briony comments, sighing.

'They probably reduced his sentence for good behaviour too,' Priya suggests. 'They go far too easy on some of these people.'

Damn straight.

'He had another conviction dating back to the eighties. Molested a little boy back then too,' Briony recalls. 'He probably just kept his head down so he could get out quickly and abuse more kids.' She visibly shudders at the thought.

'They should have locked him up and thrown away the key,' Annika states firmly.

Or murdered him. Way faster and far more efficient.

'I'm not going to look right now, but what does he look like?' I ask. I can feel the itch brewing. A new target. Two years is no kind of justice for a man like that.

'Pale, pasty old guy. Cheap navy suit. Red pocket square,' Briony says, picking up her drink and taking another sip.

My friends are gawping over this information, stunned to discover there's a paedophile in our midst. There's even talk of asking security to remove him. I sip my wine and try to act nonchalant, but I can't take it any more. I need to check this guy out.

'I'm going to the loo,' I say, placing my glass on the table and getting up. As I walk towards the toilets, I do a scan of the bar, focusing on the area Briony was glancing at, but I can't spot this pale pasty prick in his cheap suit. Damn it. I weave through the punters gathered around the bar.

'Hi, Camilla,' says a guy I met at an art show a few months ago. His name's Mungo Tuck, which has always sounded to me like it should be a brand of zany health-food snack bars, but Mungo's a painter. Fairly talented, if you like cutesy landscapes. He smiles, giving me an unsubtle appreciative look. Clearly had a few. He's

118

good-looking in a wholesome, bright-eyed, bushy-tailed kind of way. Totally not my type.

'Hey, Mungo,' I reply, aware that the two friends he's standing with are now also checking me out. Urgh. 'How are you?' I ask, rhetorically, while squeezing past him. 'Sorry, I just need to . . .' I mutter. 'Chat in a bit,' I say over my shoulder as I make my way through the throng, casting my eyes around for Miles as I go.

Where the fuck is he? I'm looking around, but I can't see him. I make my way to the toilets, even though I don't need to go. I lock myself in a cubicle and get my phone out, googling Miles Brady.

A stream of headlines appears.

Jail for paedo pianist

Pianist who performed for the Queen JAILED for indecent assaults

Concert pianist abused piano pupil who idolised him, court told

'Vile predator': judge slams pianist who preyed on pupils

The headlines are accompanied by pictures of Miles Brady. He's the worst kind of creep, because despite being pale and a bit pasty, he has kind-looking brown eyes. Slightly beady, behind glasses. He looks completely harmless. He smiles in one of the shots, posing in front of a grand piano. He seems guileless, almost sweet. If I had kids, I'd probably let them have lessons with him too.

Actually, fuck that. I'd install fucking CCTV with what I know about men, but still, I can see where the parents who hired him were coming from. He looks *nice*.

I click on one of the articles – *Pianist Miles Brady jailed for indecent assaults* – and have a read.

> INTERNATIONALLY renowned concert pianist Miles Brady has been jailed for five years after a jury found him guilty of sexual offences against three of his former music students.
>
> Brady, 53, who once performed for the Queen, was today branded a 'systematic and relentless' abuser of young boys who had looked up to him as either a gifted musician or a trusted mentor.
>
> The court heard that Brady had preyed upon three boys, aged between 8 and 14, to whom he had been providing private piano tuition in west London. Brady filmed his assaults using a camcorder and was found to be in possession of 3,500 indecent images of children, as well as a manual on how to groom minors.
>
> The defendant was previously sentenced in 1989 for sexual activity with a child he met when volunteering with a local orchestra while living in his hometown of Chester.

I scroll through the article, flicking through the others as well, picking out details, piecing together a picture of this monster. I take in various quotes.

'A dangerous and predatory abuser of children.'

'Convinced his pupils his assaults were normal.'

'Brady's victims felt lucky to have such a celebrated tutor and were scared to say anything in case the lessons stopped.'

I read an article stating that one of Brady's victims, an eight-year-old, didn't speak up about the abuse as he was 'fearful that if he said anything, it would be the end of his dreams of becoming a pianist'.

Apparently, another of Brady's victims, an eleven-year-old, was invited to his home for a 'masterclass' on Brady's personal piano, but was greeted by Brady in a pink dressing gown, 'which he took off to reveal he was naked, before abusing the boy'.

Urgh. I click through the articles, comparing them. The pink dressing gown makes a fair few appearances. It seems Brady liked to lie next to his victims in bed wearing it, while trying to coax them into touching him. It gives me the creeps. Big time. What did he think it made him look like? A giant fucking marshmallow? Mister Blobby? A cuddly Care Bear?

I snap the toilet seat closed and sit down, trying to gather myself. I can feel the rage, simmering away. Two measly years after being sentenced and he's out drinking, while those poor children's lives are wrecked. Those kids will never, ever view the world in quite the same way again. They'll never fully trust again. Or be quite as light and happy and carefree again. They have a life sentence to endure, but this twisted piece of shit is out and about, doing his thing. He'll probably keep raping and pillaging to his heart's content, destroying more lives, taking more innocence, and making the world an even darker, more horrific place.

I hate him. I really hate him. I can feel the pain, the rage swelling inside me. I want revenge. I want to kill him, I really do. He's the perfect target. He's practically fallen into my lap, like the universe has lined him up for slaughter. The temptation is intense, nagging. I want to give in, hatch a plan, and yet I know I shouldn't. I should resist.

I got sloppy with Julian's murder. I'd be putting myself in danger if I were to kill again any time soon. And it's not like Miles is my responsibility. There are plenty of bad men in the world. I can't single-handedly deal with every last abuser. At some point, I'm going to have to accept that I have to coexist with these creeps. I need to push my rage and pain down, find a way to live with it.

Sighing, I emerge from the cubicle. I eye my reflection in the mirror. I look normal. You'd never know what's going on inside. I dust my cheeks with a bit of powder and apply a fresh slick of my lipstick – Orgasm by NARS. Fuck's sake.

Funnily enough, Miles Brady is the first person I see when I come out of the toilets. I must have missed him before, but there he is, reclining in an armchair in an ugly navy suit with a red pocket square. He's sitting at a table with another old bastard, sipping whisky, laughing at something. It hits me again how normal he looks, how *nice*. He's the kind of guy you'd stop in the street and ask for directions if you were lost. The sort of man you'd imagine is a loving dad or granddad even, a caring husband. And yet he dresses up as a marshmallow and tries to get little boys to touch him. I don't know what to think. I just wanted one night off. Just one night, to hang out with my friends, have a few drinks and forget that the world is full of creeps, but I can't get away from them. They're everywhere.

As I walk back to my table, I stop and chat to Mungo again. Better my friends think I've been busy talking to him all this time than googling a paedophile in the loo. Not that they'd ever suspect that. They'd probably approve of me talking to Mungo though. He's the type they'd like to see me end up with – a sweet, attractive, posh boy. They don't really approve of my lovers.

We chat a bit about Mungo's art, his studio, and for a few moments, I allow myself to bask in the warm glow of Mungo's lovely, sheltered life; his unselfconscious privilege. I take it in, like sunshine. I gaze into his emerald-green eyes, smell his clean, fresh scent, return his friendly smile, but then the shadows come back and my thoughts start to wander, retreating back to Miles Brady, and as Mungo tells me about his upcoming exhibition, I find myself daydreaming about the ways I'd like to kill Miles.

I could hang him with the tie of his pink dressing gown. Or I could lock him up in a dungeon and leave him there with no food or water, and then, after about a week, as he's about to die of thirst, I could give him one glass of water, to keep him going. Then I could cut his arm off while he's starving to death, cook it up for him with some herbs and sauce and present it to him. I could get him to cannibalise himself to death. I read about that on Reddit recently. I'm not sure if it would work but it sounds fucking cool.

'We should hang out sometime,' Mungo suggests.

'Sure!' I reply, plastering a smile on my face. 'Sounds great.'

I tell him I should be getting back to my friends and it's only when I'm approaching our table that I realise I never gave Mungo my number. I was too preoccupied with thinking about Miles. Oh well, Mungo can find me if he wants me.

I hesitate as I sit down. Briony's got her coat on. Priya's draped a pashmina around her shoulders. A bill rests on a silver dish on the table, a few cards next to it. A waiter comes over carrying a card machine.

'I can't stay here with that creep around,' Briony explains in a hushed voice.

'We were thinking of The Cauldron,' Annika tells me, slipping on her Moncler coat.

'Sounds good,' I reply, recalling the new cocktail bar around the corner as I take my wallet out of my bag.

I glance over my shoulder to see Miles throwing his head back in laughter at something his friend has said. Asshole. I know I shouldn't kill him. I know it's too risky with the police already looking into Julian's murder. I know I shouldn't kill right now, and yet, I'm not sure I'm going to be able to resist.

Chapter Seven

I know there are nicer things I could be doing on a Saturday morning than googling paedophiles, but I can't seem to stop myself.

Curled up under a cashmere blanket on my Amode sofa with my iPad on my lap, I set to work finding out as much as possible about Miles Brady. I should just forget about him, leave it. But I don't know if I can.

I've moved on from the information about his cases. I've read enough, I don't need to torture myself. Now I'm focusing on Miles's personal life: where he lives, what health condition he suffers from, where he hangs out. I tried searching for him on Facebook, but nothing came up apart from a few links to articles about his crimes.

Nevertheless, it didn't take long to track him down. All I had to do was look up a few old guys who were at the private members' bar we went to last night. I know of a few of them. There's a washed-up actor, a former news anchor, a retired politician. I added them, and eventually, after poking around on their friends lists, I found my way to Miles's page. Turns out he's trying to reinvent himself as Giles Bradshaw. Idiot. His profile photo is of a cat prowling over the keys of a grand piano.

Hopefully the cat isn't his. The last thing I'd need after killing him would be to find a home for a poor little pussy. Giles the cat lover could have been someone else, but maybe he should have untagged himself from his friends' photos. I'd recognise that creepy, pasty face anywhere.

Now that I've found him, I have to decide what I'm going to do with him. I could kill him and make it look like a natural death or an accident. It would have to be something subtle with the whole Julian thing going on. I do like the idea of doing something more torturous, like locking him up somewhere, slowly starving him to death, forcing him to cannibalise himself Reddit-style. But I need to exercise some restraint. I shouldn't even be killing him at all and yet I can't stop thinking about it. I want him gone. I can't accept the thought of him swaggering around, a free man. His death would be justice. It might bring his victims peace. And stop him creating new ones.

My phone buzzes. It's a notification from the Met Police's Twitter account.

@metpoliceuk: Do you recognise this woman? Detectives are appealing to the public for information to identify this individual, seen with crossbow attack victim Julian Taylor on the night he was brutally murdered in Hayes on Sunday, 17th January.

Oh my God. The picture is of me and Julian, staggering down the street in Hayes. I don't look like myself, I've got my Ciara wig on and the denim cap I was wearing does a good job of concealing most of my face, but the tip of my nose is visible, my lips, the angle of my jawline. Fuck. I scroll through Twitter, browsing different accounts, but the police have only released one image. It's grainy. On first impression, you'd never think it was me, but the lips are my lips, the jawline is my jawline. My hands bead with sweat, my heart's thumping. The Met's tweet already has seventy-seven likes and forty-three retweets. It's got eighteen comments. I scroll through them:

@jonah0871: Catch this bitch

@tony5stevens: Lunatic

@claire_xx: What the fuck?! No way she killed him!

Someone's left a GIF of a Funny Yellow Guy cartoon character with flashing red lights going off around its head with the words 'Freak Alert!' *Rude*.

@jimbob_90 has written 'I'd swipe right tbh' with a shrugging emoji.

I click on to a tweet with a link to a BBC article about the photo. It's already the third most-read story on their site. What the . . . How long has this information been circulating? I check the *Daily Mail* – nothing yet – but they'll no doubt be all over this in minutes. Fuck's sake. I was beginning to think the whole thing was about to blow over since there hadn't been an update for days, but this picture is going to fire everything up. I refresh Twitter and, sure enough, there's an article from the *Sun* with the headline *Could this woman be crossbow victim's 'deadly date'?* People are going to love that. The comments are already pouring in:

@steveguillion1: Scary. Find her and give her the death penalty. #hangher

@markyboy17: deletes Tinder

@imran_named: Sorry but no way a woman did this

@sweetirishgirl: Find her, lock her up and throw away the key. Sick

@elaineDDingram: London these days. So glad I left

@needaholiday: This is what happens when you ask to go Dutch on the bill

There's more of the same. Garbage. I start to relax. It's a grainy photo that's now being used for clickbait articles. It doesn't mean anything. It's not like the police can pin me down with one blurry picture. I'm about to log off Twitter, go and make a coffee, try to forget about it, when a new comment captures my attention.

@adrianclark: Is it just me or do these two look kind of similar? Look at the face . . . SERIAL KILLER????

@adrianclark has taken my picture and posted it next to the hotel security image that was taken of me after I killed that repulsive bastard Edmond Wyatt – the sugar daddy who was beating women. The blurry image shows me in my blonde wig and fedora, strutting through the hotel lobby after I left the crime scene. Both pictures are nice and indistinct, and you can barely see anything beyond the blonde curls and the hat in the hotel shot, and on the surface, the pictures don't look particularly alike – but side by side, you can spot the similarities: the shape of my mouth is the same, and so is the jawline. Oh shit. I fucking hate Twitter. Why are people always trying to be so quick and clever on there? They're outsmarting the fucking cops. The cops I could handle.

Who is this @adrianclark? He's sharp. I click on to his page. A young guy with a cute face – wide eyes and a dimple in his chin.

Sheepskin jacket. Green hair. Three hundred and seventy-six followers. His bio reads: '21. Criminology, Newcastle University. Rat daddy.' His tweets are all about murders. He's a true-crime fanatic. He retweets criminology research too. There are pictures of his rats. Wry commentary on his life: 'My hairdresser just very firmly told me that I should chase my dreams. I mean, thanks? But my hair looks awful?' and 'When your Uber rating's 3.4 and you've never even been sick in a car. Just unlikeable then?' His tweet about me has seventeen likes already and five retweets. It's only been two minutes. There are three comments.

@bookishthings: omg . . . SAME PERSON!

@scotinengland: You could be on to something. Have @metpoliceuk connected this?!

@motorroller: Whaaaaaat?! Mind BLOWN!!! London has a serial killer!

Oh shit. Oh shit. Oh shit.

I place my iPad down. My clammy hands leave misty fingerprints on the screen. I get up. I pace around my flat. I walk over to my floor-to-ceiling window with its view over London. What the fuck am I going to do? Surely a rat-loving twenty-one-year-old with green hair isn't going to be my downfall? And yet, I'm sweating. I feel done for. The whole 'Sugar Daddy Slayer' thing blew over pretty quickly. No one came forward identifying me then – or at least, if they did, the police never followed up on it. But what about now? What if the media gets wind of this serial killer angle? What if the police investigate it? What if they already are? No one will shut up if they think there could be a serial killer on the loose. The pictures could go viral. What if someone recognises me? Sees beyond the wigs and the hats and spots the lips, the jawline. What if this is the end?

A chill sweeps through me. My heart pounds in my chest.

No. It's not going to happen as long as I stay calm and cool-headed. I look out over the city. I need to avoid being out and about as much as possible over the next few weeks. Keep a low profile. No one will suspect me at work. They wouldn't dare, but what about Jess? What if she sees those pictures and spots a likeness to me? What if she ties that together with the fact that my date's name was Julian? What if she reports me? Would she do that? Surely not. Jess and I have worked together for years. She knows me as a decent person. Surely she'd never really believe I could be a serial killer. And even if she did, would the police be able to do anything? So I look a tiny bit like those pictures, and I went on a date with a guy called Julian, what else have they got on me? There's no actual evidence tying me to the scene. I'm careful like that. And anyway, would Jess really jeopardise everything? The police wouldn't be able to charge me, I'd be released, and yet our relationship would be ruined forever. I'd get another assistant, Jess would lose her job, word would get around about what she'd done, she'd never be hired again in fashion, she wouldn't be able to keep up with the mortgage repayments on her lovely Clapham house. Her husband, Jake – an unemployed artist – wouldn't exactly be able to cover it. They'd end up having to move out, rent some shitty flat. Jess wouldn't want that. She definitely wouldn't want that.

Clouds pass over the sky. I force myself to take a deep breath. I'll probably be okay. This will blow over. But for now, I need to get the fuck out of London.

I find my phone and cancel the appointment I had at a hotel around the corner for a massage, facial, manicure and pedicure.

I'd been looking forward to it, but I can't face being in a gossipy spa right now. I can't handle having a beautician literally staring at my face, focusing on every part of it. I'm meant to be meeting the girls for brunch tomorrow, but I'll have to cancel that too. I need to lie low, or better still, get out of town. I know! I'll go home. I'll make up some shit about how my mum's sick and say I have to go back to Suffolk. Perfect. Serial killers don't go home to tend to their sick mothers at the weekend. I'll head up to Somerleyton, take a ton of pictures, update my social media. I'll cancel work on Monday, citing a family emergency, and work from home. I'll stay out of London until these pictures are old news. Hopefully a new story will come along soon and Julian will finally be history.

I click on to the Airbnb app and see if the Suffolk house I usually stay in is available tonight. It's a bit short notice, but it is out of season. I enter my dates and I'm in luck! The place is free. I make the booking and message the host, telling him I'll be there by this evening. Then I get packing.

I know I should probably just lie low in Somerleyton, but I'm surprisingly sociable for a serial killer.

I wanted company, so I invited Vanessa. She was fretting about her dissertation, but I managed to convince her that the peace and quiet would be great for her work. I told her about the private study in the cottage overlooking the windswept fields, and messaged her a picture of the desk, set within a little nook, surrounded by wooden beams. She took the bait and I picked her up from her place in my SUV. She loaded the boot with books – an optimistic amount for such a short trip, especially with someone as distracting as me, but

131

I didn't say anything. We just drove out of London, catching up, listening to songs on the radio, singing along. I'd forgotten how much I enjoy Vanessa's company. Joining in as she belted out the lyrics to 'Shake It Off' by Taylor Swift, I really did feel like I was managing to shake off the whole photo thing.

Vanessa is the last person who's ever going to recognise me from the pictures. She barely goes online, let alone browses Twitter. I think she likes to feel somewhat above all that, as though engaging with Twitter is incompatible with being intellectual. Tweeting and reading dusty old library books on Aristotle don't really go hand in hand in her world. The girl's living in another century. There's no way she'll realise she's having a weekend away with a serial killer.

We pull up outside the cottage. It does feel weirdly like coming home. The last time I was here was only a few weeks ago, when I came to 'visit the family for Christmas'. I spent a week alone, reading crime novels, working, swiping on Tinder.

The place has become so familiar to me now, with its black-latticed windows, wooden doors and brass knockers, its green picket fence. The trees in the front garden that are so verdant and green in the summer are dark and gnarled now. The sun is setting in the distance and the sky has a rosy-pink, fading blue hue.

I place my bag down on the porch and reach under the plant pot where the owner always leaves a key for me. I unlock the door.

'Wow, this place is amazing,' Vanessa says, walking through the hallway.

'Isn't it?' I reply. As far as Vanessa is concerned, this house is a holiday rental I stay in from time to time. She knows nothing about my pretend family. We've never really talked about our families, and it's nice to be here and to not have to lie. For once, I can experience Suffolk with another person, and I won't have to constantly pretend my personal life is something that it's not.

'It's gorgeous,' Vanessa says, dumping her bag by the front door and wandering through the living room.

The guy who owns it – a wealthy but kind, old Etonian country boy called Harry – has decorated the house to be completely in fitting with what you'd imagine an English country estate to look like. It's almost like a film set with its quintessential features: the old, careworn rugs across the wooden floorboards; the wicker basket containing logs of wood by the fireplace; old, creased leather sofas, and antique plates on display on the mantelpiece. The beds upstairs are rickety and a bit cheap, and the oak desk that Vanessa wants to study at later is a bit flimsy. Sometimes the furniture reminds me of the kind of thing you'd find in a doll's house. The whole place never quite feels real. It always feels like make-believe.

'It's lovely, isn't it?' I comment, as Vanessa moves from the living room to the kitchen, which is even more twee with its copper saucepans dangling from a rack, its clay pots full of utensils and jugs of dried flowers on the windowsill. It even has a string of garlic dangling down from a shelf laden with cookbooks. There's *Delia Smith's Complete Cookery Course*, a battered old edition of *Mastering the Art of French Cooking* and even an ancient copy of *Mrs Beeton's Cookery Book and Household Guide*. It wouldn't surprise me if Harry went down to his local charity shop, scooped a load of cookbooks up in his arms and bought them all for a fiver.

'It's so cosy, Camilla, I love it!' Vanessa says, stroking some dried thistle on the windowsill. 'It's so different from your London place. I didn't think this kind of place would be you!'

I shrug. 'I like a change as much as the next person.'

Vanessa smiles and looks out at the view. The sun has set more now, turning the sky a highlighter pink. I watch the fading sun fall on her face, the warm hue making her features soft and hazy, seductive like mood lighting. Unlike me, Vanessa doesn't wear much make-up. A bit of BB cream and a slick of mascara is all she bothers with.

'I've missed you,' I say, the words tumbling out of me.

I have genuinely missed her. I've missed her bad fashion sense, her cluelessness, her otherworldliness. I've missed her wild hair, her fine-featured face, her beautiful, soft femininity.

'I've missed you too,' Vanessa insists, looking away from the sunset and meeting my gaze.

Her eyes are so pretty. Chocolate brown, lined with naturally curly lashes. They're kind, honest. I wonder what she sees in mine. If she can see all the secrets and pain and hate, or if she just sees the desire.

I take a step closer and place my hand on her hip. Vanessa holds my gaze and tilts her head towards me. Her lips are soft and smooth, her kisses are so gentle and slow. Tender. Unlike Abay's kisses, or even Mr USA's. We kiss slowly, reacquainting with each other, exploring each other, until desire truly takes hold and our kisses grow in intensity, becoming rougher, hungrier. My hands roam over Vanessa's body, feeling her curves through her cotton top. She's touching me too now, her hands moving erratically over my back, pulling me into her. Vanessa always comments on how she loves my little body. She likes to make cute jokes about how I'm 'pocket-sized'. We like to marvel over each other, enjoying the novelty of each other's forms.

Vanessa runs her hands over my back and squeezes my ass. I let out a moan. She pushes me back towards the sofa, pressing me into it, until I'm lying on my back and she's crawling over me. She plants kisses on my neck and pulls off my top. I'm not wearing a bra. She reaches down between my legs. I'm already hot and wet and I moan, relishing her touch as her long, bony fingers press through the fabric of my trousers. I sigh with pleasure and reach for the hem of her baggy jumper. I want to see the beauty beneath. Vanessa has the most incredible breasts. She stops rubbing me for a second and crouches between my legs, helping me remove her top by pulling it over her head. She's wearing a purple bra with luminous blue embroidery. The colours resemble an oil spill. I don't know where Vanessa gets her underwear from, but it's godawful. She does complain that it's hard to find nice underwear for bigger breasts, but I know at least a dozen labels that do better designs than some of the stuff she wears. But still, I don't complain. I've almost grown fond of Vanessa's hideous underwear; it's like a surprisingly good present wrapped in cheap brown paper.

I reach around her back and unclip her bra, pulling it free from her shoulders and chucking it aside. Her breasts are large but shapely, gravity-defyingly pert. She has the kind of breasts that belong on a catalogue model and yet she keeps them hidden underneath her baggy clothes. I reach down between my legs, unbuttoning my trousers, wriggling free of them. I keep my Simone Pérèle knickers on. I want Vanessa to remove them. I watch Vanessa touching her breasts, massaging them, squeezing her nipples. She knows I like it when she does that. I reach inside my knickers and touch myself. Vanessa's eyes mist over as she watches me. Within seconds she's tearing off my knickers. She lowers her head to my pussy. I lose my fingers in her flowing brown hair and concentrate on the sensuous strokes of her tongue. It feels amazing.

'Get on top,' I gasp.

Vanessa looks up from between my legs. She gets up and wrestles off her jeans and knickers inelegantly, her movements clumsy and eager. I smile, watching her indelicate enthusiasm as she frees herself from her clothes. She gets on top of me. I run my fingers down the curve of her slightly rounded stomach, across her crotch and between her legs. She's already warm and slick. I dip my fingers inside her. Her eyes widen as she grinds against my hand, but that's not enough. I pull my fingers out of her and place my wet hand on her hip. She presses her groin against mine, straddling me, our thighs interlocking. She thrusts against me. I sigh as I grind back, drinking in the sight of her. Her breasts rock with each movement. The way they move is spectacular. I reach out to touch her breasts, squeezing them, tweaking her nipples. She moans with pleasure. I feel myself getting close, light-headed. Her breasts sway in my hands, her nipples hard. The pressure builds, the ecstasy overwhelming. I come hard, my pussy spasming, in freefall. I cry out as the orgasm tears through me. I feel incredible.

Vanessa doesn't come with me, but once I've caught my breath, we swap places, with her lying on the sofa and me between her legs. I suck her clit, fingering her hard. Her salty, familiar taste is as much of a homecoming as being back in this house. Vanessa grabs my head and pushes me into her as she cries out. I love it when she does that. I feel myself getting wet again and reach back between my legs, rubbing my clit. The sound of Vanessa moaning, the feel of her hand gripping my head, the taste and the warmth of her makes me come again. My orgasm is even more intense than the last – sharper, more insistent. I groan into Vanessa's pussy, sliding three, four fingers into her. She gasps and cries out, pulling my hair, bucking against my hand, coming hard. Her dark pussy wet and quaking.

We pull apart, our bodies sweaty, clammy against the leather.

'Harry would hate me if he knew what I'd done on this couch,' I joke, lying back against the cushions.

'We're probably not the first!' Vanessa says, breathily, still recovering from her orgasm.

'Eww, don't say that!' I comment.

'It's true though!' Vanessa laughs.

I roll my head lazily towards the window. It's dark outside now, the sky having turned an inky blue. I get up and close the curtains.

'Just getting some drinks,' I say, before wandering into the kitchen.

I retrieve two bottles of local ale, Brewer's Gold, from the fridge. I don't usually drink this sort of thing, except when in Suffolk. Harry knows I like it and he always leaves a few bottles for me. I thought he might not bother this time seeing as my booking was so last-minute, but he's gone to the effort regardless. So sweet of him.

I uncap the bottles and carry them back to Vanessa. I flick on the lights. She's lying on the couch, still naked, looking like something from a daydream. I hand her a bottle.

'Thanks,' she says, drawing her legs up so I can sit down.

I take a sip of the ale, relishing its rich, hoppy taste. I like to drink it directly from the bottle, feeling the cool glass against my lips.

'This is delicious,' Vanessa says, wiping foam off her lips with the back of her hand, while inspecting the label.

'It's my favourite,' I reply.

We sit there on the sofa, legs intertwined, chatting shit and drinking Brewer's Gold for the rest of the evening. London feels a million miles away, along with Julian, my picture, that greenhaired, eagle-eyed Twitter boy and everything else.

Vanessa and I have stayed at the cottage a bit longer than planned. I told Jess that my mum really needs me. I've been posting sombre pictures of the wintry Suffolk landscape to my social media accounts, saying how good it is to be back, furnishing each post with quotes like 'Having somewhere to go is home. Having someone to love is family. And having both is a blessing' and 'Family – where life begins, and where love never ends'. I know, I hate myself too.

Fuck family, I've had the time of my life here with Vanessa. We've had sex in practically every room. Even the utility room. But it hasn't been all about that. It's been quite romantic too. I took Vanessa to the pleasure gardens of the Somerleyton estate – a seventeenth-century manor with beautiful, manicured grounds. It's one of my favourite spots. We ambled through the arched paths, which look spectacular in summer when draped with wisteria but have a desolate quality to them at this time of year. We devoured cream teas in the quaint little café with its aproned waitresses and wrought-iron chairs and got so hyper from caffeine and sugary jam that we giggled like schoolgirls through the yew-hedge maze. We visited Fritton Lake too – a secluded spot surrounded by willow trees and reeds. Vanessa and I managed to persuade the man who looks after the site to let us take a rowing boat out even though it was off season. We rowed as swans glided past us. The water reflected the sky like glass and rippled as we pulled our paddles through it. We kissed in the middle of the lake, snuggling close for warmth, fending off the cool breeze that rustled through the reeds.

Last night we wandered into the village and went to an old pub for dinner, where we sat close in a quiet corner eating casserole with mashed potatoes – the most carb-rich meal I'd had in weeks. Retired locals reading the papers glanced over at us curiously, intrigued by this pair of city lesbians.

Feeling guilty for all her time off, Vanessa has been up in the study this afternoon, working on her dissertation, while I've been sitting on the sofa downstairs, catching up with emails, making work calls and checking the news. The story with my picture has been covered by all the nationals, but none of them have followed up on @adrianclark's suggestion of a serial killer, which is a major relief. I suppose until the police have confirmed it's an official line of enquiry, anything the papers say is just conjecture. I check Twitter. People are still talking about Julian's 'deadly date', but the line-up for a new celebrity reality show has been announced, an earthquake has hit California and #MondayMotivation is trending. The news cycle is moving on. People are forgetting about Julian. The whole thing is blowing over, like the winds that sweep through the fields outside.

I breathe a sigh of relief and lie back, relaxing into the sofa. A gentle breeze blows through an open window. I listen to the birds.

A few times during this trip, I've found myself daydreaming about a different kind of life. Of living out here with Vanessa. We could create our own little paradise in a world that's hell. I've realised this weekend that I like her more than I thought I did. She's a genuinely good person. I think she's finally achieved eudemonia. Being around her, I feel safe, soothed, unthreatened. I picture us lying in each other's arms in the mornings. Watching the sun rise over the verdant fields. Drinking fresh coffee. I could go freelance and write articles from home from time to time, rather than running around in London, editing. Not that I'd need to work. If I sold my Mayfair flat, we'd be set up over here for life.

If Vanessa wanted to, she could do her thing upstairs in the study, writing papers on Aristotle. We could go for long country walks every day. Abandon fashion. Live in cardigans and leggings and wellington boots. Hold hands while walking through the wheat fields like we're in an LGBT-friendly Boden ad. We could even bake our own bread. Okay, maybe I'm taking it too far. But it could be heavenly.

But my fantasies have been repeatedly interrupted by real-life intrusions. Like my phone buzzing with constant alerts from the Met Police's Twitter account. The last one was some self-congratulatory update about the good work of their staff. Sure. So good that they've let a serial killer like me get away with it for years. Keep up the good work, lads! But the tweets bring me back to reality. Life here with Vanessa would be amazing, for about two weeks, but I'd soon be craving the grit and grime of the city – the drama, the fumes, the chaos, the competition, the glamour, the power, the clothes, the chase. How long would I last before I'd be racing back with an axe slung over my shoulder, itching to chop Miles Brady's head off? Until I'd be running home begging Abay to throw me on to a bed and fuck me? Until I'd be splashing five grand on a handbag and wanting to show it off down the King's Road? I can go away for the weekend, but I can't escape myself.

On Tuesday, Vanessa and I head back to London. I can't put it off any longer without getting into serious trouble at work. Weirdly, I've never felt sadder to leave Somerleyton. Vanessa is the first person I've ever brought here, the first person I've ever shared this place with. I've tried to tell myself so many times that I'm content in my own company, but this place has been so much more enjoyable shared. The local pub, the pleasure gardens, Fritton Lake – they were nice alone, but they've actually been fun with Vanessa. I feel a weight settling around my shoulders as we drive back. Neither of us speaks. We're both pensive and resigned. As we pelt down the motorway, the sky fades like an old photograph, sepia to grey, before dissolving to black. We stop at a service station and eat sandwiches that are as stale and depressing as our mood.

'Let's see each other again, soon,' Vanessa suggests, as I finally drop her off outside her house in Balham.

She lives in a four-storey Edwardian terrace on a road where the bins are left out on the street and foxes prowl furtively in the distance. She shares her home with five other students. I've never been inside. And to be honest, I'd rather not.

Vanessa reaches over and takes my hand. Her eyes are even more tender than usual. Oh no, she's definitely got the feels. But can I blame her? I almost felt like that too, with my daydreams of a serene, sapphic Suffolk life, but I know there's a difference between daydreams and reality. I know where to draw the line. Vanessa is more naive though – hopeful, less jaded. I'll have to manage this one carefully if I don't want to hurt her. I make a mental note to distance myself gently over the next few weeks. I'll make up some stuff about work keeping me busy. Soon she'll have snapped out of this crush, she'll be back to her books, fangirling over Aristotle once more.

'Thanks for an amazing weekend,' I say, squeezing her hand and leaning in for a kiss. Even as we're kissing goodbye, I feel a stab of desire. The sex this weekend was incredible, but I pull away and let her go.

Vanessa waves over her shoulder as I steer away from the kerb and drive home.

I put the radio on. It's still tuned to Capital FM from when Vanessa had control of the dial. I'm not usually a fan of pop music, but they're playing 'Starboy' by The Weeknd and I quite like that song, so I let it play. It blends into 'Accelerate' by Christina

Aguilera – another good one. Okay, so maybe I'm not quite as highbrow as I'd like to think.

As the music fills my car and I weave through the dark streets, headlights flashing across my face, passing strangers, I begin to feel okay again. The ennui of leaving Suffolk is replaced by the familiar frantic buzz of being back in the city. London will always be where I belong, despite the rapists, the abusers, the paedos, the creeps. It will always be my home regardless of the hunt. By the time I get to Mayfair, I'm singing along to 'Fancy' by Iggy Azalea. I pull on to my road when, suddenly, an unwelcome sight takes my breath away. Literally. Iggy carries on without me as my eyes laser in on a police car waiting outside my building. Coincidence? I hope so. But I never see police cars where I live – it's a good area.

I turn the radio off. Shut up, Iggy. I need to think. I glance towards the car. An officer sitting in the driving seat meets my gaze. He glances at my car. Is he just checking me out? Or is he checking out my car, my BMW X1 SUV? A lot of men do. Policemen or otherwise.

But I wonder: has he really seen me? Has he seen through the grainy CCTV image and spotted the killer underneath? I lower my head and bite my lip, trying to hide my mouth as I pull into the car park of my building, my palms so damp with sweat that they're sliding down the steering wheel. I should have stayed in Suffolk. I should have stayed there with Vanessa forever. I should never have come back. What was I thinking? London isn't my home. London's going to destroy me. My heart's pounding as I steer through the car park and drive towards my space. The car park's dark, silent, lit with the sodium glare of dusty strip lights. I feel like I'm being watched as I take my bags from the boot and lock up, before walking towards the exit.

It's a coincidence. It's just a coincidence, I tell myself as I head towards my building. The door from the car park is next to the

142

lifts. I glance over at the concierge's desk, but he's talking to another resident and doesn't notice me. I step inside the lift and press the button for my floor. I draw in a deep, shaky breath as the doors close, taking in my reflection in their shiny metallic surface, but all I can see is my mouth, my jawline, those damning pictures blending with my face. If only I could get a new mouth. Maybe I should get filler. Except I like my lips. And anyway, that might look suspicious. I could change my hairstyle to hide my jawline better. That's worth looking into.

I'm probably overreacting though. One police car outside my building doesn't exactly mean I'm done for. London's the knife crime capital of the UK. It's worse than New York. Moped theft is happening all the time. Someone important probably had their phone snatched, made a fuss about it, and the police came out to investigate. Yep. There's no way the police have managed to track me down using some grainy picture of a girl with lips that slightly resemble mine. I run my fingers through my hair while looking at my reflection. I fix myself with a steely stare, taking another deep breath as the lift doors open.

I step out. Breathe in jasmine, rose. I turn to my front door.

There are two officers waiting outside.

Chapter Eight

'Hi . . .' I croak, giving the officers a wary, flummoxed look, as though I have no idea what they're doing here. 'Can I help you?'

'Camilla Black?' says the taller of the two.

'Yes?'

'I'm Detective Chief Inspector Wheelan, and this is my colleague, Sergeant Porter. Could we have a word?'

DCI *Wheelan*? The detective who referred to my murder as a 'brutal slaying', who said it was one of the most shocking he'd witnessed in his entire career. I saw him making a few appeals in the press for someone to come forward about the 'Sugar Daddy Slayer' years ago, but I never thought our paths would cross. I'd put him out of my mind. And yet now, he's here, right before me, standing at my front door. He looks different in person. Younger, more imposing. He looks around forty, with dark features and broad shoulders. What's he doing here? What does he want from me? My heart thuds in my chest. Has he knocked on every door or did he pick mine specifically? What does he have on me?

'Okay . . . What's this about?' I raise an eyebrow dubiously, trying to put myself in the shoes of an innocent woman who'd be completely freaked out by all this. 'How long have you been hanging around outside my flat?' I ask condescendingly.

'We'd like to speak to you,' Wheelan says, ignoring my question.

'Can you please tell me what this is about first?' I repeat huffily, as though affronted by the intrusion. An innocent woman would want to know. She wouldn't just let a couple of police officers into her Mayfair penthouse, into her life. She wouldn't let them encroach on her evening without making them justify it.

'It's about an incident nine days ago, Sunday the seventeenth. A murder,' Wheelan tells me, his eyes fixed on mine, taking everything in.

'A murder?' I baulk, heart thumping under my cashmere. 'Around here?'

'No, in west London. Hayes,' Wheelan says, still watching me closely.

I glance at his colleague. His eyes are on me too.

'Well, what are you doing around here then? Shouldn't you be questioning people over there?' I take a step towards the front door and reach into my bag for my key.

I'm getting into my stride now. I can do this. I've been acting my whole life. If these two had any real evidence on me, they'd be arresting me right now. Whatever has brought them here must be insubstantial. Flimsy. They must be trying to catch me out, sniffing out more clues. My performance is crucial.

'Can we talk inside?' Wheelan asks as I slide my key into my front door. I make a conscious effort to steady my hand.

'I don't see how I can help, but I'll try,' I tell him, sighing as I turn the key.

'Thank you,' Wheelan replies.

'This isn't about that guy who was in the papers – Julian something, is it?' I ask, trying to appear blasé, unruffled, as I push the door open.

'Yes, Julian Taylor,' Wheelan replies as he and his colleague follow me into my flat.

'Right, yes. Julian Taylor,' I say as I place my bag down by the door and flick the switch on.

My flat is flooded with light. My cleaner's been, and as usual, the light illuminates how beautifully pristine and immaculate she has left the place. It is a sight that tends to soothe me, but tonight achieves nothing.

Nevertheless, I'm curious as to what Wheelan makes of my place, but when I glance over at him, he doesn't react. His eyes wander towards my grand piano. Still nothing. His face is completely impassive. I suppose he's seen all sorts of homes in his line of work. Or else he's trained to be inexpressive. He's hardly going to ask me where I got my sofa from.

Act *casual*, I remind myself as I take my coat off and hang it up, draping it over the hanger, even though creases are the least of my worries right now.

I kick off my trainers. I consider keeping my scarf on to hide my jawline in case the officers spot my passing resemblance to the CCTV image, but that might look strange. Concealing my features might only serve to draw attention to them. Better to brave it. I unwind my scarf and hang it on the peg. I briefly consider asking the officers if they'd like a drink, before deciding that would be way too obsequious.

'So, how can I help?' I ask, walking over to the sofas. Wheelan and his colleague follow.

Even in my panicked state, I still can't help eyeing Wheelan's shoes and the sergeant's heavy, grubby-looking boots, praying they don't leave marks on my Elie Saab rug. They sit down on the sofa. I take a seat in the armchair opposite.

'Can you tell us about your connection to Julian Taylor, Ms Black?' Detective Wheelan asks, watching me with those emotionless hawk-like eyes.

'*Connection?*' I echo. 'What are you talking about?'

'How do you know Julian?' Wheelan continues, eyes almost stern now.

'I don't know him. I've read about him in the papers. I don't know him though. What makes you think I know him?'

I sound a bit hurried, panicked. I try to steady myself.

Wheelan leans forward.

'So, are you saying you've never met him?' he asks, elbows on his knees, eyeing me.

I feel like he can see right through me. His colleague sits mutely by his side, a notepad on his lap, pen poised.

'No, I've never met him!' I return Wheelan's steely gaze, even though my mind is ticking away like a broken clock, trying to figure out how they've connected me to Julian, getting nowhere.

My passing resemblance to the CCTV image is surely far too weak a link. And even if my slight similarity to the image is their lead, how did they track me down? Did someone report me? Did Jess call them and tell them about my date with a man called Julian? No way. She wouldn't do that. She just wouldn't. And even if she did do that, would it really be enough to go on? Would it really bring them here, knocking on my door? I can't work it all out, and the unease is making my palms sweat.

'What were you doing on the night of Sunday the seventeenth?' Wheelan asks. His accent is slightly northern, but I can't quite place it.

I laugh, trying to seem genuinely shocked. 'Am I a suspect or something?'

'Can you answer the question, please?' Wheelan responds.

I raise an eyebrow. A normal woman of my status in this predicament would immediately call her lawyer, except the last thing I need is for my lawyer to get wind of all this.

A silence passes between us.

'Please answer the question,' Wheelan urges me.

'I . . .' I frown, looking down at the floor, as though wracking my brains and casting my mind back to the previous weekend. 'Sunday night . . . One second.'

I pull my phone from my pocket and scan my diary, pretending I need my memory jogged.

'Nothing much, I'm afraid.' I glance up from the screen, placing my phone down on the armrest. 'I was doing what I do every Sunday night,' I tell Wheelan with a little shrug. 'I was winding down. I had some dinner. I read my book. Looked over my diary for the week ahead. Usual Sunday night stuff.'

'Right. So you were at home all evening?' Wheelan asks.

'Yes,' I lie.

'You didn't go out at all?' Wheelan reiterates.

'No!' I insist. 'I stayed in. I was going to go to the shop to get some food, but I ordered in instead. I have a bad habit of doing that at the weekends, especially on Sundays.' I allow myself a small smile. Wheelan doesn't return it.

I'm not even lying. Before Julian and I left for Hayes, while he was slipping in and out of consciousness, drugged on the sofa, I ordered sushi. I pulled him into my bedroom when the order arrived, left him slumped on the bed, probably thinking he was going to get lucky, and then I answered the door wearing only my underwear and a silk gown. Got to make sure you leave an impression when you're looking for an alibi. But in case that wasn't enough, I put my clothes back on and nipped downstairs to see if I could borrow some soya sauce from my neighbours. A retired theatre couple – totally lovely, always pleased to see me.

Then I stashed the sushi in the fridge. Bundled Julian into a cab. Brutally slayed him in Hayes.

'Where did you order from?' Wheelan asks.

'A sushi place down the road,' I respond, smiling as though this whole thing is baffling to the point of amusement.

'What's it called?'

'Musashi,' I tell him.

Wheelan's sidekick makes a note.

'Did they deliver, or did you collect?' Wheelan asks.

'They delivered.'

'To your front door? Or to the building?'

'To my front door. The concierge let them in.'

'What did you get?'

'Sushi.'

Wheelan eyes me coldly, unamused.

'Sorry. Tuna nigiri and salmon rolls. I always get the same thing.'

Wheelan nods. Sergeant Porter makes another note.

'I had to borrow soya sauce from my neighbours. They forgot to include it in the order,' I add, casually.

'Which neighbours?'

'The Hamiltons. They live at number thirty-four Maybe you can interview them? Perhaps they did it?' I snipe, my resentment at Wheelan's inquisition overriding my need to remain calm and collected.

Wheelan doesn't react. As per.

Porter makes a note. I start to relax. They seem to be buying my story.

'So you ordered sushi? What else did you do?' he asks.

'I told you, I read.' I gesture towards a novel on the coffee table. It's the type of thing I'd never normally read – a self-indulgent romance set in 1920s Paris about a troubled ballerina caught in a love triangle with a married man.

'Any good?' Wheelan asks.

I raise an eyebrow. It's as though he can tell I'm faking. Not just about Julian, but in general.

'Looking for recommendations?' I ask casually, trying not to lose it again.

Wheelan smirks. 'What's it about?'

I've read it, like I said I had. I've kept it on my coffee table in case my friends come over. They all love that book. I pretend to love it too, but really, it's bullshit. I give Wheelan a brief summary, replete with a few gushing remarks.

Sergeant Porter makes a few more notes. 'Why am I a suspect?' I ask eventually.

'We have reason to believe that Julian was in the area on the night of his death,' Wheelan explains.

Great. They must have accessed his phone records, tracked where he was that night, but I was confident that wouldn't lead them back to me. The tracking wouldn't be specific enough to place Julian right here, in my flat, or my building. It would only lead the police to the area, and there are thousands of people in Mayfair. Thousands more passing through.

'Okay, but why me?' I ask. 'I'm not a murderer – I'm sure there must be some in this area, but they're not me!'

Little does Wheelan know that in the drawer of the coffee table between us is an old Mulberry purse containing a tiny key. A spare to my garage. The garage that contains all the answers to his investigation and probably several others, too. The thought is unnerving.

'We have a witness who says they saw you with Julian,' Detective Wheelan tells me.

A witness?

'Okay, well, I'm afraid they're mistaken. I was at home, like I said,' I insist, furnishing my statement with a weary look.

'Did you leave home at any point on that Sunday?' Wheelan asks.

'I met up with my friend Eva for lunch. Got back at around three p.m. and then I stayed in. You can check with Eva if you want to. Check with my neighbours. I've got nothing to hide,' I insist, mustering the exasperation an innocent person would feel.

Secretly, I'm hoping he doesn't talk to my neighbours. The Hamiltons will back up that I popped over, but what if one of my other, less friendly, neighbours saw me with Julian? I didn't see anyone around when we returned from the bar or when we snuck out later, via the fire exit at the back. But someone could still have glimpsed us through a window. And what about the building's CCTV? What if Wheelan requests it? The thought is unnerving, although I think the building's management deletes footage after twenty-four hours if nothing untoward has gone on. I asked to see it one time when a delivery man claimed he'd dropped off a £5,000 Tommi Parzinger cabinet I'd ordered online that was nowhere to be seen.

But who did see me? Was it someone from the bar? One of the staff? I can't even remember what they looked like. I'd be surprised if they remembered me. Julian and I were just like any other punters that night. Could it have been the driver of the minicab we took to Hayes? He barely acknowledged us, and Julian was slumped head down the entire journey, with his cap on. The driver wouldn't have gone to the cops, not after the company's previous run-ins with the police. But then who was it? I can't think. *Fuck*. I should never have killed Julian. It was far too spontaneous, haphazard, arrogant. I thought too much of myself. I thought I could get away with anything, but now look at me.

'What is it that you do, Camilla?' Wheelan asks.

I'm pretty sure he already knows that.

'I work for *Couture*. I'm the editor,' I tell him.

'And how long have you worked there?'

'Around four years now.'

'Like it?'

'Yes, I love it,' I reply, although now I'm starting to really sweat. If Wheelan starts poking his nose around at work, then I'm done for. If he talks to Jess, I'm fucked. 'Is there anything else I can help with? I'm not the person you're looking for. Clearly. I was at home that night, and yet you're accusing me of having killed someone? Or having been with someone who was killed? It's ridiculous!'

'We're doing our job,' Wheelan replies, unfazed.

'I know, but I've told you what I was doing, and I'm tired. As you can see, I just got home, and I was looking forward to winding down.'

'Where were you?'

'What?'

'Where were you today, Camilla?' he asks.

'Is that relevant to your investigation?'

Wheelan's face is unmoving. He doesn't answer, he just waits for me to respond.

'I went to Suffolk for a break with my friend,' I tell him.

That sounds good. Suffolk with a friend. That's totally the kind of thing a wholesome, well-adjusted person would do.

'A close friend?'

'Yes. My friend, Vanessa.'

'Okay.'

Sergeant Porter jots that down.

'It's getting late. I need to get to bed,' I tell them, glancing towards my bedroom.

'Not ordering takeaway tonight?' Wheelan asks, a little sardonically. There's something in his dark eyes. Wryness? Mockery? Could it even be flirtation?

He's definitely not bad-looking. Is there part of him that's drawn to me, despite his antagonistic inquisition?

A moment passes between us as we hold each other's gaze. I feel something, a flicker of desire cutting through the panic, but no. I can't possibly think of Wheelan in that way. The last thing I need is to bring him any closer to my life.

'No, I'm not,' I reply.

Wheelan glances at his colleague and gives him a near-imperceptible nod.

'Okay, thanks for your time, Camilla.'

They get up to leave. I smile politely. I can't help checking Wheelan out as he turns to my door. I know I shouldn't be looking but he has got a really good body – muscular, large. I look away. I don't need any more lovers, and certainly not him. I already have Vanessa, Abay and Mr USA.

Wait.

Abay.

My heart lurches. It was him. The witness was him. He must have seen me walking down the street with Julian after all. And later, he recognised Julian's picture in the papers.

I think back to the last time I saw him, the way he was being more affectionate than usual, wanting to cuddle. Julian's body had been found at that time, but his pictures hadn't made the press yet, and neither had that grainy photo of me. There'd be no reason for Abay to have thought at that point that I had anything to do with a murder. He probably saw me and Julian together and assumed I was seeing someone else. Maybe it made him jealous, protective, and that's why he wanted to get closer than usual. And then Julian's death was all over the press and the pictures came out and Abay's desire turned to suspicion. But does he really believe I'm a killer? After all the time we've spent together, it's hard to accept. I'm always relaxed around him. He's never seen that side of me. And yet, he's the only one I can think of who would have spoken to the police. Perhaps he did it to spite me since I was never really into him.

'Lovely pictures,' Wheelan comments, pausing at the framed photographs of the Bryces on my wall.

I fake a smile. 'Thanks.'

'Your parents?'

'No, family friends,' I reply tightly. I can get away with lying to my friends about my fake family, but I'm not sure it's worth faking it with a detective.

'Right.' Wheelan frowns slightly, as though trying to figure out why I have photos of family friends on my wall but none of my family.

I smile innocently back, silently urging him to leave. To not ask anything more. I feel acutely aware of the Bryces on the wall, their warm eyes turned shrewd, their wide smiles mocking, their arms around each other's shoulders, grazing, clawing at the edges of the frames as though they want to break free. As though they're sick of being part of my world, my lies.

Wheelan's eyes are still on me, as if he's seen something. But what? I look away, feeling uneasy. How is it that I can just about keep my cool when lying about a murder, but when it comes to my fake family, I start to lose my shit?

'Here's my card. If you think of anything that might help our investigation, please get in touch,' Wheelan urges me.

I take the card. It's white with blue lettering that matches the Metropolitan Police logo. Wheelan's name is printed in bold, along with his mobile number, landline and email address. His station is the Met HQ in Victoria. His card is so different to the stylish ones I'm usually given at networking events, each one a cry for attention, a bid to appear tasteful, original.

'Thank you.' I slide the card into the back pocket of my jeans, before walking to the front door, leading Wheelan and Porter out.

I say goodbye and close the door. It clicks shut. I take a step back. I stand there, listening. Listening to the sound of the lift doors sliding open, closing, the hum of the lift as it descends down the shaft. They've gone and yet I can still smell them – a cold, slightly sweaty smell. I swear I can see footprints on my rug. I look towards my sofa, the coffee table containing the key to all my secrets. I'll have to move it somewhere much more obscure. Perhaps it's time to get rid of my garage altogether. It's too near the crime scene. The police are way too fucking close.

I walk over to the pictures of the Bryces.

'Oh, fuck off.' I sneer at their wide, warm smiles. But the words don't quite ring true.

I can't even pretend to hate them. It feels wrong. The Bryces are nothing but pure. I've been building our imaginary world for years. They've always stood for everything that's good in the world: loyalty, kindness, compassion, love, trust. I can't hate my perfect family. The fantasy is too ingrained.

I sigh, walking over to the seating area instead. I sit back down in the armchair and eye the space on the sofa where Wheelan sat. I thought he was just a standard police paper-pusher, but I clearly underestimated him. He was keen to catch me when I killed Edmond Wyatt, but I didn't give it much thought at the time. I just assumed he was useless, like the police always have been. I never thought he'd get this close. He's far too close. He knows my name. He's suspicious of me. He's been in my home.

I wonder how much he knows about me already. He called me Camilla several times, but does he know that's not my real name? If he's gone to the trouble of coming over, then he may well have gone to the effort of doing a background check. He might know that I changed my name by deed poll. And if he knows that, then he'll have been able to look up the old me. He could know everything I went through.

I pull my legs up on to the chair, wrap my arms around my knees, curl up. Wheelan probably knows me better than anyone else in London right now, and that thought is horrible. He'll already know I took my dad to court for all the horrific, unspeakable things he did to me. He might even have read the transcript of my evidence, and all the harrowing details it includes. He'll have discovered that the jury let my dad walk despite everything, believing my dad's lawyer's stance that I was a wild child making things up. Will Wheelan understand that no teenager takes their dad to court on rape and assault charges for fun, or will the reality be too much for him, like it was for the jury? Will he find it easier to write me off as a liar, a troublemaker, a lunatic? Either way, the thought of Wheelan knowing what I've been through makes me sick.

I take his card from my pocket and stare at his name: Detective Chief Inspector Glen Wheelan. I lean forward and place the card on the coffee table. I walk over to the window and look out at the city. I picture Wheelan driving back to the station, his police car one speck of light among many scattered across the London skyline. I take a deep breath, steadying myself. Gathering strength. I don't know what he knows about me, but I won't let him take me down. Just like I refused to let my dad take me down. I'll rise from this investigation like I rose from my childhood – a phoenix. Not even a phoenix: a crow, shaking the dust from her wings before breaking into flight.

Chapter Nine

Glen Wheelan.

I double-check my encryption software is working, and then I set about finding out everything I possibly can about the detective who's after me. It's pouring down outside, and sheets of rain lash against my bedroom window. The London skyline glimmers as Google generates its results.

The first page is full of articles about Wheelan having overseen a manhunt for the notorious serial killer Duncan Renwick – a violent thug of a man I'd like to have hunted down myself. A wheel clamper and security guard by day, killer by night. His modus operandi was to drive around in a van, prowling the streets until he found young, vulnerable girls walking alone or waiting at bus stops. He'd pull over, try to chat them up, and if they rejected him, he'd attack, manhandling them into the back of his van, where he'd rape them or kill them, battering them to death, slinging blows to their skulls with a hammer.

I open one of the articles. It praises Wheelan for his 'dogged pursuit' of Renwick. *Dogged pursuit.* That doesn't bode well for me. The article describes him as 'tenacious', noting that before he joined the Met two years ago, he spent a decade heading up the murder team at Greater Manchester Police, where he was personally responsible for thirty murder convictions. Thirty. Not bad.

Although it sounds better than it is. That's only three a year. How many people get murdered in Greater Manchester each year? Or go missing? Surely way more than three. For every murder Wheelan has solved, plenty more must have gone unsolved. His track record isn't that stellar. After all, he didn't manage to solve my sugar daddy slaying. And there are a few others he's missed too.

I click out of the article and browse the next page on Google. There are a few links to a recent radio interview Wheelan has done. Even talk of a book deal. Hmm. Didn't realise I'd had a minor celebrity in my home. I keep scrolling, but it's just article upon article about crimes he's solved, quotes he's given about 'horrific murders' and 'bringing justice to victims', delivering 'closure to the victim's family'. Blah-blah-fucking-blah.

I click play on Wheelan's radio interview. The sound of the recording bleeds out of my laptop speakers into my bedroom. The interviewer is irritatingly sycophantic, clearly likes a man in uniform. She giggles at pretty much every comment Wheelan makes, even ones that aren't remotely funny. It's irritating to listen to, but I do pick up on a few interesting details: such as the fact that Wheelan's only forty-two. Pretty young for someone of his rank, especially given that he's headed up a homicide team for more than ten years. He's clearly ambitious, which isn't good news for me. I keep listening. He grew up in Lancashire. Bit of a leap to have gone from sleepy Lancashire to murder squads and the Met, but each to their own. The giggling presenter starts to really grate on me. Even when talking about the murder of a twelve-year-old girl, she's giggling. Idiot. I turn it off.

I pick up Wheelan's card and google his mobile number, but of course, it doesn't deliver much, only a link to his profile on the Met site. I enter it into Facebook and Twitter, but he's not stupid. He's hardly going to have used his work mobile to set up social media profiles. *No results.* Unsurprising, but it was worth a try.

What next? I need some dirt on him. Some details. So far, I have nothing.

I try a few other searches: 'Wheelan, London'. Nothing new comes up, just more of the same. 'Glen, London'. A load of random Glens. Naturally. What else?

I want to hack him, but what can I hack? There's someone on the dark web who I've used a few times. A fifteen-year-old tech whizz from Cumbria who likes to flirt with me. He's a bit of a pain, but I don't care. He's good at what he does, and he's managed to get me into a couple of people's personal email and social media accounts a few times, when I've needed it. But I don't have Detective Wheelan's personal email address. I only have the details on this stupid card.

I type 'glen.wheelan@gmail.com' into Google, hoping something might come up. But there's nothing. I try the same with Yahoo and Hotmail, trying different formations of his name, different email-hosting sites, but still nothing. God . . .

I can't hack his work mail. It's way beyond my hacker friend's abilities, and even if it wasn't, it would immediately set alarm bells ringing at the Met. It could incriminate me far more than help me.

I feel impotent. At a dead end. I need to do something, but what? I tip my head back against the headboard of my bed, the blueish light from my laptop pouring over my face. I close my eyes and think. Just think.

Then it hits me: newspapers.

Google only delivers so much news coverage, but what if there's something on Wheelan dating back earlier? Something from his youth, back before newspapers had websites and everything was online. The internet's only been around for thirty or so years. Wheelan precedes it. Could I find something from his childhood? Gather some details about him or his family that I can't find online. It's worth a try. It's not like I have any other ideas right now.

I pay thousands for a subscription to an online newspaper archive service. It's a database of UK papers dating back a hundred years, the stories carefully tagged and as easy to search as on Google. I had a flight of fancy a few years ago that the database would help me research victims. I thought I could hunt down abusers banged up years ago, stalk them, see if they've changed their ways. I imagined wreaking vengeance on them, just when they thought they'd got away with everything, like a dark marauder appearing from nowhere, an angel of death. But I never really got around to it. The guy who sold me the subscription was a little surprised that a random woman would pay so much for a service, usually used by media companies or universities, for purely recreational purposes. If I recall correctly, I made up some bullshit excuse about researching a novel. Not that it was any of his business. If I want to spend thousands of pounds a year to browse historic news articles, that's my prerogative.

I log into the portal. It takes me a few attempts, my grasp on my login details a bit rusty, but I get in eventually.

I search for Glen Wheelan.

No Results.

Damn.

I try 'Wheelan, Lancashire'.

Twenty-nine results. What the hell?

I scan them, eyes widening. I sit up straighter.

Man stabbed wife in front of son 18 times

Croston man murdered wife in savage knife attack

'Caring and kind' mother slain in front of her son in vicious attack by estranged husband

I open the first article. A young mum – a pretty brunette – only twenty-five, attacked by a controlling husband she'd been running from. He'd shown up one night at her new home and stabbed her to oblivion, while the couple's six-year-old son looked on. Horrible.

Surely the six-year-old son wasn't Detective Wheelan? I check the date on the article and compare it to his age now. Yes, he would have been six around that time.

I read the other articles, checking to see if any of them mention Wheelan by name – a tag the search function might have missed – but I can't find the name Glen Wheelan in any of the reports. None include a picture of him either, not that he's likely to look much like his six-year-old self now. I go through all twenty-nine of the articles, even though some aren't about the murder. There are a couple from happier times. Detective Wheelan's mum, Maria, pictured at a charity fundraiser; another of her taking part in a half-marathon with her sister, Genevieve.

I google the name 'Genevieve Wheelan'. Not much comes up.

I type it into Facebook. Two results appear. One is for a woman based in Texas. Unlikely to be a relative of Wheelan's, but the other is for a woman – an attractive older lady with thick grey hair who looks mid-sixties, which would be about the right age – living in Surrey. I click on to her profile. She has 194 friends. I search her friends list for Glen's name. Nothing. He's a detective, I remind myself. He's not dumb. If he were to use Facebook, he'd surely use a fake name for his profile. I scroll through Genevieve's pictures. Her privacy settings are weak, and she has quite a few photos on show. Boring shots of weddings and barbecues and birthdays – the usual happy-family bullshit.

I'm about to click off, totally bored, when I suddenly land upon a picture of Genevieve with Wheelan. Detective fucking Wheelan. It's him. It's definitely him. He looks a few years younger, thicker hair, dressed down in shorts and a T-shirt, grinning in someone's back garden, his arm slung around Genevieve's shoulders, but it's him all right. Same eyes, same hair, same build. It's him.

Wheelan, with his aunt. The son of a man who murdered his wife. A six-year-old boy who stood by and watched. Who took all of it in, and then grew up to work in the police, heading up the murder squad at the Met. Police officers don't usually bother me much. They like to think of themselves as important, better than everyone else, but they're just the same. They want to clock off at the end of the day, go home and watch TV, get their pay cheque at the end of the month. They claim to care, but most of them just want an easy life, and a job's a job, we all grow numb after a while. But Wheelan isn't like that. He's not motivated by status or money or ego, he's motivated by justice, and that scares me. I know what that feels like. I kill bad men because they deserve it. I kill bad men because, like Wheelan, when I was young, very young, one made a stark impression on me. An irreversible impression. Damage that can't be undone. And ever since then, I've shown no mercy when it comes to hunting down men of that ilk and wiping them out. If Wheelan feels the same way about murderers that I feel about rapists, abusers, wife beaters, paedophiles and creeps, then nothing's going to stand in the way of his pursuit of Julian's killer. Which means I should be worried. Very worried.

And yet, despite my fear and anxiety, my eyelids are dropping. I glance at the clock on my bedside table: 2.34 a.m. I'm meant to be getting up for work in less than five hours. I want to go to Hayes and clear out my garage, in case Detective Wheelan finds it.

The garage contains the crossbow, and an arrow I pulled from Julian's corpse as a memento. If Wheelan discovers any of this, I'm done for. If he finds my weapons, my mementoes, and all the press cuttings I've collected over the years about my kills, he'll know everything. I want my things. I want my bag of red herrings, the gloves and scarves, and hairs, and fag butts, and toenails: all the bits of DNA-laden crap I've taken from creeps over the years.

I want to take everything – my armchair, my chest of drawers, my camping lamp – everything that might hold traces of my victims' DNA – and destroy it all. And yet I can't. For all I know, the police are on to me. They might already know more than they let on earlier. They could still be outside, waiting, like they were when I arrived back from Suffolk. They could be tracking my car. The last thing I need to do is lead them directly to my deepest darkest place. The one place where I hide nothing, where the mask is nowhere to be seen.

No. I'll have to leave it for now, and pray that this blows over, becoming yesterday's news, like all my other kills. I close my laptop and try to sleep.

Chapter Ten

Couture.

I eye the familiar sign. The gold letters are engraved in honey-coloured stone above tall plate glass panels that frame revolving doors. I walk through these doors every day. On good days, I barely register this building – pristine and imposing – with its gleaming entrance sealed from the public with an intercom system, security passes, CCTV and alarmed locks. On good days, the air-conditioned, wide marble foyer with an ostentatious flower display in the centre, soaring ceiling and twinkling chandelier barely even registers. On good days, I pound the marble with my heels, sashaying through the security barriers, arrogant, rushed, like I belong. And yet on days like today, I see it all. An outsider looking in. I see the affluence all around me and I feel like an interloper, wearing someone else's shoes, dressing up in someone else's clothes. I feel like a nobody.

I walk unsteadily in my Jimmy Choo stilettos towards the entrance, fumble in my bag for my pass, and present it to the sensor. The revolving door clicks, its latch freeing. I push my way through and try to look casual. *Couture* is my world now. My Mayfair flat is my home. London's most exclusive streets are my domain. The past was just a bad dream. The girl I used to be is dead. I take a deep breath, trying to centre myself, trying to feel strong.

I make my way across the light-filled foyer, swiping my pass against a security barrier.

'Morning, Camilla,' says a doorman who's here all the time, but whose name I don't know. He's been here for years, and the moment when it would have been appropriate for me to ask passed a long time ago.

'Morning,' I reply, forcing a smile.

I head over to the lift, my heels clacking sharply against the marble floor. My mood starts to lighten a little. I breathe in the clean air, which in the morning always smells of the bleach the night cleaners use. I step inside the glass lift, press the button for the newsroom. The doors close and the lift swoops up the shaft, lifting me higher into this bubble of luxury, a place that usually makes me feel okay, and far, far away from dead rapists and police officers. I'd probably go insane if I was knocking around my Mayfair flat all day, with nothing to do apart from have sex and get up to no good.

Couture might feel strange to me sometimes, but I'm grateful for it. It grounds me. It turns me into Camilla the editor – a force to be reckoned with. The light shifts as the lift climbs higher, growing darker as it rises further into the building, dense with offices, workers. My job may ground me, but it's also the ultimate alibi. How could a woman like me possibly be the person I am? No one would believe that someone as glamorous and poised as myself could be so depraved. My job's the perfect cover-up. Perhaps it doesn't do me any good at all. Perhaps it doesn't ground me, but simply facilitates my madness.

The lift doors ping open. The office is empty apart from a couple of early birds: Dennis, a page designer, and Anita, a sub. They glance my way as I cross the newsroom. They smile in acknowledgement, but visibly stiffen, straightening their backs.

'Morning,' I say as I stride to my office.

'Morning,' they echo.

It's 6.35 a.m. Usually, at this time, I'm showering at home, or I'm doing a workout at the gym. I'm never in the office at this time, but I've been awake since 4 a.m., when I woke in a panic, having been dreaming about being locked in a prison cell. I lay in bed as the grey, early morning light filtered through my curtains and I felt like my mind was closing in on itself. I tossed and turned and tried to get back to sleep for a bit, but it was no use. I got up, showered and got dressed, putting on a bold outfit unlike anything I'd usually wear – a red and yellow Salvatore Ferragamo shirt dress – in the hope that the bright colours might distract me from my melancholic mood. And distract others too.

I sit down at my desk and scroll through page mock-ups of the magazine on my screen. Features on luxe winter coats, ways to style the puffed sleeve trend, and Meghan Markle-style inspiration go over my head. I gaze out of my office towards Victoria, where the Met Police HQ is based, the address of which was on Detective Wheelan's card. I wonder what he's doing today. Is he doing background checks on me? Has he got any more leads?

There may be a witness who claims to have seen me with Julian, and I may have slipped up by blabbing his name in the office, but that's not enough to convict me of murder. I should be fine. I didn't leave evidence at the scene, I just didn't. I was careful about that. I may have blurted Julian's name in the office, but I'm too much of a pro to leave evidence at a murder scene. The police can tear that scene apart and they won't find a trace of me.

They'll be too busy wasting their time and resources on all the red herrings I left there – a fag butt I plucked off the patio of a known paedophile's house, the old jumper I nicked from a rapist a few years ago and kept in my garage, a glove I swiped off the table in a bar once that belonged to this asshole who wouldn't stop berating his girlfriend. I left them all on the roof of that council block, knowing the police would be all over them. Bagging them up, sending them off for forensic examination, running DNA profiles through their system, following up any potential matches, questioning suspects, seeking alibis, blah-blah-blah. And then, before they know it, someone else will have been murdered. Someone else's family will want justice and they'll have spent their budget and will be forced to move on.

I try to let my worries go. Wheelan's got close this time, too close. But he's not got anything solid on me. If he did, he'd have arrested me already and brought me to the station for questioning. He's just digging, that's all. As long as I keep my cool, it'll be fine.

I distract myself from my dark thoughts and reply to emails instead, coordinating features and sorting out the final details for a shoot later in the week. Fashion takes over and I start to feel normal again. Camilla the editor is back, while Camilla the killer is in her box. Far away, in her grotty Hayes garage where she belongs. I can hear the newsroom filling up beyond my office door as my colleagues start to arrive for work, the hum of chit-chat growing louder as I type away.

Suddenly, my office door bursts open, and Jess charges in, holding today's newspapers.

'Camilla!' she gasps. 'I didn't realise you were here.' Clearly, Anita and Dennis weren't feeling chatty.

'Just felt like getting a head start on everything after my weekend away,' I tell her.

'Oh, I see.' Jess places the newspapers down on my office table. 'How's your mum?' she asks.

For a moment, I have no idea what she's talking about.

'Oh, she's all right. Still a bit ropey but she's got my dad to look after her, she'll be fine,' I say, with a careworn smile.

'Aww, sounds tough,' Jess comments sympathetically.

'Yeah, she'll be okay though,' I insist, hollow inside.

'Good.' Jess smiles. 'My mum got some stomach bug a few weeks ago. She was bedbound for days. I went over with chicken soup and she made me watch pre-recorded *Cash in the Attic* episodes all afternoon,' she tells me, rolling her eyes indulgently.

I laugh, as though I can relate. I feel I should add something, but I can't think of a fake mum anecdote off the top of my head.

'Oh, did you hear Rayna's on the Women of the Year judging panel,' Jess says, distracting me.

'Rayna? Really?' I baulk.

'Really!' Jess confirms.

Rayna's fresh out of fashion college. She's only just released her first collection and yet she's already on the judging panel for one of the most celebrated media awards events in the country?

Jess and I exchange a look and it's clear that we're both thinking the same thing: *Nepotism.*

Jess heads out of my office. Once she's closed the door behind her, I google the Women of the Year Awards page. The event has a media category. A few editors on competitor titles have been recognised in previous years. I've always wanted to be nominated, even to win. I used to daydream about it from time to time. The awards are held at the Grosvenor Hotel, and it's an incredibly glamorous, exclusive event. I've often fantasised about picking up one of the gleaming glass trophies, grasping it, clutching an emblem representing the final stage of my metamorphosis: the moment I truly become Camilla Black. I check out the judges. The panel features half a dozen esteemed individuals, from all walks of life: philanthropy, the arts, fashion, the media, tech, politics. And there's Rayna's face. Her biography describes charity work she carried out in Moscow that I knew nothing about, before going on to detail her transition into fashion. Interesting. I decide we'll run a six-page spread on her new collection instead of the four-page spread promised, organise a shoot. I email the team to let them know, hoping Rayna might remember the gesture when compiling the shortlist.

Email sent, I retrieve a bottle of sparkling water from my office fridge and pour myself a glass. I take a sip. As I head back to my desk, I grab a few of the newspapers Jess left behind and flick through them. No stories about Julian today – at least that's something. It's just warmongering and royals and storm forecasts. I read an article in the *FT* about the 'political nervous breakdown' the country is going through and find myself momentarily distracted from my own personal crisis. I put the paper down and pick up the free local paper that I like to read instead. Jess always finds it amusing that I'm interested in the parochial goings-on of the borough, with the paper covering everything from charity fun runs to cats getting stuck up trees. Jess doesn't realise that the real reason I read the paper is to uncover weaknesses in the area that I can exploit – the dodgy minicab scandal for example, cuts to the council's CCTV funding, derelict buildings, demolition projects, that kind of thing. I flick through, but today's edition is pretty tame – a couple of concerts have been announced at the Royal Albert Hall, a socialite has launched a community centre for children with autism, a mosaic by local kids is being unveiled at Chelsea Old Town Hall. Even if my little bubble feels like it's falling apart, at least life in Mayfair is hunky-dory.

I'm about to close the paper, but an advert for a mystic offering angel readings catches my eye, and inspires me to flick through the ads. Occasionally, there's something interesting hidden among the classifieds. I found the ad for the company I rent my garage from in Hayes while flicking through the classifieds tucked away in the back of *Metro*. And I once found this ad an old lady posted where she was flogging a ton of old designer bags. I figured I may as well give her a call, and as it turned out, I managed to get my hands on a ton of vintage Chanel, Hermès and Dior at absolutely bargain prices. I know I should be working, but I'm agitated and the weird ads from psychics promising curse removals and past life regression, and the dodgy personals from lonely men who 'WLTM' pretty/carefree/nice/young single women for long-term relationships or 'fun', are making me feel marginally better about my own fucked-up life. I'm about to close the paper when another ad catches my eye.

Piano tuition in Knightsbridge

Giles Bradshaw.

An experienced piano tutor currently accepting new students in Knightsbridge.

Thirty years' experience of private tuition. Trained at the Royal Academy of Music. Has enjoyed a successful international career as a concert pianist, including performing for the Queen.

Lessons £50 for one hour.

No fucking way. I stare at the ad, my blood stilling in my veins. That fucking pervert Miles Brady is out on the hunt again, posing as his alter ego Giles Bradshaw to lure children for piano lessons and paedophilia. The shamelessness of him. So much for prison changing his ways.

I place the paper down on my desk. His advert lists his contact details. I gaze at it, thinking, tapping my toe.

I want to go after him. It would be so easy. I can see it now: I'd pose as a Chelsea mum, arrange a lesson, lure him in. He'd be like a lamb to the slaughter. It would be so easy, and yet, I can't kill again. Not now. Not now that Wheelan's on to me. He was at my flat last night, for God's sake. The police are closer than they've ever been before. Killing is the last thing I should be doing. I need to keep my head down, be discreet.

And yet . . . I look at the ad. Right before me. It's fallen into my lap, literally. Would it be so difficult to just . . . snuff Miles out? Get rid of him. Take him down. Would the police really make the connection? Wheelan doesn't have enough to arrest me for Julian's murder, never mind connect me to any other deaths. I'm hardly a top suspect. Perhaps there's a way I can get away with Miles's murder, make it work . . .

I want to do something. The thought of just sitting back and allowing that creep to prey on more kids is too much. And yet, I'd have to be careful. *So* careful. London with its anonymous crowds, labyrinthine streets and soaring crime rates may have been the ultimate hunting ground for me up until now, but if I don't play my cards right, this city could become my prison.

I pull my keys from my handbag and unlock a drawer in my desk. Inside is one of my burner phones. I turn it on and head over to my office door, twisting the lock so Jess can't interrupt me.

I dial Miles's, or 'Giles's', number. I can't resist. I want to find out where he lives, at the very least. I don't necessarily have to do anything with that information . . .

His phone rings. Two, three times. And then he picks up. I hear the husk of a throat clearing.

'Giles Bradshaw,' he says.

Slick. He must have a phone specifically for the purpose of answering calls from this ad.

'Hi, Giles, I saw your advert in the *Mayfair Chronicle*,' I tell him in a dumb-sounding high-pitched voice.

'Oh, hello. Thanks for calling,' he answers, his voice full of warmth, charm.

'No problem! Your ad looked great. Incredible that you performed for the Queen,' I gush.

'It was a long time ago, but yes, it was definitely a career highlight!' Giles replies, sounding modest.

A long time ago. Before he got banged up in a cell.

I loosen him up with a few more compliments and then start telling him about my fictional son.

'His name's Luke. His last teacher moved back home to . . .' I pluck a location out of thin air. 'Spain, so now we need to hire another. Can I ask, do you do lessons at your home? We don't have a piano in our flat unfortunately.'

'Yes, I host pupils,' Miles tells me. 'I have a grand piano.'

'Fab!' I enthuse.

I ask if I can bring Luke over for a trial lesson to see how things go. Miles is keen. I grab a pen and a Post-it and jot down his address. Belgravia. Nice.

We arrange a time and I hang up, telling him that I can't wait to introduce him to Luke.

I turn off my burner phone and look at the address scrawled on the Post-it. One step closer to Miles. I'm so close. I have a time and place to meet him. It would be so easy to take him down. I'm itching to do it. To wipe him out. Get revenge. It's so tempting and yet, it's risky. Now isn't the right time. I should leave it. I should walk away. And yet, I'm not sure I can resist.

I fold the Post-it and slip it into my handbag. For later, maybe . . .

Chapter Eleven

It's been two days now, and the police haven't been back in touch.

There have been no police cars outside my flat, no knocks on the door, no calls from Detective Wheelan. It's dying down. Wheelan's clearly moved on to another suspect. He's probably getting all excited about one of the red herrings I left at the scene, like the fag butt or that ratty old jumper. I bet he's running DNA tests on it, thinking he's on to something.

He's got nothing on me. He was just trying to intimidate me with his questions, his cold stares. Hoping he'd get something. Anything.

I shouldn't have got so panicked about everything. I should never have let his visit unnerve me so much. He's no threat to me. The police never have been, and they never will be. I've outsmarted them enough times before and I'll do it again. It's about time I started believing in myself.

It's late afternoon. I'm out of work sooner than I expected to be and the sky isn't yet as dark as it usually is when I leave the office. It's inky blue, pretty. I feel free as I walk away from the office, but I have nowhere to go, aside from home. On a normal quiet Thursday night, I might see what Abay's up to, but since he's likely the one who witnessed me with Julian and reported me to the police, that probably isn't the best idea. I could see what Vanessa's doing, call the girls, but neither option feels quite right. I know where I want to go. I want to go to Belgravia. I want to check out Miles's home. Investigate the address scrawled on the Post-it in my bag.

I just want to see where he lives. I'm not going to do anything. I don't have any weapons on me for a start. I'm wearing the Furla handbag I wore on my date with Julian. The one with the dual pockets: Camilla Black, and my shadow self. It still contains my lock-picking tools, a couple of roofies, but not much else. I couldn't take Miles down with that. Definitely not in the way I'd like to anyway.

I walk alongside Green Park on my way to Belgravia. Black cabs crawl past. Tourists pose with selfie sticks next to phone boxes. A busker strums a guitar. A man in an expensive suit checks me out as he walks past. I smile back, feeling a sense of belonging. On the surface, I'm a beautiful woman, walking through a beautiful city on a winter's afternoon. I couldn't feel more different to the insecure girl I was a few days ago, arriving at work feeling like an imposter, haunted.

I know Belgravia fairly well, but I still check Miles's street on my phone to orientate myself amongst the high pillars and tall white townhouses. When I arrive at the end of Miles's road, a man almost charges into me.

I step back, apologising.

The man simply grunts, continuing on his way. I realise with a shiver of revulsion that it's Miles himself. Pasty-faced, wearing a vile mustard-coloured blazer replete with pocket square, a striped shirt barely covering his gargantuan stomach, and beige chinos. He waddles down the road. Probably going to drink the night away at a bar. I can't imagine he'd be doing anything else. Unless he's had some more enquiries from his advert and he's heading out for an evening lesson to prey upon an innocent kid? The thought is vile. And not wholly inconceivable either.

I eye him as he approaches a turn off for another road. The sight of him is repulsive. How can he waltz around one of the nicest parts of London in his *Brideshead Revisited* clothes, shamelessly showing his face about town, despite all the things he's done? How is that justice? His victims will be traumatised. Raped as children by a grown man. Their dignity torn apart at the kind of age that makes it impossible to recover from. What are they doing now, while he swans off to while away another day? How are they coping? I know what it's like to be abused, and you don't simply bounce back. You don't forget.

I look up and down Miles's street. It's nice. Really nice. A cute Belgravia side road, lined with pretty townhouses. A sleepy, almost villagey vibe in the middle of one of the most expensive postcodes in Europe. A strange conceit. The neighbours have plant pots on their windowsills. One even has garden gnomes by their front door.

The street's quiet. Bizarrely quiet for London. Some of the houses are probably second homes. London dwellings of Russian billionaires. Or family homes that have passed through generations of old money. The downstairs curtains are drawn in quite a few of the houses, no doubt hiding expensive furniture from prying eyes. I wander over to Miles's place. His curtains are drawn too. I wonder if he lives alone. I suspect so. Who in their right mind would want to live with that creep? But what if he has an ageing mother or something? Someone old and senile who's stuck with him?

I press the bell. It bleats through the house. I'm not exactly sure what I'm trying to achieve. It's not like I'm going to kill Miles right now, and yet something compels me to investigate. Maybe it's just because I'm bored, a little restless. Or maybe I could just do with getting a bit more dirt on him.

No one answers. I hear nothing. No stirring inside.

I try again. Wait.

Nothing.

I glance around for a security system, CCTV, but Miles doesn't strike me as organised or modern enough for that. He probably thinks he's fine, safe, cruising along in his Belgravia bubble.

I know I shouldn't . . . I should turn around and head home, enjoy a quiet night in, put my feet up, lie low, and yet, I can't. I can't let Miles go. I need to hunt. I'm itching for it. It's in my nature.

I root around in my bag and find my lock-picking tools. It's not ideal to pick a lock at this time of day, when it's not quite dark yet, but the street is quiet, the houses sleepy and subdued, and Miles's lock looks like a fairly simple one. It shouldn't be too hard.

I pull on a pair of latex gloves from my bag, take out my tools and look over my shoulder a few times, before standing close to the door and sliding my tension wrench and lock pick inside. I rattle around, loosening the pins. I get the latch free in under a minute and push down on the handle.

I'm in.

Chapter Twelve

I push the door open and step inside.

Immediately, I'm hit by the stench of Miles's aftershave. Old Spice or something equally rank. I fan it away from my face as I take in his living room. It's disconcertingly ordinary. Cosy even. Miles's front room is nothing like the repulsive paedophile's lair I'd imagined. There's a grand piano, stylish, in polished mahogany. A couple of Chesterfield sofas, laden with cushions and throws. A soft carpet with a swirling pattern. A big flat-screen TV. A mantelpiece hosting framed pictures of family or friends. Tasteful art on the walls. Even a few pot plants and a vase of flowers on the coffee table.

What the hell?

For a moment, I wonder if I could be wrong about him. Could Briony have picked up on a false rumour? But no . . . I read the articles. I saw the pictures of him in the papers.

Anyway, I should know more than anyone that appearances can be deceptive. No one seeing my flashy, beautiful, sophisticated apartment would assume I'm a serial killer. I just need to dig a little deeper.

I wander into the adjoining kitchen. Miles has left a plate on the breakfast bar, scattered with toast crumbs and smeared with jam. There's a half-drunk mug of tea next to it. The kitchen has a window overlooking the garden. I peer out. There's not much to see. Unsurprisingly, Miles isn't the green-fingered type, and the garden is an uninspiring sight: a patio with uneven, loose paving stones, and a grassy expanse overgrown with weeds.

I turn away. There's a door leading off from the kitchen. I pull it open to discover a downstairs toilet. A small narrow room with a loo and a sink. Not much to see.

I head upstairs. There must be something up here. Something troubling. There must be. I refuse to believe that a long-term predator like Miles Brady has simply been reformed during a two-year stint in prison. I refuse to believe it. I *can't* believe it. If shit like that's true, and prison does work, then how am I justified in my kills? How is it okay that I murder guys like him when they can become new men after only a few years in a cell? No. Men like Miles don't change that easily. They just don't.

I open a door on the landing. Miles's bedroom. It's just as fucking normal-looking as the rest of the house. A king-sized bed, perfectly made up. Bedside tables with matching lamps. On one of the tables there's a glass of water and a pair of glasses. I walk over to it and pull open the drawers, expecting to find a stash of child porn or something equally vile, but it's filled with normal stuff: a couple of trashy novels, tweezers, medication, sleeping pills, a few pairs of thermal socks. The kind of things you'd expect to find in any old guy's bedside table.

I close the drawers and look around for some other clues, but anyone checking out this room, and this house, would truly believe that Miles Brady is completely respectable. He even has pictures on his bedroom walls of him playing the piano at various concerts, including a shot of him performing for the Queen, the occasion marked in gold lettering underneath.

I go over to his wardrobe and pull open the doors, but there's nothing weird in there either. Just shirts, jackets. I root around, but just find clothes, shoes. Normal stuff. I walk over to his chest of drawers. Open them. I root around among socks, pants, vests, jumpers. I rifle through the rest of his drawers, searching for something, anything incriminating, but there's nothing.

I check out his en suite, but there isn't anything of note there either.

Maybe I should head home. But I can't quite bring myself to leave. I feel like I'm missing something. There must be something here. There must be.

I cross the hall. There's another door. A spare room? I press down on the handle, but the door doesn't budge. It's locked. Interesting . . .

I retrieve my lock-picking set from my bag, kneel down, and set to work on the lock. I'm not as experienced at opening household mortise locks as I am at picking locks with pins, but I have the tools to do it. After five or so minutes of twisting and turning, I feel the lock loosen. I pull down on the handle and the door opens.

The room is dark, shadowy. Windowless.

I step inside. It smells chemical and strange. I feel around on the wall for a light switch. My fingers land upon one and I flick it on.

A darkroom. Miles Brady has a darkroom. There's a camera on the counter. An enlarger. A tray of developing fluid.

My stomach starts to fizz with anxiety, my heart growing tight. I have a horrible feeling I know exactly what I'm about to discover.

I peer into the enlarger, trying to view film, but none has been loaded.

I look in the trays of developing fluid for pictures, but there aren't any.

I pull open a drawer and rummage under a few packets of photo paper, spotting something underneath. I lift the packets out of the drawer and find a dozen or so pictures. The first one, on top of the pile, shows the face of a little boy. Maybe five or six. He's cute, with long eyelashes. An innocent face.

I know I'm not going to like what I'm about to see as I put the picture aside. There it is: the little boy, lying on a bed, naked, confused. Another, in which he's in a strangely sexualised pose, the look on his face tragic. He looks scared. Lost.

Rage floods through me. It makes my fingertips sweat. I'm going to destroy Miles. I knew he was rotten. I knew it. I knew prison hadn't changed him. Two years. As if. Someone needs to stop him. And that person is going to be me.

I don't want to see any more, but as I rearrange the pictures how they were, I get a glimpse of the next shot in the pile. The boy's body, battered. I take a closer look at the picture. The boy looks dead. Bruised. Rotting. His small naked body is in an unmistakable state of decay. The boy is on the floor of Miles's front room, I recognise the swirling pattern of his carpet. Miles is even worse than I could have possibly imagined.

I check out the next picture. Another shot of the boy's body. Decomposing. Taken from a different angle this time. Miles was clearly getting off on it when he took these pictures.

My heart burns with fury. I feel sick with it.

I look at another picture. A close-up of the boy's face. His cheeks are hollow, rotting.

Dare I look at another shot?

I'm shaking, the pictures fluttering in my hands. But I still look at the next photo. It's another close-up of the boy's decomposing face, this time with Miles, grinning, in shot. The sickest selfie I've ever seen. I want to hurl, but a cry pierces through my shock.

I freeze, terrified. Is Miles back? There's another cry. A few yelps. Giggles. The sounds of children playing. I breathe a sigh of relief. It must just be a neighbour's kid.

I need to get out of here though. Miles is not someone whose path I want to cross unprepared. He's far worse than I imagined. My hands are still shaking, but I force myself to take a deep breath. Bile rises in my throat.

The photos make me want to run, get out of here. Get as far away as possible. But no. That's not how I work. I want to get out of this sick bastard's lair, but I'm not just going to scarper. Not like this. I need to control myself. Prepare.

I draw in a deep breath and take a burner phone from my bag. I start taking photos of each picture. Then I put them back in the order I found them and return them to the drawer, feeling tainted from even having touched them.

I need to know who this boy is. He must have gone missing at some point. His parents are probably beside themselves with worry. Presuming these pictures are recent, I'll google missing persons stories later and see if any of the descriptions or photos match up. I check the pictures on my phone. Sharp. Clear. I put my phone back in my bag.

I check everything in the room is as I found it. I arrange the packets of paper on top of the photos in the drawer, as I found them. Then I head back into the hall, closing the door behind me.

I left my lock-picking tools in the door, and I rattle around with them, heart thumping, until I manage to turn the lock, leaving the darkroom as I found it. I take my tools and stash them back in my bag.

Scanning the hallway and glancing into Miles's bedroom, I make sure nothing's out of place, then I hurry down the stairs, pull the curtains ever so slightly aside in the living room, and check the coast is clear on the street. The children have gone. It's empty.

I slip out of the house, the door locking automatically behind me.

Heart slamming in my chest, I walk away.

Chapter Thirteen

I grab a copy of *Metro* as I cross the pavement towards my waiting car. Julian isn't on the front page today. It's just war. Corruption. Climate change.

'Morning,' my driver says, as he walks around the car, opening the door for me.

It's a different driver to the one I had the other day, but I vaguely recognise him. A mild-mannered dark-haired guy who listens to the radio quietly up front and rarely bothers with conversation. I like him.

'Morning,' I reply, smiling politely, as I get in.

I skim-read the front page and flick through, but it's just storms, migrant crossings, a movie mogul on trial for rape and sexual assault. Julian's face is nowhere in sight. He's gone. Old news. History. Like all my victims. Idly, pausing between pages, I wonder what his family will do with his body. Will they bury him or cremate him? They'd probably rather cremate him than preserve my handiwork any longer. I wonder what they'll do with his ashes. Will they be kept in an urn on the mantelpiece? Or scattered in an ocean somewhere? I prefer the urn idea. I like the thought of Julian in an urn in a suburban house, out of harm's way, a relic his mum can cry sad, self-pitying tears about over tea with her friends, while turning a blind eye to how her son behaved when he was alive – beating, raping and abusing women. Julian doesn't deserve to have his ashes scattered somewhere beautiful. Or a gravestone in some sun-dappled graveyard. No, a sad little urn is where Julian belongs.

'Nice day, isn't it?' my driver pipes up.

I've been so lost in my daydream about Julian's ashes that I've barely noticed the weather. The sky is bright, azure blue, gleaming. Too bright for me, but cool slate-grey skies aren't everyone's cup of tea.

'Gorgeous,' I reply, smiling tightly, hoping that's the end of the exchange.

Fortunately, my driver smiles politely back before returning his attention to the road. We lapse into silence as Lady Gaga pours from the car radio.

'Turn it up if you like,' I suggest.

My driver nods enthusiastically and twists the dial.

'Stupid Love' plays as we leave central London. He's taking me to an industrial estate in zone 4 where we're shooting a spread for the magazine. The theme of the shoot is romantic – ethereal floaty dresses, gentle dreamy colours, decadent hair and make-up, that kind of thing. Content for our Valentine's issue.

Bit nauseating really, but I put my own Camilla spin on it and decided we'd contrast all the soft loveliness with something bleak. I wanted the models to be shot somewhere rundown, drab, rotting, and chose a derelict old warehouse with soaring ceilings, tall windows and pitted walls. It's been vacant for over a year, since the company went bust. Maybe it's cruel of me, to make the models pose in a dump full of cobwebs and spiders, but I thought it would look good. And they're being paid a lot.

Lady Gaga bleeds into Mabel as the car hurtles down a throbbing dual carriageway, away from the city and into the outskirts. We shoot past ugly office blocks and nasty, commuter-belt new-build flats.

Eventually, the driver pulls off the main road into the industrial site. I take in the nondescript depots and warehouses, a couple of offices scattered about, offering services like B2B marketing, printing and low-rate litigation. I feel sorry for the people who work here. Their workplaces couldn't be any more different to *Couture*, with its imposing entrance, plate glass windows and central London location surrounded by hustle and bustle.

We approach the warehouse. I recognise it instantly, having seen pictures after I got one of my assistants to scout locations. It's huge – tall, red-bricked, and yet dilapidated and almost fragile-looking. Some of the windows are smashed. They're dusty. The bricks are crumbling. It'll be demolished soon, replaced with a fancy new office block. But for now, it's in its final chapter of existence, an empty vessel. Air rattling through its deserted rooms. Undisturbed.

The driver pulls up outside the warehouse. A fully made-up model with a flawless, doll-like face and wild curly hair is having an animated phone conversation by the entrance, a few feet from a massive silver SUV that belongs to Philippe, the photographer. The driver parks, and moves to get out of the car to open my door, but I tell him it's okay, and step out of the car, thanking him.

The model clocks me, and immediately starts wrapping up her conversation. She's unnerved, a little intimidated, like a lot of the models tend to be by me. They're young and they see me as a scary magazine editor, someone they need to impress. They don't realise that, not so long ago, I was a nobody.

'Hi, I'm Olivia,' the model says, stowing her phone in her jacket pocket.

Her eyes are framed by long feathery lashes, her skin dusted with pearlescent highlighter.

'Hi,' I reply.

I push the door of the warehouse open. 'Come on,' I say, holding it for her.

She reaches for the door and smiles politely as she follows me inside.

The warehouse is as vast and gloomy as I'd hoped. It smells musty, damp. It reminds me of my garage. Old pallet boxes, stacking shelves and moving trolleys have been left behind. There are a couple of rails of clothes by one of the walls. A hair and make-up station's been set up, where a couple of make-up artists diligently powder models' faces, apply mascara, smooth their hair. Philippe is setting up his lights. I spot Jess. She's sitting with a model who has a copy of what looks like her contract on her lap, which Jess appears to be patiently explaining. I head over to Philippe.

'Hi, darling,' he says, leaning in to kiss me on the cheek. He smells minty, of chewing gum.

He smiles, but it's a strained kind of smile, and even though on the best of days Philippe isn't exactly a ray of sunshine, I get the feeling something's up.

'Hey,' I reply. 'How's everything going?'

Philippe swallows a mouthful of instant coffee from a plastic cup. He winces.

'This stuff tastes like shit.'

He places the cup down and flicks a switch on his studio light. Nothing happens.

'My light isn't working,' he grumbles.

He frowns at the light through the heavy-framed specs he always wears and flicks another switch. Suddenly, light beams across the derelict space.

'Looks like it's working to me!' I laugh.

'It wasn't working before,' Philippe huffs.

A lot of people would probably find Philippe's downbeat, miserable manner unappealing, but I quite like it. Maybe because it means I don't have to pretend so much around him.

Olivia's up first. She's wearing a plunging, pale blue Oscar de la Renta gown embroidered with winding metallic leaves. She's perfect for this shoot, with her oceanic eyes and killer bone structure. She drapes herself against a stacking rack and works the camera. The shoot is a bit self-consciously edgy, but the effect is good, nonetheless.

The images start to appear on Philippe's monitor. I highlight the ones I like, discussing them with Jess as Philippe snaps away. Eventually, Olivia starts to run out of poses, and we agree we've got the shots we need. Philippe and his assistant, Wendy, begin moving their equipment to another part of the warehouse, while the make-up artists apply the finishing touches to the next model's look. Jess is hanging around by the make-up station, chatting to one of the make-up artists. I'm at a bit of a loose end so decide to head outside for a moment and have a cigarette.

I don't smoke too often. I'm not addicted, but I quite like the ritual. I smoke Treasurer cigarettes. I like withdrawing their long slender stems from the packet, pressing one between my lips as I flick my lighter and feel the golden flame, warm and bright near my face. I like the excuse smoking gives you to step away for a moment.

I wander through the warehouse, towards the hallway. The owner of the company that used to run their business here knows we're shooting today. They provided us with keys, and we paid them a fee, but they haven't cleaned the site, leaving it laden with cobwebs, squalid – just the way I wanted. The hallway is thick with dust. I walk along, leaving footprints, and discover a flight of stairs at the end of the corridor, also dusty, with cobwebs between the railings. I head up three or four flights of stairs and wander down another corridor until I find an abandoned office with a cheap desk and swivel chair. I spot an invoice on the table, with numbers in black ink fading to grey.

I head over to the office window. It's clearly been a long time since someone opened it, the windowpane thick with dust and the hinges stiff. I get it open though, pushing it wide, imagining the room gasping for air. I reach into my bag and take out a cigarette, leaning out of the window as I light up.

The warehouse is by far the tallest building in this industrial estate, and being on the fifth floor, I have a broad, expansive view of the roofs of the surrounding buildings. Most look fairly new, office blocks and warehouses with cars parked outside. I spot a couple of workers coming and going. But there are a few buildings that appear old and dilapidated, abandoned like this one. The area is an odd combination of old and new, maintained and neglected. I wonder if it makes the current workers here feel on edge, seeing the relics of businesses having gone bust so close by every day, or if they're pragmatic about it, seeing it as just business. Just life.

I inhale, exhale. My mind's blank.

I take another drag of my cigarette and think about Miles Brady. The shoot temporarily distracted me from him, but I haven't forgotten. I'm still shaken.

Last night, I risked a trip to my garage and, in the dark, dank silence, processed what I'd seen. I resolved to take Miles down. I have no other choice. But there are steps I need to take. I have to be careful, considered, one step ahead, if I'm going to come out on top. Miles presents a bigger challenge than the men I usually deal with. The stakes are higher, and I know that when we come head-to-head, it'll be different. There'll be no impulsivity. No frills. No wild rage. Just a cold, calculating entrapment.

I did some more digging. Posing as Luke's parent, I added Miles on Facebook and, within an hour, he accepted my request. I scrolled through his posts and noticed one which he'd signed off 'randymonkey', like it was a nickname, a username. It struck me as odd, almost a little obvious, as though he were hiding in plain sight. Exposing himself. Practically egging me on. I googled the username and found a profile on a bizarre nineties-style chat room called egroupchat.com. With a profile picture of the same cat I'd seen on Miles's Facebook page, I figured it must be him.

Wondering what he was up to, I joined egroupchat.com and set up a profile. I used a cartoon character avatar and called myself Robbie, claiming I was a ten-year-old boy whose interests included football, video games, skateboarding and music, adding that I was learning the guitar and piano – perfect bait for Miles, or @randy-monkey as he likes to be known. I posted a message in the chat room – 'Bored lol. Anyone wanna chat?' – and then left it and went to sleep. I figured I'd give Miles time to reply.

I take my phone out of my bag and log on to the chat room, wondering if Miles has messaged. I suck on my cigarette as I scroll through the creepy messages, which I bet are almost all from old men, and there it is: a notification from Miles.

@randymonkey: hi robbie. sucks that ur bored!! I get bored 2. What u up to?

I smirk, laughing out loud at his attempt to sound like any other young kid, the manipulative shit. But the important thing is, he took the bait. It was almost too easy.

He's mine now, and I'm going to reel him in. I'm going to set him up, like I've done with paedophile scum in the past. Make him think he's meeting a child and then disappoint him in the most brutal way imaginable. He'll get the justice he deserves.

I suck the last few drags of my cigarette, before stubbing it out on the grubby windowsill.

Chapter Fourteen

@robbie2006: hey, just got back from school. Boring day lol! How r u?

I press send on the message on the way home. I have the same driver as this morning, who came to pick me up at the end of the shoot. It went on almost all day, but I feigned a migraine mid-afternoon, telling Jess I'd spend the rest of the day working from home. Really, I wanted to be alone. I wanted to be alone so I could message Miles.

He appears online immediately. He must have been gagging for the notification. I picture him sitting in bed in his lovely Belgravia home, a self-satisfied smile playing on his lips. Dots ebb and retreat on my screen as he types.

@randymonkey: haha. Im good. Why woz it boring?

Woz? I scoff. Who says 'woz'? I bet even ten-year-olds don't say that.

I feel my driver's eyes on me and catch him looking at me in the rear-view mirror. We exchange polite smiles and then I return my attention to my phone.

@robbie2006: jus teachers doin my head in. and my team lost at five a side.

I hit send. We pull off the dual carriageway, heading back into central London. Miles types a response.

@randymonkey: damn. Hate losing. What u doing now?

@robbie2006: just at home. Playing PlayStation

My driver jerks away from a speeding car, honks his horn. My phone buzzes.

@randymonkey: u home alone?

I shake my head. Dirty bastard. Three or four messages in and he's already trying to establish how vulnerable little Robbie is.

@robbie2006: yeah are u?

@randymonkey: yeah my parents are out 2 . . .

Ha. The creep's leaving the ellipsis to see if Robbie elaborates on his living situation. I'll give him what he wants.

@robbie2006: live with my dad but he's always at work. He drives lorries. Long hours. He's out a lot. It's alright tho. I can watch as much TV as I want and stay up late lol!

I press send and gaze out of the window, picturing Miles salivating at that response. A ten-year-old boy with a dad who's a long-haul lorry driver. Could that be any more perfect for him?

@randymonkey: wow sounds cool!! Can see why ur bored lol!

I message a few more times, chatting about normal ten-year-old boy stuff: TV, football, friends. Miles plays along patiently, enduring all the tedious chit-chat, waiting for the moment he can step things up a notch. He starts asking about music, piano, as my driver pulls on to my road.

@robbie2006: gotta go. Sorry. Chat later!

I send the message and log out of the chat. Treat 'em mean, keep 'em keen.

My driver draws to a halt outside my building. I thank him, hoping he hasn't found it weird how much I've probably been sighing and shaking my head and tutting at the manipulativeness of Miles's messages. He probably thinks I'm emailing a difficult work colleague or having an argument with my boyfriend.

I get out of the car, shutting the door behind me, before crossing the pavement towards my flat. A pigeon pecking at scraps of a discarded sandwich clocks me with its beady eyes as I approach, before launching off, flapping its wings and darting away. I step forward, dodging the crusts, and spot Abay, loitering by the entrance to my building, hunched, wearing a hoodie. His hands are buried in his pockets, and he eyes me coolly.

A jittery wave of panic floods through me. My stomach lurches. Why's he here? What does he want from me? It's not like he's here to hook up. Who wants to fuck a murderer?

'You okay?' I grumble, eyeing him warily as I reach into my bag for my keys.

I step closer to the door and try to unlock it, but Abay stops me, gripping my wrist.

'Get off,' I hiss, twisting, trying to wrench my arm free. My heart pounds in my chest. 'What do you want?'

I look at him searchingly. His eyes are black.

'You mad bitch,' he spits, slowly shaking his head, wearing a disgusted scowl.

'What?' I try to pull his hand off me, but his hold is tight, vice-like. It hurts.

I look searchingly around, but none of the passers-by – office workers eager to get home – are looking in our direction. I could scream for help, but provoking Abay right now probably isn't the best idea.

'What are you doing? Let me go,' I implore him.

I yank my arm but it's no use. I feel like a puppet in the grip of a giant. He pulls me close, his face inches from mine. I smell his familiar smell: sweat, rubber. He's holding me so tightly that it's almost like a lover's embrace. So many of our encounters have started in similar ways to this – the mixture of strength and closeness, the menace, the tremor of fear. But the menace has never been real, it's never been truly vicious, it's never not been tempered by lust.

'You killed him,' Abay hisses.

I can feel his warm breath, his palm beading with sweat, slimy on my wrist. I can feel the rage in his eyes. A chill sweeps up my spine, but I keep my face impassive. I act like nothing's happened. He's the crazy one. Not me.

'You killed that guy – Julian Taylor. You shot him with a crossbow, you fucking psycho,' Abay rages.

He's so close that I can see myself reflected back in his eyes. It's the first time anyone has ever properly seen me, apart from my victims. Abay's repulsed. Repelled. Livid. And beneath the shock of being seen for who I really am is a small triumphant part of me, a twisted part that's perversely thrilled and excited. Part of me is enjoying being able to appal and enrage. I'm a bitch. I'm a lunatic. I'm a fighter. I'm me. I feel like laughing in Abay's face. I feel powerful. I've reduced a man as strong and confident and controlled as him to a manic, raging mess.

'What are you talking about?' I ask, not letting on.

'You know what I'm talking about.' Abay laughs, tightening his grip on my wrist.

I roll my eyes, trying to ignore the sting of his grip. 'I don't. You must be high or something. Leave me alone.'

I try again to pull my arm free, but Abay is so much stronger than me, and even though his palm is slick with sweat, his grip is firm. He knows, though, that all I'd need to do is raise my voice, cry out for help, and a passer-by would step in at any moment. He'd look like the bad guy. He'd look like an abuser. And I'd be the innocent, vulnerable woman.

I could scream. But I'm enjoying this exchange.

I gaze into Abay's revolted eyes. He looks colder than ever. Even the chip in his tooth looks uglier than usual – tough. I've always found his hardness sexy, but it's thrilling on a psychological level now too. We're going head-to-head. Not just physically. He might be able to overpower me that way, but he's no match for my inner darkness. I allow a small smile to creep on to my face. His eyes narrow. I know I disgust him, but I know I could push him to the very brink and he still wouldn't have it in him to hurt me. Abay puts on a front of being a hard man, but that's all it is – a front. He's had to act like that to survive, having spent his teenage years on an estate in Canning Town.

Unlike a lot of his peers, who got into gangs and are running from the police or caged in a cell, Abay's a good guy. He turned to personal training to make a decent life for himself, and he genuinely cares about it. He's not like a lot of the other personal trainers at the gym, who aren't particularly discreet when chatting about their questionable side hustles while bench-pressing. Abay works hard, never misses a session with clients, takes what he does seriously. He still remembers his life back in Nigeria. He talks about it sometimes. Some of the other guys at the gym came here when they were too young to have made any real memories of life back home, but Abay was twelve; he remembers. He's grateful to be in the UK. He wants to make the most of it. Do himself proud. Do his mum proud. That's why he keeps his head straight – not drinking, avoiding drugs, watching what he eats, rather than loading up on steroids like so many others. He goes to bed early. He even believes in God. His only vice is sex, and that's not even really a vice. It's just another form of cardio.

Abay may glare at me. He may hate me, truly hate me. I can believe that, but he wouldn't hurt me. He loves his mum and his sister; he could never hurt a woman. It's one of his rules. No wonder he's so disgusted with me. I'm a violent woman. If I were a man, he'd probably have shoved me up against the wall at this point. He'd be spitting in my face, fists raised, but I'm a psychopath he can't hit. I'm a woman capable of things he's not.

'Let go of me, Abay,' I insist, trying to yank my arm free once more.

He's rock solid, muscles tensed. He feels even bigger than the last time we saw each other, as though he's been working out even more.

'You're something else,' Abay sneers as he looms over me, his grip still tight.

Despite my panic, it occurs to me that this will be the last time Abay touches me. The thought is a little sad, but there's no point dwelling on it.

'Fuck off. I need to get home.'

'You know . . .' Abay chews his lip. 'There was always something not right about you.'

I laugh. He's right. Of course he's right. But it's not like it's news to me. Does he think I'm not aware of the hollowness? Does he think it's not a daily struggle to hide it? To erect my mask? To try to invent substance where there's nothing?

I pretend every fucking day, and it's not like I'm going to stop now.

And anyway, it's not like my hollowness was a problem for Abay a couple of weeks ago. Before he saw me with Julian, he was into me. He wanted to get closer. He wanted to cuddle. I'm sure he was entertaining the idea that we could be something more. I could tell. Our casual arrangement had evolved into something more for him. In spite of himself, he'd started to fall for the girl with the empty heart. Maybe he thought he could change me, save me.

Or maybe he simply didn't care that something about me wasn't quite right, as long as I was hot, rich, agreeable. Good in bed.

'Look, it's not my problem you developed feelings for me. I'm sorry you're hurt, but I can't force myself to feel the same way about you,' I state, trying to keep a straight face.

Abay laughs, a high-pitched crazy laugh that spills from his lips.

'Feel the same way! Ha!' He shakes his head.

I stick to my story, getting into my stride.

'Whatever. I know you wanted more. Wanting to see me all the time, trying to hold me tight. Well sorry, but I'm not interested.'

Abay laughs louder, his laugh even more high-pitched and crazy-sounding. A man and woman, both in suits, glance curiously in his direction as they walk past, but they say nothing, do nothing. We must look like some couple having a domestic; they don't want to get involved.

They pass, retreating down the street. I make another effort to wrench my arm free, but Abay steps closer, his huge imposing body casting a shadow around me, surrounding me. The body that's turned me on so many times, that still turns me on a bit even in this fucked-up situation. My senses are hardwired to want him.

'You killed that guy, admit it,' Abay insists, his voice low now.

I search his cold eyes. I know we'll never see each other again. He's dead to me already. I'm dead to him. I disgust him. Abay's the first man who's ever seen me for what I truly am, and I feel small, rotten, tainted under his cutting gaze, and yet I also feel sharp, sly, smug. I have a nihilistic urge to admit it, to tell him that I killed Julian, just to see the shock blaze through his eyes. I want to do it just for the thrill of it, and I would, to see his reaction, his impotent rage, but I'm not stupid. Abay could easily be recording this conversation on his phone. I know he wants me banged up or he wouldn't have reported me to the police in the first place. He's probably downloaded a recording app. It's probably flashing away in his pocket as we speak.

'Let me go, Abay, or I'll cause a scene.'

Abay laughs again. That crazy laugh.

'You know, I should never have fucked you,' Abay muses.

'Here we go,' I groan. 'Going to try and bring me down now, are you? Is your ego feeling a little raw? A little bruised?'

I give him a mock-sympathetic look even though part of me is a little hurt, a little bitter. Even if Abay hadn't connected me to Julian, our relationship would probably have gone this way eventually. All of my relationships with men end in hatred and violence, regardless of the precise circumstances. Gerard was the same. And Martin. If I don't play along with exactly what they want me to do, how they want me to be, they're always up in my face, brimming with rage, hissing at me, cold as ice. I gave up expecting anything different a long time ago.

'No, you're hot, all right.' Abay looks me up and down, part lascivious, part disgusted. He kisses his teeth.

'You look hot, but it's like fucking a ghost. There's nothing there,' he spits, jabbing his finger at my chest, stabbing at my heart.

I gasp.

I shrink away, startled, my gaze scattering over at the pavement. It stings where he jabbed me, and I shield my chest with my hand.

When I look back up, Abay's gone. He's walking away, not looking back.

Chapter Fifteen

I close my front door and let out a sigh of relief.

My chest still stings slightly where Abay stabbed at it. I dump my bags at the door, peel off my coat and wander over to my kitchen. I drape my coat over a seat by the breakfast bar. I open a cupboard and retrieve a bottle of wine.

I think about Abay as I pour a glass.

He knows. There are no two ways about it. Not only did he see me with Julian, but he could see it in my eyes. He recognised that I'm a monster.

I place the bottle down and take a sip, wandering over to my sofa. I sit down and gaze out of the plate glass windows, the sky darkening, the city glimmering. Abay may know what I am, but he doesn't have evidence. Nothing concrete. A feeling and a sighting don't amount to much. He can't do anything. He can't run back to Detective Wheelan claiming I'm a killer. They've already questioned me. All Abay has left is a hunch. If Wheelan bothered digging and found out how Abay knows me, it would make the whole thing look even more ridiculous. He'd look like a spurned lover, some poor rejected fool with a grudge. Abay knows better than to become the laughing stock of the local station.

I know he's livid though. He wants to expose me, but he needs something more concrete, and he knows it. He doesn't have a single thing. Julian went missing weeks ago. All fingerprints will have been analysed, all elements of the crime scene tested and assessed. And there's no one knocking on my door. Abay's right. I am a ghost.

I laugh to myself and take another sip of wine, before reaching for my iPad and tucking my legs up on the sofa.

I log on to egroupchat.com and check out the last message from Miles, sent before Abay confronted me.

@randymonkey: Awesome. Chat l8r.

L8r. What an absolute loser. Who even says that? Where does Miles even get this lingo? He probably googles 'kid slang' and makes notes, like the twisted creep he is. Fucking prick. He makes my skin crawl.

I log out of the chat room, not wanting him to see that I'm online. He's probably sitting at home right now, staring at the screen, willing Robbie's avatar to come back on. I'd bet my life that if I stay online a minute or two longer, there'll be a message pinging through. Nope. I don't have time for that now. I'll reel him in later, once I have a plan.

I need to figure out how exactly I'm going to go about killing Miles, and I need to make sure I do it subtly. I can't just let it go, not after what he did to that boy. I stayed up late, really late, after I went to Miles's place, trawling endlessly through missing persons reports about young boys. Scrolling through news articles, clicking through Google search results, browsing social media posts from distraught relatives, for hours and hours, looking for a picture or a description that might match the photos on my phone. I scrolled and scrolled and was beginning to think the search was futile. After all, Miles Brady could have killed that boy years ago, decades ago, and only just decided to develop the film. I was about to give up, when on page sixty-seven of a Google search for 'missing boy, London', I finally found a picture that matched: the same boy. Samuel Clarke, seven years old, from Harrow. He'd gone missing on the way home from school, six months ago. Not long after Miles Brady was released from prison. The sick bastard. Clearly couldn't wait to get his hands on another kid.

I googled the boy's name. Found a couple of dozen news articles, replete with imploring, pleading quotes from his parents, begging the public to get in touch with any scrap of information that might bring their son home.

Miles is sick and he definitely needs to die, but I need to be careful about it. I don't trust Abay not to be hovering about, loitering around my place, trying to catch another sighting of me with another victim. And I'm not killing Miles near Hayes; the last thing I need to do is go anywhere near my garage. Anywhere near the block where I killed Julian. I need to be discreet this time, especially with Wheelan having got so close to me.

I take another sip of wine. I need to lure him somewhere quiet, peaceful, derelict. I'm not going to get fancy with Miles's death. No Saint Sebastian shit. I got too carried away last time. It was a daydream that went too far and look where it got me. No, I need to be clinical, efficient. I need to stop showing off. There's no need for stunts or spectacles, I simply need to get rid of him. As long as Miles is dead, the rest is immaterial; it's just details.

I'll kill him quickly and easily. A few well-placed stab wounds. Maybe I'll even cut up his body and dispose of it. Incinerate it. Flush the ashes down the toilet. As long as there's no body, Miles will be just another missing person, like the little boy he took from the world. He lives alone. He has no spouse, no family, no one's likely to kick up a fuss that he's gone. His alcoholic mates will probably shrug it off. They'll probably assume he's been charged with more sick shit and been banged up again and he's too embarrassed to let them know. The only thing I need to worry about is how to get rid of Miles's body, but I'll find a way.

I know where I'm going to kill him. I probably knew deep down when I leaned out of the window earlier on today and lit up my cigarette, gazing out over the rooftops of the abandoned buildings, the office blocks, the sleepy industrial site. I knew deep down that I'd probably kill him there, maybe even in the warehouse itself. The universe put that creep in my path the night I saw him when I was out with the girls, just like the universe presented me with that advert for his piano lessons when I flicked through the local paper in my office. The universe wants Miles dead and has even presented me with a kill room. It's all aligning too perfectly. I can't ignore the signs.

I log back on to the chat room, take a sip of wine, and set about reeling Miles in. We chat about TV shows, football, favourite bands. Miles tries to get a conversation going about piano, but I feel it would be going too far if Robbie happened to be a piano enthusiast. I drop in that he has lessons at school, but his musical tastes are more Drake than Debussy. Miles went a bit quiet during that part of the conversation and I could practically feel him going on to YouTube, ears bleeding at the sound of hip hop.

Things haven't got dirty yet, but I didn't expect they would. Miles isn't a fool. He doesn't want a bit of flirty chat. He wants the real deal. He has to build up trust, get Robbie to believe he's the same as him, and then pounce. That kind of groundwork takes time.

@randymonkey: do u have a gf?

Finally. I take a sip of my wine. I knew he'd get to this question eventually.

@robbie2006: kinda. There's a girl I like. It's kind of like an on off thing.

@randymonkey: lol cool. U on atm?

@robbie2006: yeh kinda. We get off with each other sometimes u know.

@randymonkey: yeh mate.

Mate? I snort. What a dork.
@robbie2006: wbu?

@randymonkey: kind of the same. Theres a girl I know. Send pics to her. Stuff like that.

Here he goes.
@robbie2006: yeah me n my girl do that too.

@randymonkey: cool right?

@robbie2006: yeah deffo.

@randymonkey: so u send them?

I take a sip of wine.
@robbie2006: yeah sometimes.

@randymonkey: me too. I sent one last night. Wanna see?

Urghh.

@robbie2006: of u or her?

@randymonkey: me.

@robbie2006: I dunno, dude. I thought u ment her

@randymonkey: no. she'd kill me if I sent pics of her lol

@robbie2006: haha same.

I expect him to reply with some other lame comment, but he's gone quiet. I head back over to the kitchen and grab the bottle of wine, root around in one of the cupboards and find a pack of wasabi peas, which I pour into a bowl. I carry the bowl and the bottle back over to the coffee table and top up my glass. I'm about to take a sip when a message comes through. A picture. Ha! I sit tighter, bracing myself. I'm pretty sure this isn't going to be a picture of Miles's dashing smile. Or a cat pic. I open it, squinting at my screen as an engorged cock appears. Rank. I close the picture immediately.

@robbie2006: woah ok!

He types a reply. I picture him smiling to himself, sitting in his Belgravia townhouse, feeling smug.

@randymonkey: what do u think?

I pause, trying to put myself in Robbie's shoes. A real kid would be horrified right now. They'd be shocked, unsure what to say. I grab a handful of wasabi peas, crunching as I look out over the city. It's raining now. Swathes of shining raindrops sweep down.

@robbie2006: dunno man . . .

@randymonkey: do u think it's big?

Yuck. Sick cunt.
@robbie2006: I guess.

@randymonkey: show me urs then. Let's compare.

Asshole.
@robbie2006: no man, that's weird!

He's typing. I wait, wondering what justification this creep's going to come up with for getting a kid to share a picture of his penis.

@randymonkey: me n my mates show each other all the time. Don't u?

I roll my eyes. Not only does Miles want a dick pic but he also wants some kind of creepy locker room fantasy to jerk off to. I don't want to give him the satisfaction and yet I need to keep him interested, hooked. I need to reel him in.

@robbie2006: seen a few when staying at friends n stuff.

@randymonkey: ha yeh I get u. and u show ur girl?

@robbie2006: yeah sometimes.

@randymonkey: then jus send me one of the pics u send her lol. Wanna see now lol.

Lol. It's funny how whacking a 'lol' on to the end of a repulsive statement makes paedophiles somehow think they're not coming across as perverted creeps.

I toss back another handful of wasabi peas. Keep him waiting for a moment. Get him worried he's maybe gone too far.

Treat 'em mean, keep 'em keen.

My phone rings. I glance at the screen: Jess. What does she want? I let the call go to voicemail. I'm too involved with Miles right now to face talking to her.

@robbie2006: I dunno about sending that online. If we ever hang out, I'll show u.

Take the bait, Miles. Take the bait, I silently urge him. This is the jackpot. Surely, he must be punching the air right now?

@randymonkey: haha ok cool. Wen were u thinking?

I smirk. Even in the midst of Miles's excitement, he hasn't dropped his childlike-boy misspellings. What a pro.

Good question though. When am I thinking? It'll take me a few days to prepare. I need to go back to the industrial estate, find the right spot. Then I need to pick up some supplies. Maybe get a new knife, a high-powered saw, some heavy-duty plastic bags. There's quite a lot to do, but I'm also raring to go. It's Friday night. I can probably be ready by next weekend. I'm quick when I'm pumped.

I message back, suggesting we meet next Sunday. I tell Miles my dad will be away all weekend. I mention that I live in south London. I give the area of the industrial estate and tell him that I'll text him my address on the day. He's probably wondering why I'm being a bit vague, but he's clearly too delighted with his luck to question it too much. I message him the number of one of my burner phones.

I pull open the coffee table drawer, retrieving the phone. I turn it on, and there's a message there already.

Miles: Hey, it's Tom. Will be cool to meet. See u l8r.

I write a quick reply.

Me: See you later!

I log out of the chat room and put the phone aside. It's done. He's mine now. And I don't have long to wait.

My own phone flashes. Jess has sent a text. I open it.

Jess: Check your emails!!!

I raise an eyebrow. My emails? Jess usually filters my emails before they get to me, dealing with the simple queries and deleting anything irrelevant. Clearly there's something important I need to see. I click into my inbox. There are several messages, from colleagues and PRs, but the one that catches my eye is an email with the subject line: 'Women of the Year Awards Shortlist Announced!'

No way. My heart flips in nervous anticipation as I open the email. It's from the founder of the awards, a media mogul with a global empire of lifestyle magazines and newspapers. I scan the email, my eyes landing on a sentence I can barely believe is real.

> I'm delighted to let you know that you have been shortlisted in the Media category of this year's awards.

Oh my God. Oh my God! I let out a squeal, unable to contain myself. I jump up, pace around the room, buzzing, grinning, disbelieving. Then I grab my phone to call Jess.

I shake my head, delighted, shocked, as the phone rings. The Women of the Year Awards. Unbelievable.

Chapter Sixteen

I've showered, blow-dried my hair and meticulously applied a subtle but flattering amount of make-up.

Vanessa's on her way over in an Uber. After I got off the phone from Jess, I realised I wanted to do something to celebrate. I wanted to be with someone, and the only person I really want to see is Vanessa. I drift through my flat, lighting candles. I think about the long brambles of Vanessa's hair, her curves, her warm body, as the flames flicker, the mood of my sitting room growing sexy, romantic. I think of her smile. Her eyes.

I perch on the edge of the sofa and write her a text.

Me: Can't wait to see you xxx

I press send. I lie back and let my hand trail across my stomach, pull up the hem of my dress. I look at my phone, but nothing's happening. I sit up. I need to distract myself. There's no point getting too excited before Vanessa even gets here. I could go on to the chat room and wind up Miles a bit more, but that's far too much of a mood killer. I could reread the email about the Women of the Year Awards, but I've already read it about fifty times, to make sure it's real. It definitely is. According to Jess, the nominations will be announced in the press soon. She's already booking interviews, photoshoots.

This is my moment, the beginning of a new chapter. And yet, Miles is still at the back of my mind. I need to get his murder over and done with. Killing will be a lot harder to get away with if I become better known, particularly if I win. The excitement of gaining more status, fame, is tinged with sadness. If I become Woman of the Year, gone are the days of knifing paedophiles in alleyways and going on deadly dates with predators. Miles will have to be my last hurrah.

I go on to Google and browse photos from last year's awards ceremony, checking out the outfits of the nominees, wondering what I'll wear.

My intercom sounds. Vanessa's here.

I get up and glance at my reflection in the mirror above my mantelpiece. I look good. Pretty. Young. Sexy. Innocent. I smile. I'm free.

I walk over to the intercom and buzz Vanessa up, before heading to the kitchen and pouring us glasses of wine. A moment later, there's a knock at my front door.

I place the bottle on the counter and go to answer it.

I pull it open to see Vanessa standing there, in her usual laid-back student get-up. Black skinny jeans, chunky lace-up boots, an old jumper, bobbling at the sleeves. And yet, despite her casual clothes, she looks beautiful. Her cheeks have a rosy glow. Her eyes are bright. Tendrils of hair fall around her face.

'Hey,' I say, smiling, feeling genuinely happy to see her.

'Hey,' she replies, looking pleased to see me too.

I step back to allow her into the flat. She leans close, planting a kiss on my lips as she enters.

'I brought this,' she says, handing me a blue plastic corner-shop bag, which contains a bottle of something.

I pull the plastic back, scan the bottle. Cheap champagne.

'Oh, thanks!' I gush, and even though I know I'll probably find it undrinkable, I feel touched, nonetheless.

'I just poured us some wine!' I say, wandering over to the kitchen, grateful that we can drink my stuff.

'Cool.' Vanessa follows me through. I pluck a glass from the counter.

'You look great,' she comments as I turn around, handing it to her.

Her gaze wanders from my legs back up to my eyeline.

'Thanks. So do you.' I hold her gaze as she takes the glass.

She perches on a seat by the breakfast bar and looks around my flat.

'Love the candles!' She laughs. 'Very romantic.'

'I try!' I joke.

'I can never get over your flat. It's crazy,' Vanessa comments, eyeing the vast expanse, the expensive furnishings, my grand piano. Her expression is a little sad, a note of frustration and resignation in her voice.

I know how she feels. I know that feeling of denial, of being on the outside, looking in, feeling broke, stuck. That was my life for years. Half the time, I still feel like that person in spite of all my wealth.

I don't know how to reply in a way that isn't patronising, so I sit down opposite her and ask about her day. She tells me about a meeting with her supervisor, a lecture she gave, some issue with a proctor. It's kind of dull, but I nod anyway, making the right noises, admiring the way she looks in the candlelight.

'So, what are we celebrating?' she says, eventually.

I told Vanessa I had some 'good news'. I want to tell Vanessa about the Women of the Year Awards, but she still doesn't know I'm the editor of *Couture*. She believes the lie I told her when we

211

first met, that I'm in the fashion industry, working as a designer. I never wanted her knowing too much, getting too close, although she's probably beginning to figure things out by now. And if I do triumph at the Women of the Year Awards, she might end up seeing my face in the *Evening Standard*. Although given how bookish she is, how cut off from the real world, I wouldn't be too surprised if it passes her by.

'Just a work thing,' I tell her, tracing my fingers around the rim of my wine glass. 'I got some recognition at work. It feels good.' I smile, taking a sip.

Vanessa frowns slightly, questioningly, and I wonder if she's going to pry.

'Well, cheers to that!' she says, her face relaxing as she leans across the breakfast bar and clinks her glass against mine.

There are reasons I like Vanessa, and one of those reasons is that she lets me have space. She's not a snoop. She knows the right times to ask questions and when to leave something alone.

'Cheers!' I reply, grinning, clinking my glass against hers, taking a sip, holding eye contact.

She smiles, taking a sip too. She places her glass on the counter.

'Are you hungry?' I ask, feeling conscious of my hosting skills.

Vanessa has come all this way. She's not Abay. What we had was always strictly casual, at least until the end. Vanessa's not like that, though. It's not all about sex with her. And after the weekend we shared together in Suffolk, it feels wrong to simply jump into bed. That weekend wasn't just sexual, it was romantic too. I've thought about it far more than I expected I would. I've reflected on the way Vanessa laughed in the rowing boat in the middle of Fritton Lake, surrounded by swans. She joked that it was like something from *The Notebook*, while I smirked, stroking her hair away from her face, kissing her. I've thought about how it felt to sleep at night with her body next to mine, and the cute, soft whimpers she makes while she's sleeping. I've thought about the frankincense-scented moisturiser she uses and the way it smells on her skin. I didn't think my mind would dwell on such things. I thought my heart was insulated from thoughts like that, but the memories, the feelings, have cropped up, uninvited but not unwelcome. While I'm falling asleep, taking a bath, walking home from work, my mind has wandered to her.

'Yeah, I am a bit,' Vanessa replies.

'Cool,' I chirp, hoping my cleaner might have replenished the fridge.

I don't think of my cleaner as a housekeeper, but really, she is. She does more than cleaning. She keeps my flat ticking along, feeling like a home. She does the things I'm too busy trying to get away with murder to remember: she buys new towels when mine grow old, she orders bulbs for lamps when they stop working, she polishes all the crockery so that it gleams. She replenishes the cupboards and fridge with fresh food and supplies. She does the laundry, the ironing, leaves my clothes where they belong: neat and perfect in my walk-in wardrobe. I forget how many things she does. It all happens when I'm out, like magic, so that my flat's perfect and comfortable by the time I get home.

I hop off my stool and walk over to the fridge. I'm relieved upon opening it to discover fresh supplies: milk, eggs, butter, cheese, a couple of yoghurts, a packet of fillet steak, a few bags of salad, even a pack of salted caramel profiteroles.

'Fancy some steak?' I suggest, discovering a bag of green beans on one of the shelves, a pot of pepper sauce.

Vanessa turns from gazing out at the view of the city through the plate glass windows.

'Sounds perfect,' she replies.

I pull open one of the drawers in the fridge and discover a bag of carrots, some new potatoes.

I'm not the best cook in the world, but even I can fry some steaks, boil a few potatoes and green beans, heat up some pepper sauce. I root around for a frying pan while Vanessa starts talking about a political news story. I haven't read up on it as much as she has, too distracted by Miles Brady, but I can just about wing it and I chat away as I prepare the meal. I hardly ever cook in my flat, especially not for another person. I don't invite my friends round much. I could show off my flat more, but I like having my space too much.

It's different with Vanessa, though. The smell of the hot oil warming in the pan, the sizzling steaks, the sound of the bubbling potatoes, her voice. The feeling of chatting about the news over a glass of red wine at the end of the day. It tugs at my heart in a way that's deeper, more moving, more compelling than the Women of the Year Awards. Is this what I truly want? A beautiful girl. Domesticity.

I laugh at a comment Vanessa makes, and flip the steaks. They hiss, and I wonder whether I could let her in a little bit. Let her into my home. My heart. I wonder whether she'd be okay inside. She probably wouldn't mind calling my flat home, but would she want to experience the private parts of me? Could she handle it? Would she get too close? Or would she still allow me a bit of space, like she does now?

I'd need to keep parts of myself locked away, private spaces just for me. Garages of the soul. But maybe we could find a way to make it work, to lead a normal life. Maybe I'd stop wanting to kill if I had someone who loved me. Maybe the pain would abate, the rage dissipate.

Perhaps I could truly turn over a new leaf. Give up killing. Become Woman of the Year. Be with someone. Fall in love.

I push the steaks around, conscious of not overcooking or burning them.

Vanessa jumps off her stool and sidles up to me. She slips her hands around my waist, rests her head on my shoulder.

'Looks delicious,' she says, peering into the pan.

'They do, don't they?'

I move the pan off the heat and turn to face her, taking in her kind, pretty face. I want to be with her. I want to move on from my dark pastimes. I just need to get Miles out of my system – one last kill – and then I'm going to go for it. Get closer to Vanessa. Try to trust her, love her. I have a feeling we might be able to make it work. She's different. She's nothing like the controlling men I've encountered in the past, who fly into a rage if I fail to do what they want, be how they want me to be. No. Vanessa makes me feel comfortable, relaxed, safe.

I draw her closer, kissing her. I slip my fingers under the hem of her jumper, feeling her warm skin underneath. She kisses me tenderly. Her kiss isn't just lust, it's loving, comforting. Her kiss feels like home. It feels like hope.

Chapter Seventeen

My phone rings as I'm waiting for the night bus.

It's Eva. She's probably wondering why I've missed out on drinks, brunch and other social activities over the past couple of weeks. I should pick up, show I'm alive.

I answer, looking at the arrivals display, its digital times glowing in the waning evening light.

The bus I'm waiting for, the one due to take me to south-east London, is due in two minutes.

'Hey, what are you up to?' Eva asks.

'Not a lot.'

The truth is I'm already in disguise, wearing a long brown wig and a cap, no make-up, a massive ratty old coat, heels to make me look taller, and jeans. I glance nervously around, hoping my friends aren't near or planning to call in. The last thing I need is for them to see me looking weird, like this.

'Are you out?' I ask.

'I'm around the corner. At Anderson's. Where are you?' Eva asks, her voice sounding strained, tense.

What's she doing there?

'I'm . . .' I hesitate, reaching for an excuse, '. . . having a quiet night. Popped out to pick up some food,' I lie. 'What's up?'

'I need to see you. I can't really say over the phone,' Eva tells me.

I wonder what it could be. A work thing? It's hardly likely to be a man thing. Eva's like me – perpetually single, only engaging in discreet affairs she tends not to talk about. She doesn't let people in. She's not interested in silly highs and lows and dramas. She's not the kind of person to reach out either. Whatever's happened must be serious.

'Can we catch up tomorrow?' I suggest.

'Are you sure you can't meet now? It's important. I'll get you a drink,' Eva says.

I feel bad. She's clearly desperate, but I have a murder to prepare for. Miles is meeting me tomorrow. It's not like I can prepare for his kill during the day. I need the cover of darkness. And it's not like I can just pop into Anderson's. I'm in disguise. I'd have to go home and change. And I can't go to Anderson's any time soon. One of the staff might remember seeing me with Julian. Just the sight of me could jog their memory. It's not worth the risk.

'I can't. I'll call tomorrow.'

Eva sighs.

'Okay, fine. But please do. It's urgent,' she insists.

'Will do,' I reply, before saying goodbye and hanging up.

Odd. Eva hardly ever calls me. I feel a little rattled as I drop my phone into my jacket pocket. The bus arrives.

I swipe my Oyster card against the sensor and get on. I'd normally use my bank card for travelling in London, but I don't want to be tracked. I climb the stairs of the double-decker, sit on the top floor at the back, right under the CCTV camera. All the camera will see is the back of my head. I gaze out of the window as the bus begins to crawl through London. I smile to myself, relishing the feeling of being someone else, of letting the mask of Camilla Black fall and slipping into one of my shadow selves. I turn my phone off to avoid being tracked. I won't turn it on again until I'm back. For now, I'm making my way to a suburb I've never been to before. A rundown part of town. South-east London's equivalent of Hayes. I researched the area a few nights ago, with encryption software hiding my search history. I turn on my iPod and put on some music to listen to as I take in the city and watch passengers drift on and off the bus as it chugs away from Mayfair.

Eventually, I start to recognise the area from the images I've seen on Google Maps. The bus crawls down a dual carriageway. I take in a gigantic Asda across the road, sprawling car parks. A shopping estate. TK Maxx. Next. Topshop. Boots. Poundland. I turn around. Furniture depots. Trade shops for restaurants. I'm getting close. I press the bell and get off the bus.

I start walking down the side of the dual carriageway towards the hardware store I found online. There are hardware stores closer to me than this, but I'm hardly going to go and buy a ton of supplies for a murder somewhere local. I thought I'd come to this part of town instead. The store is open late, and the area is busy and built-up enough that people come and go, and my purchases won't stand out. And given that I'm in disguise, even if I am caught on CCTV, I won't look enough like myself for the police to do anything about it. As well as my wig and cap, I'm wearing a massive scarf that practically comes up to my ears, which will hide my mouth and jawline.

I head into the store. It's quiet. There are a couple of builder types inside, picking up supplies. The store isn't well-staffed. It's cold. They even have self-service tills. A teenager restacking a display of nuts and bolts barely even glances in my direction. There are a few other customers, a couple by the looks of it, standing by a display of indoor plants, looking as though they're trying to decide which to buy. The store smells of wood shavings and polish. I grab a trolley and wheel it through the aisles.

I pick up a couple of random things: a roll of wallpaper, a pot plant, a pack of brushes. Padding purchases to make the more sinister items I need stand out less. When I'm finished, I wheel my trolley towards the more exciting stuff. Power saws. I want the most expensive one. It boasts of a 'high-speed motor' which 'makes the most demanding cuts with ease'. I picture Miles's flesh buzzing off its blades, but a woman splashing out on a top-of-the-range power saw in this part of town might raise a few eyebrows. The cashier might remember me or casually ask a question. Better to stick to one of the mid-range saws instead. They should still cut through bone and flesh, and that's the most important thing. I pick up a few other things I might need: a torch, plastic gloves, heavy-duty waste bags, and a few other random bits – nuts and bolts, masking tape, adhesive – to make it look like I'm doing a spot of DIY rather than slaughtering someone.

I head to the self-service tills, hoping I can get away with scanning my items myself, even though I've picked up quite a few things The shop assistant who was stacking the shelves is now sweeping up soil from a knocked-over pot plant. I keep my head down, affecting a bored, disinterested demeanour as I start scanning my items. I definitely have too many items for the small bagging area, but I carry on anyway. I'll do two loads. I scan my kill stuff first, to get it over with. The shop assistant glances my way, but carries on sweeping. I feel almost sorry for the guy. Saturday night and he's stuck sweeping the floor of a cold hardware store in one of the grottiest parts of the city.

I feel tense as I scan my power saw, worried that someone's going to tap on my shoulder, say something, but nobody does. I bag it up, breathing a sigh of relief. Once I've scanned everything, I pay with cash – untraceable.

The machine spits out my change. I briefly consider leaving it for the poor sod who works here, but I can't risk him remembering me. I scoop the coins up, dump them in my coat pocket, gather my bags and keep my head down as I leave the store. I cross the car park and emerge on to the main road. My stuff's pretty heavy but I wander down the road, looking out for a cab. After ten minutes of walking, laden with bags, I stop to deposit the purchases I won't need in someone's wheelie bin. I glance around. There are no cabs passing by. It would take five seconds to hail a taxi in Mayfair, but out here it's dull and residential, it's just cars and buses and vans. Sighing, I check my bearings on my burner phone and head in the direction of the nearest restaurants. I lug my stuff as I walk along the pavement, head down, wishing I could have used my SUV for this, then finally, a cab appears, its orange light glowing in the darkness. I flag it down.

I keep my head lowered as I get inside and deposit my bags on the back seat. I give the driver my destination from under my cap: a street in central London. Not too close to where I live, but close enough. The driver nods, disinterested, pulling away from the kerb. I fasten my seat belt and gaze out of the window as the cab passes down the dual carriageway, leaving the shopping development behind. I let my mind wander, thinking about tomorrow, Miles.

I imagine the perfect kill, mentally practising my moves in my fantasy of how I want things to go. I'll text Miles the address of the estate, tell him I'm hanging out at the warehouse. It's the kind of thing a boy would do, right? Explore some derelict old building. Then once Miles arrives, I'll approach him from behind, slip a needle into his neck and give him a measure of sedative to the jugular. By the time he wakes, he'll be bound up. I'll torture him for a while, have a bit of fun with him as I make him confess to some of the things he's done. I'll make him pay for his crimes, feel the pain he deserves. Then, when I've had enough, I'll finish him off: saw him into pieces, bag him up. The industrial site's not far from the river. It might take a few trips, but I could carry the bags to the water's edge, weigh them down with loose bricks from the estate, and toss them in. All traces of Miles would disappear and the children of London would finally be safe.

As we get closer to the city, I turn my regular phone back on. A text comes through from Vanessa, saying she misses me and asking what I'm up to. If I'm free.

I feel warm inside, excited, all thoughts of Miles gone in a heartbeat. Thoughts of last night flit through my mind: kissing in the kitchen, having dinner together, sleeping together in my bed. Unlike Abay, I didn't want her to go straight after sex. I wanted her to stick around.

I text to say I've been doing some errands. She replies instantly, asking if I want to come over. *Come over?* We've never met at her place. She lives in a student house. The thought of going there has never appealed, and yet, I get the feeling she's trying to share her life with me, like I've been sharing mine with her. This isn't about convenience or luxury, it's about opening up. And I want to do that with her.

I shouldn't go over right now, with a power saw in tow, but I do want to see her. She probably wouldn't notice. I doubt she'd give my hardware-store shopping bags too much thought.

I text back, saying I'm on my way, and ask the driver to make a detour.

The car crawls through the suburban south London streets as Vanessa and I message, giddy with excitement at seeing each other even after just one day apart. I can feel myself changing. My preoccupation with murder is turning into a preoccupation with Vanessa. My bloodlust is becoming something different. The world is full of bad men, and for so long, I've felt a nagging obligation to fix it. Even just a little bit, here and there, but when I think about Vanessa, I don't feel the weight of the world resting quite so heavily on my shoulders any more. It doesn't feel like my burden.

I almost wish I didn't have to kill Miles, and yet, I can't quite let him go. I know too much. I've come too far already. I'm too invested. Just one more kill, and then I'm done. Then I'm going to be with Vanessa. Give this happiness thing a shot.

I ask the driver to drop me off at the end of her street. After I've paid, I get out and loiter until he's out of sight. A group of pissed girls, who look like students dressed for a night on the town, spill out of one of the houses. I keep my head down as they pass me, tripping down the road, all linked arms, giddy laughs and high heels.

Once they've gone, I check no one else is around and pull off my cap. I yank off my wig and dump both in a nearby bin. I run my fingers through my flattened, matted hair and head to Vanessa's. I'm clearly not looking my best. I'm dressed down, no make-up. Without make-up, my face is pale and unremarkable. I have the kind of face that's like a blank canvas – it can be made to look striking, but it can also be completely forgettable.

Vanessa's never seen me like this before. I've always made an effort around her. I've always been Camilla, but tonight I'm creeping into my shadow self. I'm an in-between version. Hopefully it won't matter though. Vanessa and I are beyond focusing solely on each other's looks. I feel just about comfortable showing her this side of myself, the mask slightly askew.

I walk up her front drive. Her house is a four-storey Victorian townhouse that was probably once a salubrious family home, now rough around the edges. The windowsills are rotting, the tiles on the doorstep are chipped, the paint on the door is cracked and peeling. I tap the knocker, hoping Vanessa answers and not one of her housemates. I clear my throat as I wait. I hear footsteps pounding the staircase. A blurry figure moves behind bubbled glass panels.

The door opens. It's Vanessa.

'Hey!' She smiles widely.

She's wearing her hair down, and it falls in beautiful waves over her shoulders. She leans in to kiss me. She doesn't seem to notice or care how I look. She seems happy I'm here.

'Come in!' She takes my hand and pulls me inside. I grin, girlishly, surprising myself.

I take in my surroundings as she closes the door behind me. The hallway is lined with woodchip wallpaper and horribly cheap, industrial-style blue carpet. The house smells musty, a little damp. I spot a kitchen down the hallway, hear voices. Laughter. I worry she's going to introduce me to her housemates, but she doesn't.

She clocks my bags.

'DIY stuff.' I roll my eyes.

She reaches for them. I tense up, but she takes hold of the handles, raising an eyebrow at me.

I release my grip.

'Heavy!' Vanessa comments as she takes the bags from me.

'Yeah,' I reply, willing her not to look inside, not to ask too many questions.

'I'll leave them here,' she says, placing the bags under a coat rail, amid a jumble of shoes.

'Okay,' I reply. I'd prefer to keep my eye on them, but I can't say that.

Vanessa takes my hand and leads me up a narrow staircase to her bedroom. As we head up the stairs, I notice she's painted her toenails – a garish glittering green shade that I'd never dream of wearing but that's so her.

'So this is my humble abode!' she says, beckoning me into the room with a slightly nervous laugh.

I take in her room. It's big. A large bay window frames a desk. There are books everywhere. Bookcases overflowing, books stacked in piles on the desk, towering on her bedside table. She has a small wardrobe. A shaggy rug. An antique-effect mirror with a string of fairy lights draped around its frame. Pot plants. Loads of them. Tall ones. Spider plants. Cacti on the desk and dotted along the windowsill. There's a sofa, a throw slung over it. A book open on the armrest, pages down. There are cushions on the bed, arranged prettily, as though in expectation of a visitor. A candle flickers on the bedside table and the room smells of wax and vanilla. It's homely. Cute.

There are no pictures of family on the walls. Maybe the reason Vanessa never pries too much about my family is because she doesn't want me to pry in return. Maybe her family isn't exactly ideal either.

'Oh, it's nice!' I insist, meaning it.

Vanessa shrugs. 'It's all right. I like it.'

'I like it too,' I tell her, peeling off my coat, draping it on the sofa.

Vanessa clocks the ratty old jumper I'm wearing. A cheap one from my disguise wardrobe. The kind of thing *she'd* normally wear, not me.

'You're looking casual today,' she comments.

'Oh, yeah.' I shrug, not bothering to explain further.

Vanessa steps towards me, tracing her hand over the front of my jumper. I feel a tremor of excitement at her touch. Our eyes meet. I sweep my hands around her, over her back, draw her in. I run my fingers through her soft hair as we kiss. We fall back on to the bed, amongst the cushions.

'I've missed you,' Vanessa murmurs, kissing my neck.

I kiss her hungrily, my hands tangling in her hair. I want her, but it's more than just lust.

'Let's go away together,' I blurt out, breathily, between kisses.

'Suffolk?' Vanessa says, slipping her fingers underneath the hem of my top.

'No, further away. Somewhere hot.'

224

'Sounds heavenly,' she replies, nuzzling back into my neck.

I can't tell if she's on board or if she thinks I'm daydreaming.

I take hold of her chin, draw her face level with mine, gaze into her eyes.

'I mean it. I want to go away with you. I'll pay for everything. Don't worry about that. I just want to get away. I want to be with you.'

My voice cracks unexpectedly and I feel raw, almost embarrassed.

Abay was wrong. I do have a heart. I can feel it. I can feel it pounding. A sharpness inside. A need. It's not all-consuming. It's not the stuff of sonnets or ballads or Hollywood movies, but it's something. A stirring.

Vanessa smiles, softly, tenderly. 'Okay. Let's do it. I want to be with you too.'

I smile, pulling her close.

Chapter Eighteen

It's getting dark by the time I arrive at the industrial estate. The atmosphere of the place couldn't be any more different to the last time I was here, pulling up in a chauffeured car. There are no office workers, no lights on. It's creepy, eerily quiet.

I walk towards the warehouse. It was a bustling photography set before, brimming with models. Now it's derelict, laced with shadows. I jump, eyes darting around, thinking I hear the scuttling of a rat, but I can't see anything. It's probably just the wind. Or in my mind.

I wonder what Miles will make of this place. It's hardly inviting. Will he be freaked out? Will he turn around and leave? And yet I suspect his dark motivations will override any misgivings. He'll go for it.

I remember where the fire exit is located from the last time I was here, and bypass the front door. I creep around the back of the building, glancing over my shoulder. I have a weird feeling, like I'm about to be disturbed, as though I'm being watched. I'm on edge. But I need to get this done. I need it to go my way.

I take a wrench from my bag and set to work jimmying open the fire exit door. It's stiff but I get it there. The door creaks as I pull it open and slip inside.

Inside, amid the cold, dank air, I breathe a sigh of relief. The building is silent, still, undisturbed. I stand still for a moment, letting its quietness sink into me, calming my nerves. I'm here now, in this dark, abandoned space. It's just me and the empty rooms. I feel my mask fall away as I flick on my torch and make my way deeper inside.

I head into one of the office rooms and cast the beam of my torch around. It contains an abandoned desk, a few chairs. It'll do.

I get ready. I unpack my bag, retrieving the photos. I printed out the photographs I took of the shots I found in Miles's dark room – the hideous pictures of him and his child victim, Samuel Clarke. I want him to be confronted with his crimes before he goes down, so he knows he's getting the justice he deserves.

I place my torch on the desk and set to work pinning the pictures to the office walls. The grisly images still disgust me. I try not to focus too hard on them. Instead, I imagine the look of shock and horror that will descend upon Miles's face when it dawns on him that he's been set up. It's going to be good. Really good.

My mind wanders to Vanessa too. Being on holiday with her once this is done.

I think of clear blue sea in a hot part of the world. I picture her in a bikini lying on a towel on white sand. I wonder whether she'll read Aristotle on the beach, or whether she'll opt for something lighter. I wonder what that would be. I imagine our arms draped around each other's bodies in a beach hut, the sound of waves ebbing against the shore, lulling us to sleep at night. I wonder if she'll still be wearing that sparkly green nail varnish. I think of the sea lapping against her toes as I put the final pictures up, sunlight twinkling off the glitter.

We stayed up late last night, researching where to go, coordinating our diaries. We set a date. Tomorrow, I'll book the time off work and pay for the flights. Soon, this fantasy will become reality.

But for now, I need to get this out of the way. Bring Miles to justice. Stop him from preying on any more kids. Once this is over, then I can have some reprieve. Kick back in the sun. Calm down. Be free.

My burner phone buzzes, its screen flashing in the dull room.

Miles: Not far now.

I check the time. It's 5.45 p.m. Not long to go. I type a reply.

Robbie: Cool!

I flash my torch around the room. A gory spectacle. Not long now.

I take my phone and slip out of the room, and head down the corridor towards the entrance of the warehouse. I sit in a stairwell, lurking in the shadows. Dressed in black, I blend into the darkness. My heart beats heavily in my chest. I'm excited. A little nervous. Thoughts of Vanessa momentarily elude me. The countdown's on. He'll be here soon.

I gave Miles the address of the estate. Soon he'll be wandering in, confused, expecting a suburban house.

I wait a little while, listening out, staring at my phone. It buzzes into the silence:

Miles: Were ur place?!

Ha. Still trying to sound like a kid, even though, in his eyes, the game is nearly up. As far as Miles is concerned, he's about to meet a little boy, a boy who'll be shocked and terrified when he realises he's been lied to, manipulated. Does Miles plan to pretend to be the father of his alias, Tom? Does he plan to make up some lies to temporarily put Robbie at ease before escalating things, or will he get nasty straight away?

Robbie: I'm hanging out in this cool old place. Come have a look! The warehouse at the back with the red door.

Miles: Ok lol.

My heart thuds harder. He's coming.

I get up and creep towards the door. I peer through a nearby window, and in the darkness, I can make him out. He's walking towards the warehouse. He's wearing a baby-pink shirt, like the shade of the dressing gown he'd wear when trying to get children to touch him. Classic.

I stand flush against the wall, heart pounding, ready to pounce the moment he enters.

I hear his footsteps.

Here goes.

Chapter Nineteen

'Robbie?' Miles says, his voice pitched higher than a grown man's should be. He's clearly still pretending to be a kid.

He's keeping the act up, right up until the very last moment.

The door begins opening. I hold my breath. Adrenaline surges through me.

I step back into the shadows. As the door opens, I spot a dark sleeve, no pink shirt in sight. I freeze.

The door opens further. I back away. The figure steps forward. I spot the barrel of a gun. A face in the darkness. Not Miles.

It's Wheelan, his eyes cold, challenging, victorious in the dim light.

Wheelan . . .

'Get down on your knees, Camilla,' he barks, pointing his gun at me.

Miles stands behind him, wide-eyed, watching, flanked by officers.

Wheelan paces closer.

'I said get down,' he repeats, his voice hard, loud.

My heart pounds, Wheelan's gun is unnerving me, but I back away towards my kill room.

'What have I done?' I ask, my voice light, weirdly quiet.

Officers pour in behind Wheelan, infiltrating the darkness, flashing torches around, filling the dusty space.

'Get down!' Wheelan screams as I back away further, deeper into the warehouse, towards the room I was just in.

Wheelan follows, just like I hoped he would. A few of his colleagues accompany him. I recognise Sergeant Porter among them. He casts his torch around. It lands on the photo of Miles grinning with Samuel Clarke's corpse.

Wheelan's gaze follows. I observe his face, captivated. He frowns. Shock, disgust and rage descend upon his features. His lips part, his jaw drops. I note the way his shoulders sag, the grip on his gun loosening.

Smirking, I enjoy the fleeting seconds of him having forgotten all about me.

I had a feeling this might happen.

I knew today could go either way. I knew that either Miles would be my prey, or I'd be Wheelan's.

I'm not stupid. I've been aware that Wheelan was getting close. Far too close.

I had my suspicions. There was something off about Miles from the beginning. He was tempting as prey, but ever so slightly too convenient. He practically fell into my lap. I couldn't decide if it was just good fortune – the universe lining him up for slaughter, or if something else was going on. I replayed the night in the bar when I first saw him over and over in my head that evening when I got home.

I recalled the way Briony had mentioned him the moment he'd arrived with a pointed gasp, keeping us all on tenterhooks with her dramatic story about his abuse. I was immediately hooked. Appalled. I went straight to the toilets. Googled him. Began imagining how I'd like him to die, plotting how I'd kill him. I reflected on how smug he'd looked. How free he'd seemed. How irritating it had been.

The next day I'd found him on Facebook. It was easy enough to do. And then the advert for his piano lessons appeared in my local paper, drawing me even closer to him. The leads were almost too easy to stumble upon.

When Wheelan paid a visit to my flat, questioning me about Julian with his penetrating, unnerving gaze, it was clear he was trying to figure me out, get the measure of me; I could tell he was on to me.

I wasn't sure if he had it in him or not to set me up, but I did consider it. As I took in his tenacious track record of catching serial killers and his deep-seated motivations for ensnaring them, it didn't seem impossible that he could be up to something. Something far smarter than I'd ever usually give the police credit for.

When I saw the post on Miles's Facebook page signed off with a nickname that linked directly to a profile on a dodgy chat room, I started to become wary. If I was being set up, then it was a sophisticated sting. Wheelan had clearly grasped my methods. He understood that I research my prey, dig deep into their backgrounds, reel them in. And so, to catch me, to prove my guilt, all he needed was to plant a predator in my path to draw me in. I figured he'd collaborated with Briony, who I sensed had suspicions about me.

But all this time, I couldn't be sure if it was all in my head. If I was right, then Wheelan was good. Very good. But he didn't quite have me worked out as well as he thought he did. He'd underestimated the sheer extent of my distrust. He'd underestimated my instincts and how calculating I can be.

And so I set to work reeling Miles in, messaging him in the chat room, playing right into Wheelan's hands. I imagined him salivating, rubbing his palms together, unable to wait to get his hands on me. Little did he know that I was preparing to set *him* up.

I don't think Wheelan expected me to break into Miles's home. That was the spanner in the works. That was when I found the photos of Miles's child victim, Samuel Clarke. At that point, I knew Wheelan had no idea who he was dealing with in Miles. He knew Miles was a convicted paedophile who'd done his time. But he clearly didn't realise Miles was a killer. Wheelan would never have colluded with Miles on a sting if he'd known that. He'd never let a killer walk free.

I knew the moment I saw the pictures of Miles with that poor boy that Wheelan would want him sent down for life.

I had moments of doubt. Moments when I thought that maybe I was being paranoid and that Wheelan had nothing to do with any of it. Part of me hoped that Miles would turn out to be a regular creep, an easy kill. But I sensed that wasn't the case when Eva called in a panic last night, desperate to talk to me, as though she wanted to warn me about something. I figured she wanted to give me a heads-up about Briony. I wasn't sure, but I sensed that might be it.

And then tonight, as I arrived at the estate, I noticed a few vehicles, which I suspected were unmarked police cars, parked along the road with people inside. I spotted a few CCTV cameras in the area that I didn't remember seeing before. I was sure I was being monitored. That undercover officers were on standby, waiting for me. I knew I was right not to have brought my power saw with me, and all the heavy-duty bags I'd hoped to wrap Miles's body in. I'd left them down the road, stashed in an alleyway, to retrieve later if the coast somehow turned out to be clear and Miles ended up being a regular victim.

I dropped the knife I had on me into a gutter before entering the warehouse, disappointed that I wouldn't get to use it. I'd been hoping I'd get to kill Miles. I wanted to see him die.

Wheelan was betting on my bloodlust. I figured his plan was to ambush me when Miles was due to arrive, just like he has done.

He no doubt thought he'd catch me with incriminating weapons, ready to kill, in an irrefutably damning situation. He probably hoped he'd find evidence linking me to other kills. A knife with the DNA of another victim on it, perhaps. Or a trophy from a murder. Maybe the key to my garage. He planned to arrest me, haul me to the station, break me down with questioning. Destroy me. But he underestimated me.

I knew Wheelan was far too close. Which was why I cleared out my garage in the middle of the night. I cleaned it from top to bottom, every last inch of it, before handing the keys over to a new owner. I wiped down every last trophy I took from my victims – the watch, cock ring, a pair of cufflinks – and tossed them into the Thames. I disposed of every strange possession I own. Every last weapon. Every last wig. Every last burner phone. And now I'm clean. Not a trace of my murderous past remains.

Wheelan's got nothing on me. He thought he'd bring me down tonight, but if anything, I'm coming out of this a hero. I've exposed a child killer, helped bring him to justice. Even Wheelan's got to give me some begrudging respect for that.

'What . . . What is this?' Wheelan gasps.

'I think it's Miles you should be arresting, Wheelan, not me. I've done nothing wrong.'

Wheelan stares at me, eyes wide, his face gaping with shock.

'Go. Arrest him,' he orders his colleagues.

He turns back to me, his face contorted as he struggles to process what I've done.

'Where . . . Where did you get these pictures?' he asks, flummoxed.

'I think you should be talking to Miles about these pictures, not me,' I state. I'm hardly going to admit to breaking and entering.

My nerves are turning to exhilaration now. The look on Wheelan's face is priceless. I've outsmarted him. Now it's me that's smirking.

'What did you think you'd find here, Wheelan?' I ask.

He stares at me, dumbstruck. The other officers are just as aghast.

'Put your gun down!' I tut.

'I know what you do, Camilla. I know who you are,' Wheelan insists, his focus coming back, the menace returning to his eyes.

I scoff. I'm no longer scared of him. He has nothing on me. I've outsmarted him. I've won.

'It's funny you say that, Wheelan, because I don't think you have a *clue* who I am.'

Chapter Twenty

The waves lap against the shore, the sea shimmering into the distance. The sun beams down on me and Vanessa, making our skin warm, golden. She's sitting next to me, reading a crime novel, unaware of the irony. Her toes are still painted green and they glitter in the hot sunlight, just like I imagined.

I take a sip of my cocktail and lean back in my lounger, closing my eyes. I think of Wheelan. He went full steam ahead with his investigation into Miles, launching a search on Miles's house in Belgravia and a countryside estate he owned in Sussex. Further evidence relating to Samuel Clarke's disappearance was found, including more photographs, a lock of hair and even human remains. Miles is going down for a very long time and Wheelan has taken the credit. The truly tragic case, finally solved, has exploded in the press, and Wheelan's a national hero.

I don't care. I'll let him have it. Deep down, he and I both know Miles is a loser's prize. Wheelan wanted me and he knows he's never going to get me. He grilled me over the photographs, asking how I'd obtained them, but I didn't have to say a word. I simply responded, 'No comment.' Always no comment. My lawyer backed me up during questioning and has warned Wheelan and the Met against harassing me. Wheelan would be a fool to cross paths with me again.

The police have nothing on me, and I've got nothing but good things to look forward to now. A future with Vanessa. The Woman of the Year Award, which Jess is convinced I'm going to win. She says she's heard 'rumours'. She even advised me to start thinking about what I'm going to say in my winner speech while I'm away.

My future's looking bright. Wheelan's history. I'm not going to be hounded by him any more. He wouldn't dare.

A waiter from the luxury, beach-facing hotel we're staying at approaches, topping up my drink.

I thank him, still blissed out from the sun.

I see he's left a few crisp daily newspapers from back home on the table next to me. The Samuel Clarke story is still front-page news.

I reach for one and flick through. There's nothing new, just horrible sordid details. I'm about to close the paper when another article catches my eye.

Child rapist released after serving just HALF of sentence

I read it, taking in the details. A predator from Yorkshire who raped a neighbour's daughter repeatedly during the 1990s. Released early after serving just five years of a ten-year sentence because his parole board declared him 'suitable for release'. The article goes into detail about his offences. They started when the girl was just six. The predator knew his victim's family well. He'd lock her up in his garage and subject her to horrific ordeals under the guise of babysitting.

A spasm of rage floods through me. Five years! Five years for violating a little girl. Ruining her innocence. Blighting the rest of her life.

My heart beats faster. *Five years.* That's nothing. That's not justice. Memories flash through my mind. My childhood. Up north. My father binding me in our garage. Assaulting me. Leaving me for days.

'Hey, what's up?'

Vanessa touches my arm. I flinch. Her voice feels far away.

I look up. Her eyes are soft, concerned.

'Sorry. I was miles away. It's nothing, just the news.'

'Okay . . .' Vanessa replies, looking a little bemused.

I close the paper. Put it back down. Try to push the story out of my mind.

Vanessa smiles. I try to focus on her. Beautiful Vanessa with her smooth skin and her dark hair tumbling over her shoulders. The sea, twinkling into the distance. The sound of the waves breaking on the shore.

I'm thousands of miles from Yorkshire. From England. That rapist is not my problem. There will always be men like him. Always. There will always be injustice. It's not my responsibility. I don't need to kill every predator. I don't. That phase of my life is over.

And yet the itch is there. The urge. The dark impulse. The *need*. I'm worried it always will be.

Vanessa weaves her fingers through mine. I squeeze her hand and smile back at her, not wanting to let go. Not wanting to give in.

ACKNOWLEDGEMENTS

First of all, I'd like to thank my editor, Leodora Darlington at Amazon Publishing, for championing *Pretty Evil*. I'm very lucky to work with such a talented and supportive editor and to know that my work is in such safe hands. I was so happy when *Pretty Evil* found a home with Amazon and the experience of working with Leodora and Amazon Publishing has been absolutely fantastic.

I could not have hoped for a better developmental editor than Russel McLean. Having been worried I might be asked to soften Camilla, I was so relieved when it turned out that Russel had no intention of doing this! He completely understood and appreciated Camilla's dark nature and what I was trying to achieve with her. Russel's feedback on the book was incredible and truly helped me to take it up a level. Thank you so much for your insights and enthusiasm for *Pretty Evil*, Russel!

Thank you as well to Gemma Wain for the exceptional proofread of this book. The attention to detail and astute observations have made the novel feel incredibly polished and cohesive. I'm very grateful.

A huge thank you to my agent Rukhsana Yasmin at The Good Literary Agency, who immediately saw the potential of *Pretty Evil* and completely understood Camilla. The novel is not for the fainthearted and I so appreciate Rukhsana instinctively knowing that it needed to be bold and edgy to be true to Camilla's nature. I could not have toned the novel down while staying authentic to Camilla's mindset and it was great to find an agent who understood that and shared my vision for the book. Everything lined up for *Pretty Evil* once I signed with Rukhsana. She has wholeheartedly championed the novel since the moment she first read it while being a great source of support and encouragement to me. Thank you so much, Rukhsana!

I'd also like to thank Stuart Gibbon from GIB Consultancy. I turned to Stuart many times during the writing of *Pretty Evil*, picking his brains as a former police detective. Stuart considered all my niche and macabre questions with a great deal of care and consideration, enabling me to strengthen the novel and make Camilla's world darkly believable. Thank you, Stuart.

I'd also like to thank the amazing authors Eoghan Egan, Sophia Spiers, Ritu Bhathal and Susannah Wise, for their support, camaraderie and feedback. Thank you so much!

Before writing this book, I'd had my own difficult MeToo experiences. I channelled some of the trauma I felt into Camilla and redirected the emotions into something creative and productive. It's times like this that I truly feel like a writer. I want to thank whatever twist of fate gave me my creativity because it's pulled me through some of the hardest times and enabled good things to come out of bad circumstances. Camilla is the dark angel who helped me rise up and I hope she will move and entertain my readers, as she did me (while not encouraging any of us to be serial killers!).

Thank YOU for reading this book. I hope you enjoyed it.

ABOUT THE AUTHOR

Zoe Rosi has a background in journalism and copywriting. She worked as a reporter for local and national newspapers before moving into the fashion industry as a copywriter. Zoe had four romantic comedies published before writing her debut thriller. It was while working as a fashion copywriter that Zoe had the idea for *Pretty Evil*, which she describes as *The Devil Wears Prada* meets *American Psycho*.

Printed in Great Britain
by Amazon

23289924R00142